# LAWYER GEISHA PINK

## Jonathan Miller

*COOL*
TITLES

COOL
T I T L E S

Published by
Cool Titles
439 N. Canon Dr., Suite 200
Beverly Hills, CA 90210
www.cooltitles.com

The Library of Congress Cataloging-in-Publication Data Applied For

Jonathan Miller—
Lawyer Geisha Pink

p.     cm
ISBN 978-1-935270-10-2
1. Mystery  2. Southwest  3. Legal  I. Title
2011

Printed in the United States of America

1 3 5 7 9 10 8 6 4 2

Book editing and design by White Horse Enterprises, Inc.

For interviews or information regarding special discounts for bulk purchases,
please contact cindy@cooltitles.com

Distribution to the Trade: Pathway Book Service,
www.pathwaybook.com, pbs@pathwaybook.com, 1-800-345-6665

*A portion of the author's proceeds will be donated to Japanese quake relief.*
*www.globalgiving.org/projects/japan-earthquake-tsunami-relief*

## Other Books by Jonathan Miller

## DEDICATION

To Jenny, who gave Jen Song her spirit,
and most especially to Marie,
who gave Jen Song her heart.

# Full Court Press

SHE'D BEEN A GOOD person, right?

Jen Song figured she had about one and a half seconds left to live. Or could she hold on for the full two? She wasn't very good at math, especially when calculating the speed of falling bodies. She hurtled down toward the ground floor of the courthouse atrium at an alarming rate of speed. You couldn't hit terminal velocity after only a hundred feet, could you?

Time slowed to a crawl the instant she was thrown off the balcony. Einstein had never studied the mental speeds of falling brain cells, but gravity certainly affected the speed of her thought waves right now.

Jen had hoped to make a good impression on the other lawyers in the courthouse, once she was finally admitted to the bar. Well, she was about to leave a big red impression on the tan tiles of the courthouse floor. Perhaps, she'd even leave a dent. She'd always wondered about the density of her skull.

Then again, Jen couldn't calculate her lateral velocity, the side-to-side movement of the fall. Gusts from the air conditioning vents buffeted her in both directions, especially as a police helicopter hovered just outside the window. She might just hit the upright glass disk sculpture, a relief of Lady Justice holding her scales. That disk stood in the direct center of a tile mosaic that was arranged to look like the points of a compass.

A warm gust blew her outward, toward a sharp metal edge that circled the rim of the glass sculpture below. The sculpture stood a head taller than Jen, maybe six feet. If Jen's skull hit the metal directly (she shuddered to use the phrase "head on"), the disk might slice her in half.

Another disk, this one about three feet wide, still lay below her on the fifth floor. That disk glistened like an unstable sun rotating at an unwieldy speed. It blinded her with its reflected light.

Why was that other disk, the rotating disk, suddenly so very important to her? She blinked. The light must have shifted as the disk on the fifth floor was now gone. Or was it ever there at all?

Jen's eyes took it all in. Albuquerque's Second Judicial District Courthouse really showed its age. Jen descended head first, passing window after window of the glass atrium. Outside, she could barely make out the granite over-thrust of the Sandia Mountains. The mountains had turned blood red in the late afternoon sun.

Jen had once faked her own death, and now she felt like the girl who cried wolf. Death didn't have a sense of humor, but it did have a way of getting even.

When she was little, she thought God himself lived on top of the Sandia Crest. There was a thunderstorm on top of the crest, so perhaps she wasn't wrong. In any event, she would soon meet God personally.

Well, perhaps not God. Not considering *her* life.

Since she had become a lawyer, Jen had tried to clean up her language and avoid her childhood use of the words "like" and "totally," but in an instant she would be like totally dead. Susie. Oh, Susie. This was all for you.

"I'm so sorry."

Not the best last words, but good enough. Jen was falling pretty fast. It pretty much looked like death, for real. . . .

Unless. . . .

The golden disk blinked at her again.

"I've got to head toward the light." She knew this in her heart. But how?

Her life over the last few months was now flashing before her. It was too late. As her flashback began, she felt a loss of control. Laser Geisha Pink was taking over again. . . .

# Laser Geisha Gold
# Three Months Earlier

"I, JEN SONG. . . . "

Jen Song stood up very straight, taking her oath with the other soon-to-be lawyers in the grand courtroom of the New Mexico Supreme Court. The building was an ancient adobe ranch that was way too cramped for all the new lawyers and their tastefully dressed guests. One could almost imagine cowboys arguing with conquistadors over cattle poaching out there in the lobby. Jen wondered if Billy the Kid's public defender ever filed a writ of habeas corpus at the clerk's window on the first floor.

Jen never imagined that she'd ever take an oath like this, especially dressed in the Brooks Brothers business suit that she bought at the outlet mall south of Santa Fe. The blue pinstriped skirt actually extended all the way past her knees. Jen had been a drug courier, accused murderer, legal secretary, and a waitress at a gentleman's club in her previous lives. Even worse, she had faked her own death and spent a week on the run pretending to be an Eskimo stripper.

Those were stories for another time.

In just a few seconds—assuming she could sign the two syllables of her name—she would be a real live lawyer. No money had passed hands to get her to the courthouse. She had achieved this fair and square. Thanks to the "Not-for-the-Top" scholarship sponsored by the late Korean American attorney and famed University of New Mexico (UNM) alumna, Mary Han, she'd also done it without incurring too much debt.

She still had to wait a year after passing the bar, of course.

"As a precaution," the letter from the Board of Bar Commissioners insisted. "Jen Song needs a year of supervised probation to prove herself worthy of admission."

The Board never spelled out their reasons. Thankfully, her long time therapist, Dr. Mary Ann Romero, wrote a detailed letter. "With the proper medication and therapy, Jen Song will prove to be an invaluable member of the New Mexico Bar."

Not just valuable, *invaluable.*

Dr. Romero had treated the Supreme Court Chief Justice's daughter when she had been committed to the state hospital for "exhaustion," so her word was gold.

Jen's half-sister, Luna, was in the first row, and pointed toward the front of the room, indicating that Jen had better turn her attention on the speaker. Luna was the child of their shared Hispanic father, and had the features of a fortyish *telenovela* star. She was dressed in her usual stylish black suit from the Santa Fe outlet, and her hair was held back in a severe bun.

Jen had clerked for District Court Judge Luna Cruz for the last year, and Luna had written a letter detailing Jen's metamorphosis. She then had written another one. The third letter must have done the trick, as Jen's former fiancé, Dan Shepard, had written his own letter.

"You have too many issues Jen," he had said to her when breaking up. "I don't know who you are. *You* don't even know who you are." Dan prided himself on his intellect. He once told her "You're smarter than I thought you were, but you're not as smart as I'd think you were, if I thought you were smart."

What did that even mean?

Jen wondered what he had put in his letter. She hoped he had lied. Dan was nowhere to be found today; perhaps he didn't really believe whatever it was that he had said.

While Dan and Luna had called in every favor, even Governor Diana Crater weighed in. Jen's mother was a nurse, and Diana was a former patient of hers. Jen was so pleased when Diana, too, jumped on the Jen Song bandwagon.

In her probationary year, Jen did everything right: volunteering at battered women's shelters, assisting with mentally ill and homeless patients at the UNM clinic—and working diligently on Diana's campaign. For Luna, Jen ghost-wrote the definitive decision on the use of urine samples in drunken driving cases that even the United States Supreme Court had quoted in a landmark decision. Jen was a poster child for redemption.

Luna pointed again and Jen reluctantly turned her head. The Chief Justice of the Supreme Court kept talking . . . and talking. No one listened, of course. This was about new lawyers, not the old lawyers. The Chief Justice was a petite Latina who looked more like a grandmother than a senior court official. She had even baked some of the cookies for the reception herself. Unfortunately, her speech must have been written by one of her clerks. It was a string of one cliché after another.

"The quality of mercy is not strained," the chief judge said, taking off her glasses. A few people in the front row nodded.

"The koala tea of mercy is not strained," Jen said to herself, giggling.

The judge must have heard her, because she now looked directly at Jen. "Judge not, lest ye be judged."

"Whatever," Jen said under her breath. The Chief Justice now turned back to face the audience, and Jen also turned her eyes to scan the galley. In a corner, she saw her mother, Chan Wol Song, and her own six-year-old daughter, Denise. Denise was part Asian, part Hispanic and part whatever else her late father had brought to the table. She could pass for a dark-haired Disney princess, except for her blank expression.

Denise held Chan Wol's hand as if she was a blind girl who was seeking guidance. Jen's mother had gone by "Nurse Song" her entire adult life; even her own family called her that—just like how Sting's mother called him "Sting."

Nurse Song lifted Denise's hand to imitate a wave to her mother. Denise's hand was limp; her heart wasn't in it, much less her hand. Jen didn't know how to feel. Would her daughter wave to her on her own?

Jen didn't know what else to do but wave back. Denise's blank eyes had already moved on to something else, toward a commotion in the back of the room.

A few years ago Jen had lost custody of her daughter after an angry dispute with the late father's family. It had all been a pack of lies, but even Jen conceded that Nurse Song was a more appropriate caregiver for a young special needs girl.

Nurse Song had once run a group home. After her house burnt down she moved into the group home as a sort of den mother. When funding ran out, she kept living there with

Denise as her only charge. At six, Denise had never spoken. It was agreed by many that Jen might finally be a bona fide lawyer, but she was certainly no nurse, and definitely not a mother.

Jen's father was nowhere to be seen, as usual. Her other half-sister, Selena, was present, but pre-occupied. Selena looked like a younger clone of Luna, even imitating her dark business suit, but one that showed a lot more leg. Selena was in her first year of law school at the University of Colorado at Boulder.

Luna pointed a third time toward the speaker. Jen again tried to focus on the Chief Justice as the grandmother continued talking about growing up in Espanola, blah, blah, blah. By this time, all of the soon-to-be lawyers had stopped focusing. Jen's attention deficit disorder had spread to the entire room of baby lawyers like chicken pox. Then the audience turned away from the Chief Justice as someone entered the courtroom while hastily turning off a ringing cell phone.

"That's Susie Song!" someone whispered in the loudest whisper in history. "The girl golfer!"

Now, no one in the audience was looking at the Chief Justice.

"What the hell is she doing here?" another whispered back.

"She's playing in an exhibition in Albuquerque," someone else said. "With the men."

"I think she's a cousin of that Asian chick. The murderer."

Susie was nearly six feet tall and towered over the people seated in the gallery. She wore her standard outfit: a blue golf shirt with her sponsor's corporate logo, and a baseball cap with the logo of an Asian company. Susie looked like a tomboy, tall and lean, and her shirt was billowy, as if cut for a man, not a girl. Her only teen-aged female affectation was a small gold pendant of the cartoon characters, the Laser Geishas. Jen had given it to Susie at her last appearance in New Mexico, at the Lyon Open.

"I can't believe she came," Jen said out loud. "Susie Freaking Song. Here for Jen Song, her poor relation."

"Be quiet," Jen's neighbor, a serious Navajo, muttered under his breath. "My whole family is here."

Jen turned to face the gallery. The Supreme Court Justice now quoted her own mother's exhortation about "great power and great responsibility," as if talking to the next generation of Spider-men, as opposed to attorneys.

"Next she'll quote Superman," Jen muttered.

And sure enough, the Chief Justice said something about fighting for truth, justice, and the American way. Someone in the gallery giggled.

Susie and Jen made eye contact. Susie waved, gave Jen a thumbs-up, and flashed her million-dollar smile. Susie was Laser Geisha Gold.

Jen sighed as she looked at her cousin. Susie was everything Jen wished she could be, and a few things that Jen could barely imagine. Jen finally had a future, but as a lawyer over thirty she already sensed her limitations. She would only go so far in this life.

On the other hand, Susie had the whole world waiting for her, and not just this world. Aliens probably booked Susie to appear on the sides of their flying saucers. The seventeen-year-old was more conglomerate than teenager.

"So, go out there and live long and prosper!"

That sounded logical. When it became obvious that the Chief Justice had no more clichés to spout, the new lawyers gave a hearty cheer.

"Do we have any motions?" the Chief Justice asked.

Members of the audience "motioned in" their friends, relatives, and employees. The process took a few minutes. Jen was the last, of course. After some hesitation, Luna stood up. "I am very proud to move my dear friend and half-sister—well to me she's a full sister—Jen Song, a.k.a. Chan Wol Song, named after her esteemed mother, to be admitted to the rolls of membership of the Bar of New Mexico."

Jen found that despite her innate cynicism, she had a tear in her eye. Jen looked for Susie, but she had disappeared. Had she even been here at all?

No one embraced Jen as they left the courtroom and headed for the reception outside, but Jen heard murmurings about several after-parties sponsored by the biggest movers and shakers.

One lawyer mentioned Ten Thousand Waves, the famed Japanese bathhouse in the Santa Fe foothills. He mentioned the words "clothing" and "optional" in his talk of hot sake and cold plunges. That sure smacked of the appearance of impropriety. Jen then overheard the same irritating man bragging about his firm's party that night. "We're going to the top of the Sandia Peak Tram tonight, the whole firm. We're going to the bar there to determine how altitude affects the absorption of alcohol. It's an experiment. You wanna come, Jen?"

"I totally hate heights," Jen said to the man, way too loud. "I think I'd rather die than go up there."

"I'll keep that in mind," a voice behind her said. When she turned around, she didn't see a soul.

# Santa Claus?

JEN LOOKED AROUND the park in front of the courthouse for Susie, but the girl was still nowhere to be seen. The little park was unusually lush for Santa Fe; it felt like the San Antonio River Walk in fall. Jen watched an orange leaf fall lazily from a tree and land in the sharp current of a creek, which promptly crushed the leaf against a rock. That had to mean something, didn't it?

Jen eventually found Susie signing autographs for the handful of young girls who had attended the ceremony for some distant relative. The entire village had come down from Northern New Mexico to see one of their own become a lawyer. Must be nice. Once Susie started, it was like a feeding frenzy and everyone tried to get a bite of her. Her fans weren't just young girls, though. Susie may have looked like a tom-boy, but older men responded to her as well. Many senior partners at the big law firms begged her for an autograph.

"It's for my granddaughter. She loves you," one said. He was a dead ringer for former Vice President Dick Cheney. "When do you turn eighteen?"

"New Year's Eve," Susie said. "Do you want to come to my party? I like *older* men."

"Dick" laughed. He had a vacant stare as he scanned Susie's body. Jen recognized that stare; she'd received it herself a few times when she'd worked her way through law school waitressing at the Ends Zone, a bar in Albuquerque.

Susie smiled, but Jen couldn't tell if the smile was real.

"You were robbed on the ninth hole," one man said, referring to a questionable call from this morning. "But you'll get them next week."

"Thank you, but this isn't about me. That's my favorite cousin," Susie said in a stage whisper, pointing at Jen. "She's like my sister. She's a lawyer now after all these years. You should get her autograph, not mine!"

Jen took a deep breath, but Susie's "entourage" said nothing. Jen felt lonelier than before.

A vaguely familiar lawyer came over and introduced himself as Claus Heydrich. Claus was in his forties, and with his beard he resembled Santa Claus. Well, he could be Santa Claus's business manager in a blue polyester suit and red tie. Claus was fat enough that his polyester had become a few sizes too small for him. Jen had met him when she attended a lecture Claus had given about his relief work in third world countries. Claus pointed to a mixed-race family over by the river. "There's *my* fan club," he said. "I'm probably going to adopt a few more before we're done. Families are addictive."

"I wouldn't know," Jen said. Claus had three gigantic sons who were pushing and shoving each other. The sons were Pacific Islanders of some sort. Samoan, perhaps, although they looked like they were of mixed heritage. America still had military bases out at Pearl Harbor, right? These boys looked like they could each withstand a direct hit. One shoved the other nearly over the edge of the lawn into the little creek, and then laughed about it.

"Boys, behave," Claus yelled. "Or I'll ground you for the big game next week."

The boys immediately straightened up, and pretended to be perfect gentlemen. They waited until their father returned his attention to Jen before sneaking in punches again.

Claus hugged Jen a little too hard. "Congratulations."

"Thank you," Jen said, pleased that someone was glad to see her. She looked at her family and sighed. "Maybe you can adopt me, too."

Claus laughed. "You look like you're doing just fine. It's good to see your family here."

"Right." Jen looked at her family, such as it was. Luna spoke intently on her iPhone, and Denise tugged on Nurse Song's hand, silently begging to leave. It was time to change the subject.

"Do you know someone who is being admitted today?"

"Well, actually, I am the admittee," Claus smiled. "I was here on a waiver from Utah with Menaul & Eubank," he said, referring to one of the big firms in Albuquerque. "I was there on contract writing briefs. Now that I'm starting my own civil firm, the Bar said I'd have to get my own license. I even had to take the bar again. I'm now admitted in seven states and three countries."

"That's way cool about starting your own firm. Do you need anybody?"

Claus smiled. "Well, I'm always looking for new talent. I'll be doing civil litigation and civil rights like I did in Utah. I kept my hand in it all over the world. Once, I sued the government of American Samoa and won millions. Unfortunately, the award was reversed on appeal. I've probably written a hundred briefs in my life. It will be good to keep fighting for the little guy. I love legal writing."

Jen smiled. A hundred briefs. Jen liked the law and liked writing, but hated legal writing with a passion. She had nearly every learning disability known to man, and could barely make it through a case caption before forgetting whether "versus" was abbreviated by "v" or "vs."

"Do you have a business card?" Claus asked.

"Not yet," Jen said.

Claus smiled. "Here then, feel free to take mine. Let's keep in touch."

He handed her a glossy card, with an imprint of the scales of justice in a circle.

A circle with the scales of justice? She thought of the sculpture in the atrium of the District Court building in Albuquerque, a giant glass disk with a relief sculpture of the scales. She suddenly formed an image of her head hitting that sculpture, as if falling from above.

"That hasn't happened yet," Jen said. A chill passed through her body.

"What?" Claus asked. "You look like you've just seen a ghost."

"My own," she said. "I didn't mean to say that out loud. I just had one of those visions. I get them every once in a while."

"You sure you're all right?"

"Don't worry, I'm fine."

Claus smiled. "I told my kids I would take them to the new exhibit at the International Folk Art Museum. I've got to go before my triplets start tackling the lawyers."

On a far part of the lawn, the boys now practiced the latest blocking drills. She overheard one lawyer, who was apparently a sports agent, try to convince them to stay and play for the UNM Lobos, who were suffering through yet another abysmal season.

Claus touched her arm. "Keep my offer in my mind."

"I will."

Claus hurried back to his kids. Maybe working with a man like Claus could be a good thing. It might be good to leave Luna's womb and spread her own wings.

"Jen, save me!" Susie yelled. All Jen could see of Susie amidst the autograph hunters was the top of her cap with the strange Asian logo.

Jen didn't know what she was supposed to do, but wandered over anyway. "She's got to go," Jen said. "She's got this thing she needs to do."

The line of autograph seekers politely turned away, but not before someone recognized Jen. "That's that girl who was the murderer!"

The crowd dispersed at once, as if Jen might suddenly go on a rampage with her new bar card. Jen's redemption hadn't been total, after all. The Board of Bar Commissioners might have reluctantly accepted her, but the rank and file certainly had not.

"Thank you Jen, you saved my life." Susie gave Jen a big hug. "I'm so proud of you. I really want you to be my lawyer someday."

Nurse Song took a picture of Jen, Selena, and Luna together. The "Laser Geisha Girls," they called themselves.

"Laser Geisha!" they all yelled.

Susie frowned. In that instant, Jen saw the loneliness in the girl's eyes. "You know they let me guest star on the cartoon," Susie said. "Well, they used my voice. I was Laser Geisha Gold."

"I didn't realize that you wanted to be one of us, Susie," Jen said.

They took another picture, this one with Susie.

"Be careful what you wish for," Jen said. "What did Groucho Marx say about not wanting to join any club that would have him as a member?"

# Red or Green

JEN'S RAG-TAG ENTOURAGE wandered into the crooked adobe streets of downtown Santa Fe, pretending to like each other. It was two o'clock, still time for a late lunch with the sophisticated set who were just waking up in their second homes in the foothills. Luna knew of a place that made "seventy dollar burritos."

Even seventy *cent* burritos sounded great to Jen. The aspen trees high on the Sangre De Cristo Mountains turned gold off to the west. The highest peak, Santa Fe Mountain, even had a dusting of snow on top, so it looked like a southwestern version of Japan's highest mountain, Mount Fuji.

Feeling confident, Jen approached her daughter and gave her a hug under Nurse Song's watchful eyes. It felt like hugging a corpse. Why couldn't Denise talk? Jen feared she was the world's worst mother and it was all her fault. Jen released her embrace, and Denise scurried back to her grandma. Becoming a lawyer hadn't cured everything in Jen's life.

Jen forced herself to get all of the emotional crap out of her life for one brief moment and fill her body, her mind and her soul with a single emotion. Pride. The feeling ended abruptly. A photographer jumped up out of the bank of the Santa Fe River. He must have been hiding underwater, waiting for this one shot. He managed one photo of Susie before Jen chased him off.

Susie's phone rang the Olympic theme, even though golf wasn't an Olympic sport. Susie talked briefly with someone and then said, "Fuck them! Fuck them all."

Jen didn't know Laser Geisha Gold was capable of swearing. Nurse Song held little Denise's ears.

Susie threw her phone down in disgust. Even though it was stainless steel, the sheer force of her throw caused the phone to break apart. Nurse Song picked up the phone and managed to put it together before she handed it back to Susie. Nurse Song had experience at putting things back together.

"What's wrong, Susie?" she asked.

"My mom," Susie said. "She's breaking into my trust account again. A boob job or maybe a face-lift to go with her lip job."

Jen said nothing and felt self-conscious. She'd had a discrete boob job after she gave birth to Denise. She certainly didn't want to bring that up now.

"Are you sure?" Nurse Song asked. Susie's mom was her sister. Never close, Nurse Song was always amazed at her sibling's lack of ethics.

"I hate my mom." Susie frowned. "Why can't I be a grown-up already?"

No one knew how much money Susie made. Golfing was the tip of a very big iceberg. She had a modeling contract, an endorsement with a cosmetics company, her own line of golf wear, and even an anime comic book for the Asian market.

Jen had never met her aunt, Jae Lee Song. Her mom had told her stories, but Jen didn't know what to believe. The woman couldn't be all bad if she had raised a girl like Susie. No one knew the identity of Susie's dad. It might have been a virgin birth for all she knew. There were rumors that Susie's dad was a certain promiscuous half-Asian golf superstar. Susie sure didn't get her God given talents from her mother.

Susie turned toward Nurse Song and grabbed her by both arms in her powerful grip. "Nurse Song, will you be my mother?"

Denise scurried behind her grandmother. Nurse Song was taken aback. "What?"

"Just for a few months," Susie said. "I turn eighteen on New Year's Eve. You were so good to me five years ago when I went into treatment back when you ran that group home. I like you so much better than my own mom. That whore."

Treatment? When had Susie gone through treatment? Suddenly it made sense. Susie must have been one of the girls at Nurse Song's treatment home. That would explain why the two seemed so close.

"Why didn't you tell me?" Jen asked her mother.

"Susie has a right to privacy," Nurse Song said, exasperated that Jen was ruining a private conversation. "I don't tell her your secrets. Or my secrets, either."

Susie looked quite vulnerable. She didn't look seventeen anymore—more like twelve. She hugged Nurse Song.

"Please think about it," Susie said. She then took a piece of paper from her purse and scribbled on it. "It says: I divorce my mom, Jae Lee Song, and want to be adopted by Chan Wol Song."

Susie turned to Luna. "You're a judge, will you sign it?"

Luna couldn't tell whether Susie was serious, but she signed the bottom of the scrap of paper as Judge Luna Cruz. "I don't know if this makes it valid or not," Luna said.

"I don't care," Susie said.

Jen wondered if Susie didn't care if it was valid, or didn't care who her mother was.

In the midst of Jen's wondering, Susie's phone rang again. But this time she squealed when she recognized the number.

The angst of the immediate past faded instantly. Perhaps Susie had ADD, just like Jen. Jen had once squealed like that when she was seventeen. It had to be a boy on the other end. But what kind of boy could possibly measure up to Susie?

Susie hung up moments later. "That was my boyfriend, Hal Lyon. *The* Hal Lyon, Sir Ian Lyon's son. You know the one they nicknamed 'Prince Hal?' We're going up in a balloon tomorrow at the balloon fiesta."

Jen shuddered involuntarily. She was no fan of anything that left the ground.

Susie looked at Jen and held her hand in a tight grip. "Please come with us. This is my special gift to you, okay? You can't say no. It would mean so much to me!"

Jen said nothing to her cousin. Instead, a shiver ran down her spine and she developed a sharp pain in her stomach.

"I'll think about it," Jen said. "I have a fear of heights. What was that Alfred Hitchcock film? *Psycho*?"

"*Vertigo*," Luna said.

# The Lawyer's Line

JEN WAS NOT THE focus of attention during her celebration lunch, Susie was. Susie talked about traveling the world to play golf, and did her best to make it sound like a summer internship. Jen asked questions about celebrities that Susie had met.

"They're just like other people," Susie said. "Some are nice. Some are jerks. Some are evil. I wish I had your life, Jen. It must be exciting to be a lawyer."

Jen nodded, turned her head and munched on a burrito filled with some kind of exotic game. Was it a caribou burrito? "I don't know how exciting it will be," she said between bites.

Susie then talked about her favorite TV show, a funny legal show set in New Mexico that no one else had actually watched. Jen kept her eyes on her food. She felt hungry for something else, but didn't quite know what it was. At the earliest possible moment, she excused herself. She needed to do something before the day ended.

"I'll see you tomorrow," Susie said. "I'm only here for a few days and I want to share the balloon experience with you."

Jen gave her a dubious look.

The others were still eating dessert when Jen left. It was just three-thirty, but traffic already crawled out of downtown Santa Fe. Perhaps the drivers wanted to peer inside the galleries while driving past them. Once Jen was southbound on I-25, she deliberately drove a hundred miles an hour back to Albuquerque, daring the cops to give her a ticket so she could fight it in court with her newly minted status as a lawyer.

Moments later, she passed the first Albuquerque exit, Tramway Boulevard. The Tram itself was only a few miles up the road at the base of the Sandia Mountains.

Jen was tempted to meet her fellow new lawyers at the tram party, as these were people who could give her a job. But, the prospect of flying a thousand feet above the earth for the tram's fifteen minute ascent was too much. She kept heading south.

She made it the additional ten miles into downtown at a brisk pace. She parked at her bank, which was near the courthouse, so she could get her parking validated. Money was still tight, after all. The scholarship money had run out a long time ago. Once she graduated she'd been on her own. She hurried over to the District Courthouse and its unique architecture: the bottom pretended to be adobe, the middle was classic generic office building, and the flat blue circular roof was a bad architectural joke.

Inside, two lines passed through the metal detectors, one for attorneys and one for non-attorneys. The non-attorney line contained defendants and their families. One convenience store clerk in a "Quick Stop" shirt with the name DANTE embroidered on it mumbled, "I'm not even supposed to be here today!"

The wands showed no mercy that afternoon. One kid made the wand beep twice, once for wearing a Metallica T-shirt, then again for his Pittsburgh Steelers baseball cap. The guards must be on orange alert.

Jen smiled. She walked past everyone and got in the second line, the attorney's line.

"Am I allowed to bring hair gel in?" a woman at the front of the non-attorney line asked. "Is this like the airport?"

Jen took out her fresh new Bar ID card. "I'm an attorney," she said out loud. She began to walk but the wands beeped like crazy. Jen had a phone with her, she had her keys, she even had hair gel, but with that magic laminated attorney card, the guard reluctantly waved her through.

She looked back at the line and just couldn't resist. "Oops, I forgot something."

She walked out the exit door, and then returned and walked past the hundred or so people who were waiting in line.

She once again flashed her ID. "I'm an attorney," she said for the second time in as many minutes. She then opened her purse and revealed hair gel. "I can bring hair gel into the building, too!"

"Are you going to do this all day?" the guard asked.

"I'm going to do this for the rest of my life!" Jen said.

She shuddered when she realized that in her vision, she would die in this very building. She had better enjoy it while she could.

✝

Jen rode the elevator up to Luna's chambers, where Jen shared a small office with the bailiff. She was surprised to find someone else there. The woman was taking Jen's possessions off the desk and putting them into a brown paper bag.

"What's going on?" Jen asked. "I'm going to call security."

"Didn't the judge tell you?"

It took Jen a moment to recognize Mia, a girl who had worked with her at the Ends Zone, but had turned to dancing once she realized waitressing only paid so much. Mia had once been the state champion in the pole vault, but was working her way through college dancing around a different kind of pole.

"Tell me what?"

Mia sat down in Jen's chair. "That I'm her new intern."

Jen should have known this was going to happen, now that she was a real lawyer.

"But you're a dancer."

Mia smiled. "Not any more, although maybe I still am on weekends. Law is just like one long lap dance from Lady Justice—lots of grinding, a little tease, and it's very expensive. Unfortunately, with law you don't always have a happy ending."

That night Jen went back to her small house near the law school on Stanford Street. She often reflected that the namesake of her street was Stanford University, the alma mater of both Michelle Wie and Tiger Woods. This street did face a golf course, but it certainly wasn't Palo Alto. Some of the middle class homes were little more than large bungalows with xeriscaped lawns.

Her own little adobe bungalow was ancient. Jen wondered if Coronado, the explorer himself, had built it for his caddy. She called her place Coronado's Caddy Shack. Jen might have been a lawyer, but inside the Caddy Shack it still looked like a teenager's home, with a doll collection and posters of Japanese anime. Jen only had one picture of herself with Denise.

Jen microwaved a cup of Lime Chili Shrimp noodles. She bristled at the spelling of the word "chili." Here in New Mexico the word was written as "chile," the way it was supposed to be spelled. The noodles weren't bad, though she wondered exactly how the cup's maltodextrin, soya lecitihin, sodium carbonate, desmodium insinuate, and desmodium granulate would react with the chemicals from her medicine cabinet.

The labels on her various meds all said to "take after eating." Jen took so many pills, some for her brain, some for her thyroid, that she often confused herself. She downed her latest pill with a tap water chaser.

So this is the glamorous life of a lawyer?

Jen wanted to wait up and see the latest episode of the Geishas, but she drifted off to sleep. Her eyes had closed for only a moment, when her allegedly "smart" phone played the Laser Geishas' cartoon theme song, which sounded like a techno version of The Beatle's "I Wanna Hold Your Hand" sung by Yoko Ono. Jen jumped at the noise.

Does someone actually care about me, she wondered as she picked up the phone.

"Hi. It's Susie."

"Susie. *The* Susie?"

"I insist that you join Ian and me for ballooning. It'll be an adventure."

Jen felt nauseous. "Sure. I'll, ah . . . be your ground crew."

"No, you're going to go flying whether you like it or not."

# Bastard Ballooning

JEN WAS BARELY AWAKE when a vehicle honked for her the next morning. After putting on jeans and an oversized Geishas sweatshirt, she hurried out to find a black vehicle labeled LYON AEROSPACE MOUNTAIN LYON in Old English lettering. Jen didn't know cars very well and wasn't sure if it was a Hummer, an Escalade, or a drone vehicle used in the latter days of the Afghan war. Jen didn't even know if there were humans inside until Susie bounded out to let Jen in. Once settled on the Mountain Lyon's plush seats, Jen fell fast asleep.

"Wake up, we're there!" Susie said.

Jen awoke as they turned off the I-25 frontage road onto Balloon Fiesta Boulevard. It was still before dawn, and the sun struggled to rise over the massive Sandia Crest to the east. Why couldn't balloons ascend at a civilized hour?

Susie handed her an energy drink, her own private brand, Fast Song. "You'll want to be up for this."

Jen gulped it down, and felt the rush of ginseng, taurine, and caffeine. Had she remembered to take her pills this morning?

Too late.

Nearly a hundred thousand spectators inched their cars into the park. Traffic on I-25 was backed up for miles. Luckily, the Mountain Lyon eased into the VIP lane on the main boulevard that led into the fiesta grounds, and proceeded past the angry stares of the other divers.

Kinda like being in the lawyer's line at court, Jen thought, although Sir Ian Lyon, an eccentric billionaire, was more powerful than any lawyer.

Now that her eyes were relatively open, she could see that the Mountain Lyon, on the inside, looked almost like a space vehicle. Pimp my rocket and all that. The windows were bulletproof and there were TV antennas and a satellite dish on top. The Mountain Lyon could easily chase down alien motherships from *Independence Day,* rather than mere hot-air balloons.

"This vehicle was in a commercial once," Susie said with a smile. "Our driver, Jean Claude, used to do stunt driving."

"It was a bull fighting commercial," Jean Claude said.

Jen vaguely remembered an ad that involved a vehicle facing down a bull. She saw a puncture in the right door. Sometimes the bull didn't always lose.

As if to demonstrate his prowess, Jean Claude took the vehicle onto the median to pass a few cars as they headed due west into the heart of the fiesta grounds. They were headed straight toward Albuquerque's dormant volcanoes a few miles west on the mesa and could see the three rocky cones that jutted out of the desert rim. Jen shivered as the first rays of dawn illuminated the third cone. The volcano stood less than two hundred feet high, but from her perspective deep in the valley it was hard to judge height. To her, it was an island in a sea of darkness.

Ed Hobbs, her old boss, had been murdered on top of that very volcano. The state had charged her with the crime, but thankfully, Luna cleared her of the charges. She was innocent. Well, she was not guilty. She really could not remember what happened that night.

Jen forced herself to look in every direction, except toward the volcano. Now that the light was coming up there was much to see. Balloon Fiesta could pass for a nylon zoo about to awake for the morning feeding. The zoo metaphor really worked. They passed balloons shaped like a cow, a parrot, and even a baboon that advertised a local car dealership. YOU'LL GO APE FOR OUR DEALS, the balloon's banner declared.

Jen wished she could have brought Denise, just to see the baboon balloon. Last year, she and her mom had taken Denise here. Denise had pointed up at the balloons in wonder. It was one of the few times Jen had seen her daughter show a reaction to anything.

The Mountain Lyon went over a bump and flew into the air for a second. Jen screeched involuntarily. She felt uneasy even a few inches off the ground. Jen knocked on the wall of the Mountain Lyon, testing it. It didn't seem especially solid. The walls were thin, as if a defense contractor who was trying to save a few dollars had built them.

Still, Jen wouldn't mind staying inside here where it was safe on *terra firma*, rather than risking her life in a rickety gondola. No, Jen knew she'd have to suck it up. If she was going to get over her fear of heights, she would have to do it the hard way. She had never actually been up in a balloon, even though she was a New Mexico native. It was always too crowded, or too early. This almost felt like a rite of passage, just like taking the bar exam. You've got to face your fears, head on, right?

Jen's reverie was interrupted by a girlish giggle. "Hal, that sounds nasty," a girlish voice giggled.

Jen looked at Susie as she played footsie with Hal Lyon, the legendary Prince Hal, while he whispered in her ear. He was seventeen, the eccentric billionaire's son. Hal's eyes were vaguely Asian, the only thing he inherited from his dead mother, a bar girl from Bangkok. Other than his eyes, he looked every inch his father's son. He stood six-foot-five, wore a rugby shirt from one of his father's teams, and the cap for the Asian company that sponsored Susie. Prince Hal spoke with an English accent that would sound perfect in the stands at a championship Quidditch match at Hogwarts. Jen wondered how anything could sound nasty spoken in a voice like that.

Susie gave her boyfriend a slight punch in his shoulder.

"That hurt," Hal whined, then smiled. "Hurt me more."

Susie wore tight sweat pants, which revealed the curve of her long, muscular legs. Jen thought Luna had been athletic, but Susie took it to another level. It would take a self-confident young man not to be intimidated by Susie's physique, or worry that Susie could crush him in a most unfortunate accident. Susie's arms were lean, but those arms propelled a golf ball more than three hundred yards.

Luckily, Hal didn't know fear. The Rugby shirt was no prop, he certainly knew his way around a scrum, or whatever it was that rugby players did. His father, Sir Ian, was famous for letting his boy literally swim with sharks as a tool to build self-esteem.

The fact that Hal knew he was a "billionaire to be" didn't exactly hurt his self-consciousness with the ladies. Despite Internet rumors of the Lyon family's luck with women, Hal only had eyes for Susie. Even if Susie and Hal hadn't switched to discrete snuggling, Jen would have felt like a third wheel. She pretended to look away, but couldn't help glancing back. She had been a horny seventeen-year-old too, but she had never dated princes.

Jen glanced at Jean Claude. He was built more like a bodyguard than a driver, and looked to have a mix of Middle Eastern and European ancestry. Jean Claude dropped that he'd learned to drive tanks for the French Foreign Legion, and in addition to stunt driving, had worked as a race car driver and who knows what else. A tattoo of the Ghost Rider graced his bicep; the writing underneath was in fiery Arabic.

"For my probation, I work for Sir Ian," he said. Jean Claude now looked straight ahead, ignoring the strange shapes of the balloons around him. He nearly ran over the ground crew for the baboon balloon, all of whom were wearing gorilla masks.

After some more free-wheeling, he parked the Mountain Lyon on a field. "*Allez, allez,*" Jean Claude said.

They all scurried out into the cold morning air. The sun was just beginning to rise, and to the east, the rectangular Sandia Crest was backlit, like an eclipse. On the east side of the park, a line of wooden kiosks stretched nearly half a mile. These stores sold cheap green chile burritos and balloon trinkets, but they looked especially fragile in the cold wind. Despite the early hour, the park had the look of a state fair, however in the chill, it felt like the state fair of Siberia.

"Where's your dad's balloon?" Susie asked.

"I don't know," Hal replied. "I think it got moved to the other side of the field."

Jean Claude looked at a map, but didn't seem to have his bearings this early in the morning. As they wandered, looking for the assigned spot, several tourists snapped pictures until

Jean Claude shouted obscenities in French and flashed the bicep with the Ghost Rider tattoo. The tourists hurried to hide behind a balloon.

After a few more minutes of exploring and more choice French obscenities, Jean Claude finally found the Lyons' launch spot on a far corner of Balloon Fiesta Park. The balloon's thin fabric was laid out over a wide flat area, as if it was a picnic table for the gods.

"*Voila!*" he said.

Around them, balloons inflated slowly with each blast of flame. Jen smiled as she saw the shapes of nearby balloons. One imitated a giant inflated cow jumping over a green-cheese moon. Another looked perfectly normal as it inflated, until she noticed a fabric version of the Red Baron's airplane crashing through it. It took a moment for Jen to realize that the Red Baron's plane was part of the balloon. CURSE YOU RED BARON was the caption on the balloon. The balloon's sponsor was Red Baron Realty.

Jen jumped when she heard an explosion, and then covered her ears. "Was that a bomb?"

Susie laughed. "It's just the balloons being inflated by the propane jets."

"Balloons scare me," Jen said.

Hal kissed Susie on the lips. Susie giggled, slipped him some tongue, then turned her head away from him.

"Not here." She pretended to slap him.

"Tonight at my party," he said. "I've known you for a *year*. I can't wait forever."

"Maybe you won't have to wait forever," she said with a smile, looking back at him.

Jen noticed the look in Susie's eyes. Jen knew that look.

Susie was going to give it up to Hal for the first time tonight. Jen shook her head.

They noticed her staring. Susie nodded her head. "You've got to ask Jen. She's my—"

Susie was about to say cousin, but instead she said, "Jen's my friend."

Hal sized up Jen. Over thirty, Jen felt like a piece of meat at a butcher shop that was way past its expiration date. After a few moments he smiled. Apparently she'd passed Hal's test. Maybe it was the boob job.

"You can come to my party tonight, too," he said at last.

"Well, it's my father's company party, but he's really cool. It'll be positively smashing."

"I'll think about it," Jen said politely. She didn't like being a third wheel.

"You'll have a smashing time," said Hal. He apparently loved the word.

A crew-member handed them breakfast burritos with green chile. Jen gulped hers down in three bites. This burrito was far better than the one in Santa Fe yesterday. She savored the moment.

"Your father needs to speak with you, *monsieur!*" Jean Claude said as he pointed at a tall bearded man coming toward them.

Suddenly there was another blast of propane, right next to her ear. She cringed like it was another near-miss bombing. She stumbled around for a moment, punch drunk.

"Watch where you're walking!" someone yelled. She had stepped on the balloon fabric. Startled, Jen tripped and fell over backward, but the big, bearded man caught her before she hit the ground. Then he offered his hand to her.

"Jen Song, esquire," Sir Ian Lyon said. "*Enchante.*"

No one had ever been enchanted with her before.

Jen was impressed by Sir Ian, who was nearly as tall and youthful as his son. With his long blond hair and goatee he could indeed pass for a lion, although most certainly not a cowardly one. His face was slightly sun burnt, as if he had just come back from crossing the Sahara.

Sir Ian was born out of time. He had been too late to be one of the great English explorers, like Stanley or Livingstone. He actually looked perfectly natural in his safari outfit. Were those faded blood stains on it? Jen didn't want to know.

"Sir Ian Lyon, I presume," she said.

"You presume correctly," he said in his charming voice. "Your reputation precedes you."

"None of it is true," Jen said, blushing slightly. "Well, almost none of it."

As Sir Ian returned to the balloon crew to oversee the final preparations, Jen wandered around the Balloon Fiesta. It was still chilly in the dawn. She smiled when she saw that a Japanese network had a "Laser Geishas" balloon. The balloon was of a traditional shape, but had a picture of the Laser Geishas flying overhead. The three originals, Pink, Blue, and Green, and the new one, Gold, were chasing the villainous Laser Geisha Black. Laser Geisha Black was the "geisha gone wild."

"Laser Geisha Pink," Jen said absentmindedly, doing an imitation of the Laser Geisha's famed name check.

"Laser Geisha Gold," a voice replied. Jen turned around and was surprised to find Susie right behind her.

"I love the Laser Geishas," said Susie. "They're like supposed to be for kids, but I think they're totally cool."

"They're my only friends some days," Jen said, suddenly regretting acting so needy in front of her glamorous cousin.

The two cousins had begun walking west, to check out other balloons, when Jean Claude placed a big hand on Susie's shoulder.

"*Mademoiselle* Song, it's time for lift off."

Jen instinctively shuddered, but walked back to the balloon with Susie. She noticed a very big security guard armed with a semi-automatic weapon patrolling the perimeter of the balloon. In addition to Jean Claude, Sir Ian employed Snape, an Englishman with a shaved head who could pass for a soccer hooligan of a second division team. When a gawker tried to approach, Snape pantomimed head-butting the man. The gawker scampered away.

Snape muttered a few angry sentences, but the only intelligible word was "bollocks."

"I have to pay other people to be mean for me," Sir Ian said with a shrug. "'Money changes everything.' Who said that? Shakespeare? Dickens?"

"Cindy Lauper," Jen said with a smile.

"I'm starting to like you already," Sir Ian said.

Jen had dated older men before. Denise's late father, Paul Dellagio, was certainly no spring chicken. She had some serious daddy issues, of course, but Sir Ian didn't come across as a father figure. Sir Ian was a handsome, classy man, who just happened to be twice her age.

"I've heard you've never flown before," Sir Ian said. "As one of the more recent immigrants to my country would say, 'you're like a virgin.'"

"*Touched for the very first time,*" she sang. Then, "I have a 'fear of flying.' Wasn't that a book by Erica Jong? I don't read much these days."

"That's the pity," Sir Ian said. "I don't know if they publish crap because that's all people read, or people don't read because they publish crap."

Sir Ian smiled a toothy grin. Like a lion, he could easily tear gazelle flesh with his bite. "My first impression was indeed correct. I like you already. Time for you to see my new balloon. It will make you feel all 'shiny and new.'"

Sir Ian's shiny and new balloon had almost fully inflated to become a golden lion's head. That made sense as his company was Lyonshead. But the gondola looked vaguely like a pink heart.

"Lion. Heart," Sir Ian said with a smile. "Supposedly my family line goes all the way back to Richard the Lionheart."

"Really?"

Sir Ian laughed. "Well, back to his bastard son. I think he had a fling with a chambermaid and that's where we come from. We actually had the DNA tests done to prove it. But you must admit that Lyon Heart Ballooning sounds much better than 'Bastard Ballooning.'"

He laughed. Sir Ian put his hand on her shoulder, a touch too familiar, but Jen didn't mind

"I like you already, too," Jen said with a big smile.

And what was there not to smile about? This sixty-year-old billionaire, the seventh richest man in the world, was flirting with her. His wife, the Bangkok bar girl, had died under mysterious circumstances after falling out of a balloon over the North Atlantic. Some speculated that she had been pushed. The danger made him even sexier to Jen.

If a guy like that could go with a bar girl, why couldn't he go for a lawyer like her?

A cool breeze roared in from the west, and the balloons ruffled in the wind. One nearly blew over. Jen found herself huddling against Sir Ian and found she felt comfortable there.

Susie and Hal got into the balloon first, with Sir Ian at the controls. As Susie climbed into the basket, Jen noticed visible panty lines through her tight sweats. The girl wore thong panties over that muscular ass of hers. Hal grabbed it while his father wasn't looking. Susie smiled.

Yes, Prince Hal had definitely found his princess.

After some garbled announcements, the balloonists began preparations for their mass ascension, while a cheer rose from the hundreds of people who had already scrambled into the gondolas. Then moments later, one balloon lifted into the air to another cheer.

Snape said something in cockney. Jen only made out the word "wanker," which apparently was a not good word.

Hundreds of beautiful balloons now flew over her head, blotting out the sun that had finally made it over the Sandia Crest. Jen covered her ears. The sound of the propane blasters was deafening.

As the balloon slowly rose above the ground, Susie's face betrayed a moment of fear. She put her arm around Hal. He put his arm around Susie's and whispered something that looked to Jen like "I'll protect you." She never had been all that good at lip reading.

A photographer tried to take a picture of this magic moment, but Jean Claude went over to the photographer and smashed the camera. Then Jean Claude shouted at him furiously in French.

As the balloon ascended higher, Jen watched the fear in Susie's face turn to delight. She did indeed look like she was touched for the very first time.

Sir Ian waved down to her from the gondola.

Jen smiled. "We're not in Kansas anymore," she said.

"Kansas?" Jean Claude said. "The wind's blowing west. Maybe they will make Arizona."

He had a little blood on his hands; some part of the camera must have nicked his fist. He wiped it on his shirt. Other stains were there already.

"Let's do it, *mademoiselle*."

"Do what?"

"Chase!" he said. "*Allez! Allez!*"

As if on cue, Snape blew a fox hunting horn.

Jen followed Jean Claude into the car to a cacophony of horns, as the chase vehicles started to leave the parking lot.

Suddenly Jen saw something to the west, now that the light was finally illuminating the mesa. The entire crowd at Balloon Fiesta Park, all hundred thousand of them, gave a loud gasp. The supposedly dormant volcano off in the distance wasn't so dormant any more. Thick, black smoke emerged from the cone.

Sir Ian's balloon headed right for the center of the dome. Jen swore she heard Susie scream.

# Volcano Virgin

"CAN'T YOU GO ANY faster?" Jen asked Jean Claude. She instantly regretted her question. He could and did. Jen sat in the front seat of the chase vehicle next to Jean Claude. She still had not figured out how to fasten the seat belts in the Mountain Lyon. Locking the belt in two different places was beyond the capabilities of her panicked mind right now.

Every bump in the road catapulted her into the air, and nearly into orbit. She almost landed in Jean Claude's lap on several occasions. Jen had vowed never to be on a lap again, so she now grabbed the side handle as if her life depended on it.

Jean Claude must have raced tanks in the Foreign Legion. He maneuvered the big vehicle like an extension of his burly tattooed arms. He knew a short cut through an arroyo and smashed through a barbed wire fence, beating the other vehicles onto the freeway.

Jen's phone rang. "Keep following us!" Susie said. "I'm afraid of the volcano, and Sir Ian is heading for it on purpose."

Jen hoped an eruption wouldn't happen, but she had failed geology at least once.

"This volcano has been dormant for seventy thousand years and counting," Jen replied. "I'm sure it's not really going to erupt."

Jen had heard of hell freezing over, but a dormant volcano erupting suddenly after seventy thousand years belonged in the same category. That was absolutely ridiculous. Just like her becoming a lawyer, right? Jen wanted to keep talking, but Sir Ian released a blast of hot air that nearly deafened her through the phone.

Most of the other balloons in the fiesta had managed to shift direction. They now headed south, toward the wide open spaces of the golf course near her home. But the Laser Geisha balloon followed the Lyonshead balloon as it headed straight toward the volcano. It was almost as if the volcano was a magnet. The smoke grew thicker and thicker. Would it take a virgin sacrifice to stop the smoke?

The Lyonshead lost some altitude; perhaps Sir Ian could avoid the trees and land on a sand bar in the Rio Grande. The water would stop any lava flow. Maybe.

Jean Claude took the Mountain Lyon through roads that ran along muddy irrigation ditches. He nearly flipped the car into one ditch, but somehow righted the vehicle just in time by a strategic lean to the left.

Jen prayed with every bump. "I'm sorry, Lord. For everything."

The vehicle landed with a big splash in the muddy water. The windshield was suddenly covered with mud.

"*Merde,*" Jean Claude said.

Jen sniffed cow shit in the distance as they entered an incorporated village called Los Ranchos de Albuquerque, a rural oasis within the suburban sprawl. Suddenly, the Lyonshead lifted up over the Rio but kept heading due west, toward the smoke.

Susie called again. "We're still heading right for the volcano. On purpose. Sir Ian is showing off." Another blast of hot air came through the phone and the line died.

"Sir Ian isn't afraid of anything," Jean Claude laughed. "Not always a good thing."

Jen didn't know if she could really smell the sulfurous fumes from the volcano, but she sure smelled something. A black plume of smoke floated to the west and formed a backward leaning mushroom cloud. At least the volcano wouldn't erupt in this direction. Jen smiled that the smoke blew in the opposite direction, until she realized that meant the prevailing wind would carry the balloon toward the caldera, the collapsed mouth of the volcano.

Sir Ian still had time to land in the Open Space surrounding the volcano; but instead, the balloon suddenly shot up even higher.

"Are they going to be all right?" Jen said.

"*Je ne sais pas*," said Jean Claude. "I don't know."

Jean Claude shifted into another gear and the Mountain Lyon smashed through another fence of another *rancho*. He then drove through several ditches before he came upon a large barrier that looked as if it might have guarded the beaches of his native Normandy. Jen was sure that he would attempt to take the Mountain Lyon right through the barrier, but instead he saw an opening to the right.

The balloon kept heading west. Jean Claude kept pace, even though he had to zigzag through city streets to get there. After a few more turns, he plunged the Mountain Lyon right into the muddy waters of the Rio.

"Can this thing swim?" Jen asked.

The water lay maybe two feet deep. The Mountain Lyon plowed right through like a tank, but its walls began to buckle under the water pressure. Some water seeped through the puncture on her side. Jen didn't know whether she felt exhilarated or panicked.

Jean Claude smiled and flexed his tattooed bicep. "Ghost Rider," he said.

"Aren't you worried that your boss might get a little pissed about your driving?" Jen asked.

"*Tant pis*," Jean Claude said. "*Je ne regrette rien.* Sir Ian can pay for it. All of it."

Apparently this had happened before. The Mountain Lyon did have several dents visible from the inside. Jen wondered what other rivers it had crossed. There was now a small puddle under her feet.

After smashing through some sand bars, Jean Claude took the Mountain Lyon up the banks of the Rio on the west side, and then negotiated through a few jogging paths. He nearly ran over a jogger and a roller-blader or two.

Jean Claude then found a west-bound dirt road, and pushed the vehicle up to ninety on a road that usually handled dirt bikes. Jen wondered how many checks Sir Ian had written on Jean Claude's behalf.

The Lyonshead floated too high to land in the Open Space in front of the volcano. Jen wondered if the volcano had some kind of tractor beam.

Jean Claude maneuvered the Mountain Lyon through a few more fences. He now took it on an even bumpier dirt road through Petroglyph National Park. The earth rumbled beneath her feet and Jen shuddered to think what would happen if the

Mountain Lyon started a landslide of the black volcanic rock. Many of them had ancient Native American petroglyphs, primitive line paintings with religious significance on the side. It would surely create an international incident.

Jean Claude wouldn't care. Sir Ian would just write another check.

Jen lost the balloon for a second in the smoke. "There it is!" she shouted.

The phone rang. "Jen, are you still there?" Susie yelled.

Another blast.

"Susie!"

Jen looked at her phone. The call had ended. The balloon floated even closer to the volcano summit. The plume of smoke bent back even further.

"Hurry!" Jen shouted at Jean Claude.

Jean Claude now abandoned the dirt road and switched to driving cross-country over the rocky mesa. Jen wished that she had worn a cast-iron bra.

The Lyonshead reached the airspace over the top of the caldera, maybe fifty feet above it. Sir Ian lowered the Lyonshead down slowly.

Jen punched in the number. "Susie!"

"Don't worry," said Jean Claude. "Sir Ian knows—"

Time stopped. Jean Claude didn't finish the sentence. What was he going to say? "Sir Ian knows what he is doing?" Well, did he?

"We won't make it," Jen said.

"*Que sera sera.* What will be, will be," Jean Claude replied.

The Mountain Lyon crashed through more brush, and finally Jean Claude took the vehicle onto the relative smoothness of a dirt road that circled the volcano. There was an ambulance marked LYON RESCUE already parked at the base of the volcano. How did the ambulance get here before the chase vehicle? They must have known this was Sir Ian's final destination and taken the freeway.

Jean Claude parked the Mountain Lyon next to the ambulance. The steep mountainside of volcanic rock would defy any direct assault. Jean Claude hurried out of the Mountain Lyon, and Jen followed.

"Susie!" Jen yelled into her phone again, unsure whether it was on. The Lyonshead was now directly above them, but soon passed them by.

Suddenly, a body fell out of the gondola and into the caldera. Jen didn't know if she actually heard the thud when it landed. She thought maybe she did.

Jen winced. Did they just throw Susie out as ballast to save their own lives?

The balloon rose over the cone. The volcano then emitted two quick blasts of smoke—the devil's farts. The balloon lifted up just in time as the smoke increased even further. Then the balloon disappeared into the smoke behind it.

"Where did it go?" Jen asked.

"*Je ne sais pas,*" Jean Claude said. He didn't move.

The wind shifted and they could now see the Lyonshead safe and sound on the other side of the volcano. But, Jen could not see Susie through all the smog.

Jen sniffed the smoke again. It smelled like . . . rubber. The tires!

"*Allez! Allez!*" Jean Claude yelled.

Jen heard vehicles roar up the access road, Paseo del Volcan. A TV news crew pulled up behind them. Sir Ian had probably alerted the media for this very occasion.

The balloon landed on firm ground and Susie was now visible. She waved to Jen. Sir Ian's private army grabbed the tethers and pulled the big balloon to the ground.

Susie jumped off. She glowed with sweat, but it was a good glow, like she'd been on the ultimate roller coaster and wanted to get back in line.

"That was totally cool," she said, hugging Jen. "You should do it."

Hal followed her off the gondola. They kissed as if danger was an aphrodisiac. He grabbed her ass one more time, and she snuggled even closer to him.

Instead of putting the balloon away, Sir Ian attached a tether to a mooring post in the ground. Apparently, someone had dug this into the earth years ago, as if anticipating this very balloon race.

"Jen, you really need to see the summit," Sir Ian said. "In fact, I quite insist on it." He smiled a sneaky smile.

Jen knew something was up—the mooring post out here, the fact that Susie smiled so broadly. Even Jean Claude seemed in on the act. Jen realized this entire chase was for her benefit.

"Don't worry," Sir Ian said in his BBC voice. "I'll keep the balloon tethered during our entire ascent; firmly tethered at all times."

Hal giggled, as if "firmly tethered" was part of his plan for Susie tonight.

Jen had another moment of panic, but Susie stared at her with anticipation. "C'mon Jen. It'll be fun. You need to lighten up. Besides, it's a surprise!"

Jen didn't want to look like a wimp in front of Susie, so she agreed. Sir Ian helped her into the gondola and in the process accidentally brushed her rear end. Perhaps not so accidentally, but Jen didn't mind.

"I fly into volcanoes every Saturday," he said. "Actually, I did for real. Once. It was when I had a ballooning show on a nature channel."

Jen had seen the show, once, and forced a smile. He knew what he was doing, right? The balloon inched upward with every gust of wind. Jen made it a point not to look down. Instead, she kept her eyes focused on Sir Ian's leonine smile. Who said the English had bad teeth?

Jen knew a big surprise awaited her, but she didn't know why she was so uneasy. The smoke was dying down. Whatever it was, Jen would pretend to be pleased. The balloon slowly rose above the hundred-foot mark. Jen smiled. The Laser Geisha balloon had drifted closer and from this viewpoint, Laser Geisha Black dominated the scene. Jen shivered.

As if on cue, the balloon rotated, as if the good Laser Geishas had pushed Black away. Jen waved to the two Japanese women flying the balloon. They waved back and took her picture as if she was someone famous. Then she remembered that Sir Ian was actually the famous one. She wasn't famous. Yet.

"Laser Geisha!" Jen yelled to them.

"Laser Geisha," they yelled back. They then shouted something in Japanese, and Sir Ian yelled something back, also in Japanese, before the Laser Geisha balloon lifted higher.

Jen turned her attention to Sir Ian's ruddy face. Not a hair of his sandy beard moved in the wind. She should enjoy this, she thought. When would she get the chance to fly over an active volcano with a dashing explorer again?

Jen could now see that the smoke coming from the caldera wasn't actually coming from deep in the recesses of hell. Instead, tires were burning in some kind of a pattern. The balloon rose to the top of the tether, and was now about two hundred feet in the air, the smoking caldera to the west. Jen could now make out the tire pattern clearly. It spelled out SONG in block letters.

"It was my boy's idea," Sir Ian said. "He had wanted it to spell 'Susie,' but we only had enough tires for four letters. It's actually better this way. 'Song' could refer to you as well.

Jen smiled. The Lyons were incredibly charming people. No one had ever spelled out her family name on top of a volcano before.

She hugged Sir Ian. "That is way cool." She held him tight; she was still terrified of heights, tether or no tether. Was he hugging her back a bit too hard? Oh well, she didn't mind. She broke the embrace for another look down.

There was something next to the "G."

It was a body. A dead body?

*Déjà freaking vu.*

Jen fainted.

# Ring of Fire

WHEN JEN AWOKE, HER eyes were momentarily blinded by the desert sunlight. She felt dizzy, and wasn't sure if she still floated in the air. The ground did not feel sturdy enough. It was as if the earth turned just a bit too fast. She took another deep breath and the earth slowed, and finally stopped. Jen carefully moved her arms to feel a blanket, and then reached further to find dry New Mexico dirt. She breathed a sigh of relief.

Susie face now blocked the sun. "Jen, are you all right? It was just a joke."

"What?"

"Sir Ian made a joke about sacrificing a virgin. It wasn't a real body."

It took another second for Jen to catch up. "A virgin?"

Sir Ian smiled. "Do you have something against virgins? Or volcanoes?"

Jen stared at him. Did he know? Did Sir Ian know that she had once been accused of murdering Ed Hobbs on top of that very volcano? Maybe he did know. He had access to infinite information. In his own book, the aptly named *Lyon Hearted*, he claimed that he had become a billionaire by knowing everything about everyone.

Jen frowned. "It's just the stress of being a new lawyer. I'm not myself these days."

She forced herself to sit up. A gust of wind nearly blew her back down before she anchored herself with her hands. She took a deep breath. She didn't want her new friends to see her fragility, so she forced herself to become a statue.

"Calm down," she whispered to herself. "Calm down."

Jen now forced herself to stand up. She wobbled for a second, as if her head now orbited the earth faster than her legs. Finally, after a few shaky steps, she could stand up straight.

"I need a drink," she said. "I'm totally thirsty."

Sir Ian handed her a crystal glass. Jen expected water and gulped at the contents like she was dying of thirst.

"Jen!" Susie shouted. "It's champagne! Wait for the toast! Be civilized."

Jen's mouth was no stranger to alcohol, even though she gave it up during the pendency of her murder charges and had never resumed drinking. She wasn't technically an alcoholic, but with all her medication a drink could be a very bad thing. Still, one drink wouldn't hurt her, right? She took another sip, then chugged the whole glass. By the time she reached the bottom, she felt soothed. This was some good stuff.

In light of the heat and stress, her blood alcohol limit left her mildly impaired. Sir Ian laughed and poured her another drink. One more wouldn't hurt.

"To early morning eruptions!" Sir Ian said in a toast.

Sir Ian went to the center of the circle of people. "I expect to see you all tonight at our party. The annual Lyon Aerospace Balloon Blow-out." He looked at Jen. "And no fainting allowed!"

Jen smiled after she downed another toast, but refused a third. Had she made it to point zero eight yet? The legal limit? "I'll be there," she said, forcing a smile.

"Oh by the way," Sir Ian added with a mischievous smile, "my critics have accused me of being unoriginal. I say that I know when a good idea truly works. Tonight's theme is a variation of an old classic, a pajama party. Just like at the Playboy Mansion. But our balloons are filled with hot air rather than silicone."

Jen and Susie looked at each other. Jen had long since tossed her collection of lingerie. Susie's outfits all had to pass muster with the LPGA tour.

"I don't have a thing to wear," Susie said.

"That could be the least of your problems," Jen said, noticing Hal had already opened another bottle of the expensive champagne and took a swig, as if downing a Mountain Dew. He looked like he was pre-emptively celebrating something.

Susie nodded and looked warily at Jen. "Could we go now? There's something I need to talk to you about."

# My Susie Q

HAL WENT UP INTO the balloon with his father for another tethered flight. Jen could see they were having a private conversation a hundred feet above the earth. Then the argument turned heated. Sir Ian grabbed his son and it looked like he might throw him out before the two made up with a hug.

Sir Ian's gigantic helicopter now landed behind them. Lyon Aerospace got its start in helicopters, although helicopters weren't the best business venture in today's economy.

When they found a spot alone, Susie sat with Jen. "While you were out, you kept saying 'Pink, don't.' What's that about?"

"It's weird," Jen said. "Sometimes I imagine that I am one of the Laser Geishas."

"I do too," Susie replied. "Well, geisha girl, you could be my *mama-san* tonight."

"What do you mean?"

Before, Susie could expand, Jean Claude came over. "*Mademoiselles*, we need to get back to the city," he said. The cousins reluctantly got back in the Mountain Lyon, sitting in the backseat as Jean Claude drove.

"Try not to kill us, okay?" Jen said.

"Remember, I don't work for you, *mademoiselle*," he said to Jen. "I work for Sir Ian."

"Well Sir Ian said you were to take me anywhere I want to go," Susie said. "So for today, at least, you work for me."

Jean Claude made a phone call and spoke quickly into the phone in French. He frowned when he hung up. "Where to *mes amies*?"

Jean Claude eased the vehicle onto the pavement of Paseo del Volcan, the access road back to the interstate. The motor raced too much, like a wild animal being forced back into its cage at the zoo. The vehicle was shaking; maybe the rough chase had taken its toll. After a few anxious moments, the Mountain Lyon entered I-40, and headed east. Jean Claude gunned it up to a hundred.

"I was a Grand Prix driver," he said. "I only crashed once."

Jen wanted to tell him to slow down again, but she knew it was useless to tell Jean Claude anything. What had he said? *"Je ne regrette rien."*

Jen regretted just about everything about that morning. No, she regretted absolutely everything. She had started to sober up and regrets flowed through her bloodstream. She hadn't even drunk that much.

Susie moved closer to Jen. "I really need to talk to you before the party."

"Sure."

"Let's meet around five o'clock. We need to get some things before tonight."

Jen tried to read Susie. What did the poor girl need? Why would she need Jen for anything? She was Susie Freaking Song. She had everything

"Is something wrong?" Jen asked.

"I'm worried and I need to talk to someone about the birds and the bees."

"The birds and the bees?" Jen took another look at Susie. Then everything dawned on her. Susie was probably a virgin. Duh, Jen thought. Of course she was. Susie had been protected her entire life. She spent most of her time on tour and didn't go to high school. Jen assumed that Susie had a private tutor. Boys her own age were probably afraid of her, and rightfully so. She could bench more than they could. Older men would be terrified to hit on her since she was underage. It would take a perfect storm like Prince Hal.

But why would anyone look to Jen for advice about sex? Jen had made every mistake in the book, and then some. She'd been a battered woman and an unwed mother. Her last beau, Dan, had fled to Hollywood without her. He still carried a torch for Luna.

Susie giggled. "You know how you're supposed to sacrifice a virgin, well that might change, real soon."

Jen smiled. "I'll talk to you about the birds and the bees tonight. I know about both of them."

"Thank you," Susie said. "I can't talk to my mom. Not any more. She knows too much. And I'm too embarrassed to talk to *your* mom. I need someone like a *peer*."

"A peer?"

"Yeah. A peer. Like the peer counseling they had at my middle school. I miss having people to talk to like I had when I went to public school in Arizona. Now I'm alone all the time."

"I'll be your peer," Jen said. "But let's do something while we talk."

"So we'll go shopping tonight, right?" Susie asked.

"Definitely," Jen said.

Jean Claude dropped Susie off at her hotel, the Hyatt downtown, the one with a red pyramid roof. After Susie left Jen's anxiety returned with a vengeance. Just sitting in this vehicle made her uptight.

Jean Claude looked at her. "*Mademoiselle?*"

Jen looked west. The last fumes of the volcano smoke had vanished into the crisp October sky. Way in the distance, Jen could spot Sir Ian flying off to his next event in his helicopter. Jen looked down at her shaking hands. The fake body on the volcano had affected her far more than she had supposed.

"I think I better see my doctor," Jen said to Jean Claude. "The volcano upset my stomach."

"Should I take you to the hospital?"

"My doctor doesn't usually work at the hospital."

# Thorazine Diary

DR. MARY ANN ROMERO picked up on the first ring. She quickly agreed to see Jen at the UNM Mental Health Clinic. "That time of the month?" Dr. Romero asked.

"Not really," Jen said. Jen usually saw Dr. Romero Mondays at noon and Wednesdays after work. Jen had qualified for mental health care back when she was indigent, and no one had bothered to charge her since then.

Now that I'm a real lawyer I'll have to start paying, Jen thought, frowning. She didn't know if that was a good trade: a real job for losing mental health coverage. Health care coverage could be expensive.

Jen didn't want Jean Claude to drop her off in front of the UNM Mental Health Clinic. Instead, she insisted he leave her in front of the traffic circle by the Bill Richardson Pavilion on the UNM North campus, two blocks away.

The hospital complex was gigantic, with multiple buildings that housed nearly every specialist known to medicine. It was famed as a trauma center. If you had an accident, UNM was the place for you. Jen had visited a friend in the hospital there once after the friend was hit by a car driven by a drunk driver. Jen hoped she would never have to go there again.

"What is the problem, *mademoiselle*?" Jean Claude asked.

"I've got a bad thyroid. I don't know how you say thyroid in French."

She wasn't exactly sure what a thyroid did in English either. She just took some medicine for it every day—at least that's what she thought. Or maybe it was for gout, whatever that was.

Jean Claude shrugged. He had no doubt contracted far worse diseases as a Legionnaire.

"*C'est la vie*." he said with a smile. Such is life.

Jen exited the main parking lot, dodged a speeding ambulance and walked the two blocks uphill to the clinic. This was Jen's neighborhood, adjacent to the prestigious UNM law and medical schools. It was an interesting area. The streets were named after colleges and the neighborhood had a vague college town feel, as many of the newer faculty members lived here.

The location of the clinic had been very convenient during law school. She could go to evidence class from eleven to noon, then see Dr. Romero and make it back for her one o'clock. Her daughter, Denise, lived with Nurse Song in the former group home on the other side of the university golf course. Her mom told one joke a year, and bragged that she had bought the old place "for a song," when state funding ran out and the place was decommissioned.

Considering the problems with parking at UNM, especially at the law school, Jen didn't worry about her fellow students knowing that she went to the mental health clinic. One classmate joked that he had to park at the University of Arizona Law School, then fly to UNM for class. Not that her classmates talked to her much anyway, her being an accused murderer and all.

Jen just muttered something about "getting something from her car," when her fellow students asked her why she walked so far away between classes.

The clinic itself could be clinically depressed. It was off Columbia Street. The pinkish paint was peeling, the bricks crumbling, the grass dying. A few young people smoked furiously outside, mumbling to themselves. They were the grad students who were doing internships analyzing people like Jen. A few graduate students actually became mental patients themselves, sometimes shifting from one role to another and then back at the end of every semester.

As she walked toward the building, Jen recognized Claus, the lawyer who reminded her of Santa. He even wore a red University of Utah sweatshirt, the fabric straining against his belly, which completed the image. He headed into the parking lot holding his young son's hand, as if comforting him after a tough trip to the dentist with the promise of the tooth fairy that night.

The boy looked as if he was about ten, and while he resembled Claus, he looked partly Native American with his long ponytail. Jen wasn't much at guessing diagnoses like other members of her family had been. Claus gave his son a hug.

Why hadn't my father ever given me a hug like that? Jen thought. If he had, I probably wouldn't be here right now.

The boy stayed put, like an obedient puppy. Claus hurried over to her, as much as a man of his girth could hurry.

Jen was a bit embarrassed. "Hi Claus. I'm here checking on the files of one of my criminal clients," she said.

Would he buy it?

Thankfully Claus didn't look at her directly. His son started moving again—performing various ballet moves as he walked, even twirling on his toes.

"It's my son," he said sheepishly. "I guess he's got seventh son syndrome."

Jen smiled. "I'm sure he'll be just fine."

"Think about my offer, Jen," he said. "We can team up on cases. Join forces, so to speak. That's so exciting that you know Susie Song. I bet she needs legal work every once in a while."

Jen laughed. "I think Susie's got everything under control."

Up ahead she saw the Laser Geisha balloon. The Japanese women must have tried to do a second ascent, or else had managed to stay aloft long enough to find a softer landing. The balloonists tried to land in the golf course, but the golfers shook their clubs like angry townsfolk in a monster movie, trying to scare the balloon away. But the balloon floated downward anyway. It had literally run out of hot air.

"Nothing can stay up forever," Claus said. "What goes up must come down."

Claus smiled. Jen blushed. She'd had two men smile at her on the same day.

Claus then hurried back to the boy and produced a lollipop from thin air. Whatever angst the boy had, his seventh son syndrome vanished with the treat.

Why couldn't I have had a dad like that? Jen thought again.

Jen had to press a button in the clinic door to get in the building. Inside, the grim faced guard looked through a window, recognized her, and buzzed her in.

"Hey Jen!" the pretty receptionist shouted at her. "Guess it's that time of the month."

Jen frowned. Why did everyone keep saying that?

"*Song sung blue!*" sang a long-time janitor. He was an African American man who did a surprisingly good imitation of Neil Diamond.

Jen felt like a regular walking into the bar on the TV show *Cheers*. This was not necessarily a good feeling to have at a mental hospital. Jen sat in a hard plastic chair in the grim waiting room in a corner, apart from the other patients. She saw a few people in orange jump-suits issued by the Metropolitan Detention Center. Another man, a dead ringer for a biblical prophet like Jeremiah, snarled at her.

"I know you," Jeremiah said. "You're Jen Song. We met last month."

She shook her head. He must have mistaken her for someone else.

Someone tapped on her on the shoulder, and Jen opened her eyes. She must have dozed off. Dr. Romero had finally emerged. The doctor wore business attire, a cheap knock off of Luna's dark Santa Fe outlet Brooks Brothers suit. She was dressed for success, even on a Saturday. "I've got our usual room," she said.

They retired into Dr. Romero's cramped office on the second floor. Every patient nodded at them as they passed. You know, everybody here really did know her. Why couldn't the lawyers treat her so nicely?

Inside, the office lacked windows. Dr. Romero threw down her pager in disgust. She actually broke the pager.

"Just as well," she said. "I never knew psychotics could be so needy." She then turned to Jen. "No offense."

"None taken," Jen said. "I guess."

They sat in silence for a moment, during which Jen felt self-conscious. The doctor looked at her expectantly, then down at the broken shards of her pager. Jen knew she should say something to justify the doctor's expense on her behalf.

"Well?" the doctor asked. "What caused it today?"

"The volcano, I guess. I was in Sir Ian's balloon, and we were right above it. I think it's finally time for me to deal with it. Deal with what really happened that night, and on the other nights."

Dr. Romero nodded. She pointed at the peeling walls. "You can tell they've painted over the walls in bits and pieces, but it's uneven."

"So?" Jen asked. Was the wall supposed to mean something? Jen noticed for the first time that the doctor's diploma from New Mexico Highlands hung in a precarious position, as if it was strategically placed to cover something up. Jen frowned. Dr. Romero had gone to New Mexico Highlands undergrad. It was an excellent school, particularly in psychology and social work. Still, Jen wanted to be treated by someone who had gone to Harvard, Yale, or at least Cornell.

"I do think we're going to resolve something, once and for all," the doctor said. "Unlike the wall, no more patchwork. Jen, there are some things you really need to know about yourself."

"I know my family has a history of mental illness on my mother's side." Jen remembered that her mother had told her about her grandmother, Un Chong, who had been institutionalized back in the day when the science of mental health wasn't an exact science.

"We're talking about you, though," the doctor said. "Let's focus on your issues."

"I know I was molested as a child at a camp up in Taos."

"You remember telling me that the next day you were rappelling off the climbing wall after the other girls had left? The counselor purposely dropped you almost to the ground and warned you never to tell what happened the night before."

Jen searched her thoughts. It was all so vague. "That was scarier than the incident itself." She stared at the uneven diploma. "I'm kinda blocked right now. I don't know if I can talk about it, but I want to try. I know something is wrong."

Dr. Romero stood, and went to a metal file cabinet with three large drawers. Jen noticed markings on the cabinet. One drawer was labeled "A to L," another "M to Z". The bottom drawer had one marking on it: "Jen Song."

"I have a whole drawer dedicated to me?"

"Those are just my files here," Dr. Romero said, trying to be friendly. "You should see what I keep in the archives in the main file room on the south campus."

Jen didn't know whether she should laugh or not. "So what's going on?"

"You really don't remember?"

"Bits and pieces," Jen said. "I kinda know why I freaked out at the volcano just now. There was a fake dead body on the caldera that brought back the memory of Ed Hobbs, my old boss. And I guess Adam Marin, my boyfriend. He died up there, too."

"That's a good start," Dr. Romero said. "How well do you remember what happened?"

"I know it has something to do with my fear of heights from that day at summer camp. I've been blocking it out, just like you've been telling me I'm supposed to do. That is what I'm supposed to do, right?"

"That's been your treatment plan, yes."

"But I want to explore what happened that night, the night on the volcano."

Dr. Romero smiled. "Are you sure?"

That's what her father had always said when he was about to tell her bad news. She shivered for a moment, but then nodded. "I'm sure."

Dr. Romero took a deep breath, as if girding for combat. "I'll hypnotize you again."

Again?

Jen felt uneasy. She remembered that she came here every day during law school, but she was a bit vague on what happened. Yes, she had been hypnotized a lot in the beginning. But this last year, clerking for Luna while waiting for the Bar results, she just did straight therapy, right?

Why was her memory so hazy?

Jen's anxiety increased. She wasn't sure she wanted to know what had happened.

"One thing, and this is really important. This is totally confidential? You won't tell the Bar?"

Dr. Romero smiled. "Everything here is confidential unless you state you are about to commit a *pending* crime. As for the past, the charges against you were dropped with prejudice. No one can bring them up again. I think it would be good for you finally to reconcile with your past, so you can get closure."

Jen looked down at her purse. She frowned.

"The Thorazine that you prescribe for me," Jen said. "And the other drugs. They're not for my thyroid, are they?"

# Hypnotherapy

IT TOOK A LONG time for the hypnosis to take its hold on Jen. There were a few knocks on the door that nearly jolted her out, but Jen finally crossed over. Dr. Romero said something about opening a door at the bottom of the stairs, and she forced herself through to the other side.

On the other side of the door, Jen stood in darkness for a moment, and then fireworks went off. Instead of revealing a crumbling clinic office, the light of the fireworks revealed the top of the volcano on that fateful Fourth of July.

Jen shivered as if the night wind suddenly blew into the office. Jen now floated above the scene, looking downward. There was something about the light in her vision. It was a garish, two-dimensional light that made her feel she was in an anime cartoon.

"I see dead people," she said out loud. The very late Ed Hobbs was there, looking very much alive, even in his anime state. Her former friend, the late Sandrina, stood there as well. At six feet tall, with blonde hair flowing down her back, Sandrina had looked like a cartoon even in real life.

And right below her, she saw her younger self, wearing a tight Laser Geisha Pink tank top.

"Man, I was trashy back then," Jen said to herself.

The people below could not see or hear her.

More fireworks exploded overhead, and she shuddered as a boom rocked the summit.

Down below, on the caldera, Sandrina stripped down to her bra, revealing massive mountains of her own. Hobbs undressed down to his underwear and lay on a down comforter. He was fat. Two words, Jen said to herself. "Sit-ups."

Sandrina approached the fat man. She had a detached look, as if she was counting dollar bills on each fold of Hobbs's flesh. Hobbs turned to the younger Jen. He now took off his underwear and looked even *less* impressive naked.

"Jen," he said, "there's something I want you to try."

"Don't do it," Jen yelled to her younger self. "Don't!"

Younger Jen walked slowly toward the naked man. Jen tried to read her younger self's expression, but failed. What had she been thinking?

"Put your hands around my neck," he said. "And squeeze until I can barely breathe."

Sandrina mounted Hobbs down below. "Come on Jenita," she said in her slurred Brazilian accent. "It'll be fun. Just like they do in Rio."

Jen could now read her doppelganger's mind and vivid memories of Hobbs hitting her, Hobbs nearly raping her, and warning her not to say anything flooded into her brain. But it wasn't just Hobbs; it was all the men in her past, all the way back to the evil camp counselor who nearly dropped her. Hobbs wasn't Hobbs anymore. He was all of them. Hobbs's face morphed into every face all at once, one after the other.

Jen then realized something else; the woman down below wasn't her younger self any more. The woman had transformed into Laser Geisha Pink herself in all her animated glory. Laser Geisha Pink had Jen's face, but now wore the pink kimono outfit straight from the cartoon.

Pink put her hands around the man's neck and squeezed, and then squeezed tighter.

"It's all in fun!" Sandrina said. "But don't go too far."

Hobbs turned blue in the firelight and signaled he wanted to stop.

Pink kept squeezing.

"You might want to stop." Sandrina said. "He's turning blue."

Pink kept squeezing.

Why didn't I stop? Floating Jen asked. Why did I keep going?

She tried to play defense lawyer as Pink's hands continued their work. Battered woman syndrome? Hobbs had abused her, physically and mentally. No one could deny that she didn't use all the cards in her deck.

Irresistible impulse? The chorus of old boyfriends continued their chant. "Harder! Harder!"

At that moment Pink vanished, and a younger Jen took her place again, back in that silly tank top. She released her grip, astonished at her own power.

It was too late. Way too late. Hobbs lay there dead. Totally dead.

✝

"Do you want to keep going?" a voice asked from beneath the volcano.

It took Jen a moment to realize that the voice belonged to Dr. Romero. Jen opened her eyes to see herself in the office, standing right next to the doctor. Dr. Romero held her hand in reassurance. The grip felt warm. The rest of Jen's body was cold.

"There's more?"

# Trancing With The Stars

JEN HAD A CHOICE. She could slip back into the trance and relive more memories, or break the spell and come back up for air. It wasn't much of a choice.

"Bring me back," Jen cried, as much as someone can cry in a hypnotized trance. "And this time, I want to remember everything."

It took just as long to come back as it did to put her under. The mental door back to reality kept slamming in her face, and would not let her out. Once Jen finally reached a semblance of consciousness, she opened her eyes.

"What's going on?" It took her a moment for her eyes to adjust to the light.

"Wait a moment for it all to sink in," Dr. Romero said.

Jen noticed that Dr. Romero had bottled water on her counter. She grabbed it and chugged it. The volcano had made her thirsty.

"This has happened before?" Jen asked. "Me freaking out?"

"Several times."

"And I come here?"

"You come here twice a week. You know that."

"Duh. I mean I come here after my little breakdowns?"

"You come here once a month and it's usually on a Saturday afternoon, like this time. I can set my watch by you."

Jen racked her brain. She did have a few foggy recollections of getting hypnotized. So that was what everyone meant when they shouted it was "that time of the month."

Jen also remembered when the doctor "presented" her as a case study, the "patient of the month," to a weekly roundtable. Jen explained to the table that she didn't know why she was there. The people at the table took notes as if she was the professor.

That day, for some reason, Jen talked about her life, starting from that day at camp. She didn't know if she made it to the Hobbs incident before they sent her out of the room. She never learned what her diagnosis was, although someone muttered something about her having some, but not all, of the symptoms of dissociative identity disorder. Why couldn't she remember? What had the doctor done to her? Had she asked the doctor to do this?

"I'll remember this time?" Jen asked.

"Are you sure you want to remember the truth?"

Jen took a deep breath. Several years had passed since the incident. She had finished law school. Jesus Christ, she was a bona fide lawyer. She knew she could look anyone in the eye, even Jack Nicholson, and handle the truth.

"I don't want to faint in a balloon again. I want to remember."

Dr. Romero sighed. "Then you'll remember," she said. "We can come back for the rest some other time."

"The rest?" Jen asked. "You mean there's *more*?"

"As I said, you've had a few other psychotic breaks. I can put you back under if you want to explore them this instant, but I would advise against it."

Psychotic breaks did not sound like sunny moments on the beach, not when she was starting her grown up career. "I'm good, thanks," Jen said. "I'm good right now."

"I wouldn't say that," Dr. Romero replied. "You're not totally good right now. I don't think you fully understand how deep the psychosis goes."

"I think someone said something about dissociative something or other, what used to be called multiple personalities."

"You only seem to have one alternate personality, Laser Geisha Pink."

"Well, I got that going for me." Jen stood up.

"Although there was a short period when you also assumed the identity of Nastia, an Eskimo."

"*Inupiat*," Jen said. "There's a difference.

"You told me there was a real woman named Nastia, and that your sub-conscious—"

"That was a tough period of my life. I even faked my own death because I wanted a fresh start and needed to be someone else for a while, someone who wasn't afraid of her own shadow."

"Well, Nastia hasn't asserted herself in quite some time." Jen hadn't thought of Nastia as a distinct personality, but she felt a little more comfortable in her own skin. She liked being Jen Song again.

"Does anyone know? About me? About my turning into a cartoon character?"

"You don't actually become a real cartoon character, you just assume her personality," Dr. Romero said. "The Board of

Bar Examiners had some concerns, of course. They put you under my care for a year. You do remember that?"

"Duh," Jen said again. She knew she came here to the clinic for a reason. She just hadn't realized that her trips to Dr. Romero had been *mandatory*. "So am I a murderer?"

Dr. Romero tried to put on her best doctor face and use her best doctor voice. "Murder is a legal term," she said. "Jen, you *were* mentally ill. Had your case gone to trial, you would have been found not guilty by reason of insanity, and I would have offered my expert opinion that you should not be held legally responsible for your actions."

"A lawyer who's not legally responsible for her actions. That's kinda funny."

"As I said, you *were* mentally ill at the time of the Hobbs incident. I don't consider you a danger to yourself or others now, so I don't think you should be committed to an institution."

"That's nice to know. So am I a serial killer?"

"I wouldn't say that three deaths make you a serial killer."

"Three?" Jen was thunderstruck.

"All done under exceptional circumstances."

"Like what?'

"They all tend to involve heights. Because of the camp incident, the dangling from the wall when you were very little, you suffer from acrophobia, and that can trigger the onset of this other personality, the one you call Pink. The switch to other personalities generally involves interaction with men who have violently and/or sexually assaulted you. But now, even with your meds, that's not going to happen anymore."

"Are you sure?"

"Yes, even with your meds, you passed your competency and sanity tests with flying colors."

"So am I a good guy or a bad guy? Am I Jen Song or Laser Geisha Pink?"

The doctor said nothing for a moment. Then, "Which one do you want to be?"

Jen didn't have to think. "I want to be the good guy, of course. I want to be the hero. But am I? Am I going to kill anyone again?"

"No, Jen, you won't." Dr. Romero said.

"Even if I'm in these exceptional situations?"

"As long as you keep taking your meds, you'll be fine." Dr. Romero said. "And avoid certain circumstances."

"Like rapists in high places."

"Well, any stressful situation. As long as you stay away from those stimuli you should be fine and be able to function within normal parameters. You'll make a fine lawyer. I've staked my clinical reputation on it."

Jen took another look around the crumbling room. The diplomas and the feminist artwork could only hide a few of the cracks and pieces of the uneven paintwork. The room looked like the maintenance had been done by the patients, as opposed to skilled workers.

"That doesn't reassure me."

"It's all I have for you."

"I just hope it's enough."

# Mother's Day

JEN WALKED SLOWLY OVER to the law school on the south side of
Stanford Avenue, a two-lane street with man-made speed
bumps to slow drivers who were taking the short cut to class.
The little adobe law campus was nestled against the UNM
North golf course like a country club.

Jen only lived a few blocks away, but didn't want to walk
home so soon to sit alone in the Caddy Shack with her demons.
She sat on a bench in the law school parking lot, with a soothing view of the golf course, and used her to phone to Google
herself. After a few clicks, she read the stories of the Hobbs
murder and how she had been a suspect. There was nothing
about the more recent case where she had faked her death except for one simple correction on page D-2 where the *Albuquerque Journal* regretted its error in stating she was dead.

She then typed in "Jen Song" and "law school," and found
an article in the student paper and a nasty letter to the editor
that she had written, but nothing else. Thankfully, a domestic
violence scandal involving a local artist had pushed her off the
front page.

Jen tried to remember her days here at UNM. She had lived in an iron bubble. She didn't talk in class and the few times professors called on her, she had the right answer most of the time. Jen looked up from her phone and out onto the golf course. She liked this oasis of relative greenery here in the high desert, although the nine holes of UNM North hardly constituted a world-class course. As a foursome of young women passed by, laughing, Jen wished she could have been a star like Susie. The young women teed off and moved on.

Still curious, Jen picked up her phone again and googled Sir Ian. He was a billionaire, many times over, and an Oxford grad from one of the colleges that was named after a saint. He had then gone on to Cal Tech. Sir Ian had made his fortune in aerospace, and was now looking to become the leading owner of space technology. He was single, according to the gossip mags, and supposedly distraught after his wife's ballooning accident.

"I would love to be a billionaire," she said. Didn't there used to be a show about marrying billionaires?

The phone felt heavy in her hand. Jen couldn't concentrate, and she had an urge to check on her daughter. The former group home now occupied by her mother and Denise was within walking distance. It was, in fact, just on the other side of the golf course, so she hoofed over there, taking the dirt trail that skirted the perimeter. As she passed the Pamela Minzner Court of Appeals Building, she realized that the thirty foot high south wall could pass for a stucco version of the monolith in the movie *2001: A Space Odyssey*. She desperately wished the monolith could be a doorway to another dimension.

As she came to the leafy street on the south edge, she didn't know what she wanted to say to her daughter. "I'm sorry," seemed so inadequate. Perhaps "I love you," was better. Or maybe, "Can you forgive me?"

Jen knocked on the door of the home, a small adobe building behind a cancer recovery center. The group home had been the land of misfit toys, and housed children with various mental and emotional afflictions who had no place to go. Now Nurse Song had the place all to herself, but couldn't figure out what to do with it. It was still technically zoned as a "group home," even though the group consisted of two people, Nurse Song and Denise.

During the dispute with Denise's late father's family, both sides had stipulated that Denise would stay with Nurse Song pending final resolution. After six years, final resolution was nowhere in sight.

Jen knocked again. Nothing. She knocked louder. She really wanted to see her daughter.

Her mother finally came out. "She's napping. She can't see you now. Why do you always come here on Saturdays when you know she's napping?"

Jen shuddered. This must be another part of her ritual. She would go to therapy and then reach out to her daughter. This monthly custom meant that she loved Denise, and that was a good thing, right?

"Tell Denise I love—"

Before Jen could say more, her phone rang, and the Laser Geisha theme song sounded more urgent than usual. She must have hit the volume key while she was under hypnosis.

"Please go," her mother said. "It's not the right time."

The song repeated, faster and louder, as if God definitely wanted her to answer it.

"Hello?" Jen spoke into the phone.

"Jen, it's me." It was Susie. "We still on for the night? I need to talk with you like right now. It's really important."

"I'm near the UNM golf course," Jen said as she walked away from the group home, squeezed through a notch in the fence and went back across the course.

"Golf course?" said Susie. "That's one of the things I want to talk to you about. I'll meet you in the front parking lot."

# Swing for the Stars

IT WAS ONLY A few hundred yards walk around the edge of the course, but Jen was surprised to find the black and gold hunk of metal that was the Mountain Lyon already waiting in the parking lot. The new dents from this morning's adventure were obvious.

The stucco of the monolith that formed the west wall of the Court of Appeals Building had now turned pink in the setting sun. Still, plenty of golfers were trying to sneak in a few practice holes before the sun set. Jean Claude exited the vehicle and performed a quick recon of the area. Satisfied that the coast was clear, he knocked on the back side window.

Jen expected Susie to exit the vehicle in her standard polo shirt and baseball cap, but instead she emerged in a hooded sweatshirt and the world's biggest sunglasses. With her imposing height, under the sweatshirt she looked more like a male boxer hiding a black eye than a teenaged female golfer. Thankfully, Albuquerque was filled with aspiring fighters who jogged around the golf course all the time between fights. No one gave her a second glance.

Even so, a few golfers exiting into the parking lot did recognize her, but one look from Jean Claude and a pat on his sidearm silenced them instantly. If the French army had had even ten soldiers like Jean Claude, they would have had a far better reputation. They certainly would have won at Waterloo.

The three walked onto the trail around the golf course, which began on the far side of the parking lot and proceeded counter-clockwise to the north. The course was only slightly greener than the trail, so it was hard tell where the golfer's domain ended and the runners' territory began. A sign on the trail warned PROCEED AT YOUR OWN RISK. For Jen's taste, this public golf course was a bit too public.

"Sir Ian wants to become one of my sponsors," Susie said. "One of his aerospace companies wants to switch over and manufacture golf clubs. Swords into plowshares, or whatever it is."

"Planes into golf clubs," Jen said. She felt a little cocky hanging with Susie, even though they were cousins. "Does *Pepe Le Pew* have to follow us?"

Jean Claude swore at her under his breath in French.

"It's cool as long as we walk where he can see us," Susie said. "I guess we can walk out and then double-back."

"We're going to have to double-back eventually; the trail gets kinda sketchy on the other side."

"Sketchy?" Susie asked. "You mean it's hard to follow or the people there are suspect?"

"Both."

Susie and Jen kept walking on the dirt trail that wound around the slightly battered public course. Jen had trouble keeping up with her cousin's long strides. They passed a relatively famous mixed martial arts (MMA) fighter in his TapouT sweatshirt, but he was so into his own workout that he didn't bother to glance at Jen and Susie. Susie finally felt safe enough to take off her hood, and revealed that she was indeed wearing her famous cap.

Bad move.

A golfer teeing off on the third hole recognized her immediately. "Susie Song!"

Susie grimaced.

"How do I keep from slicing, Susie?" he yelled.

"Just keep your eye on the ball," she said. "Don't look at me when you swing."

"You want to swing for us?" he asked. There was the slightest hint of a leer in his voice

Susie pretended to ignore it, and walked over to the tee. Jean Claude moved closer, just in case.

The golfer was a middle-aged man, who was playing with his wife. Susie borrowed one of the man's clubs and nodded at him. "Keep your eye on the ball."

She swung that famous swing of hers and the ball sailed three hundred yards into the course. It nearly hit the law school.

"You're so beautiful," he said.

"Well, so are you," she laughed.

For a moment the dude smiled as if he had a chance.

"I've got to go," she said. "Keep swinging for the stars."

"You're amazing, Susie," the man said. His wife looked like she wanted to punch him.

Susie hurried back to the trail just as Jean Claude was about to lose his patience. "We probably better double-back," she said.

"Does this happen regularly?" Jen asked.

"This is one of the good days. Sometimes I have to do something like that twenty times an hour. Most golfers are cool. Once they see me hit, they don't bother me at all."

"You get off on that, don't you? Flirting with older guys."

"Maybe I have daddy issues, since I never knew my dad. Besides that, I told you, I'm totally alone. I have no friends my own age. I can't even go to a mall. Little girls treat me like a rock star."

"You are a rock star."

"I'm just me."

They sat on a stone bench near a bubbling water fountain on the north end of the course, close to the bustling traffic of Indian School Road. There was an amazing New Mexico sunset to the west. The clouds looked like red battle cruisers out of *Star Wars*.

Jean Claude kept his fifty-foot perimeter, and continually scanned to see if there were any hostiles nearby. Past the green of the golf course oasis, Susie and Jen scanned the high desert to the west. There were no trees that they could see stretching toward Arizona. Jen grimaced when she saw the volcano.

Susie didn't notice Jen's momentary discomfort. Instead, she glanced to make sure Jean Claude was out of ear-shot before beginning.

"You would think the golf course is the only place I'm really happy," Susie said. "The rest of my life is so complicated. Here, all I have to do is put a silly ball into a hole."

Susie paused. Off in the distance, the middle-aged man searched for Susie's ball.

"Really? I've always been a square peg in a triangular hole," Jen said. "But you, I mean, you're Susie Song. Talk about being perfect for something, for fitting in."

Susie frowned. "I don't know. Golf is my sanctuary, but it's a crappy one. I totally hate golf. Why did God have to make me good at something I hate? I like volleyball, basketball, all of those. But I'm too slow and clumsy. I mean, I was almost six feet tall when I was twelve."

"I can relate to the slow and clumsy part," Jen said. "So what do you want to do with your life?"

Susie thought. "Well, it's cool that you're finally a lawyer. That might be something, helping people out."

"I don't know how cool it is," Jen said. "I don't think you want to be a lawyer. It's a lot less exciting than you think. What do you really want to do, Susie?"

"I want to direct."

"What?"

"It's what actresses say when they get too old. I guess I'm sorta like an actress in a way."

"Are you kidding?"

"I don't know. I always liked to draw, cartoons and stuff. That's why I was so glad that we worked out a sponsorship with the Laser Geisha people. I would love to have my own production company doing animation, you know, make cartoons for little girls all over the world."

"Well you'll be able to do that with all your money."

"I only have money if I golf. Well, I only have money if I *win* at golf. And actually *I* don't have any money at all. I think all my millions are swimming around somewhere in the saline waters of my mom's newest boobs."

Jen covered her own chest with her arms.

Susie sighed. "I missed the cut yesterday in Sir Ian's tournament. I swung a little too hard, and it went into the rough. Not once, but like three times. I mean, everyone says I've got so much potential. What's potential anyway? You can't live on potential. You actually have to put the ball in the hole eighteen times a day for four days straight. And suppose no matter how hard you try, the ball doesn't want to go in that little hole?"

"Are you seeing anybody?" Jen asked. "For your issues?"

"You heard I did treatment when your mom ran that program. I stayed at the house over there." She pointed at the house on the south side of the golf course. I wasn't famous yet, although I'd won a few junior amateurs in Tucson and all of a sudden every one anointed me the golden child. I didn't feel worthy, so after a few anxiety attacks and some cutting incidents, I ended up over there."

Jen now noticed several scars on Susie's muscular forearm. Most were healed, but some looked fairly recent.

"My mom used to be a workaholic," Jen said. "But now, Denise is like the daughter she never had. My mom ignored me, so I think she's trying to make it up with Denise."

"She made it up with me, too." Susie looked at the home. "Do you want to go over there?"

"That might not be a good idea," Jen said. "Nurse Song doesn't like Denise's routine interrupted."

Jen tried to see a troubled teen trapped in Susie's tall, elegant body, but couldn't. Susie was still a rock star to her.

"I wish I had your problems," Jen said.

"No you don't," said Susie. "And no, I can't see anybody normal. Guys my age freak out if I show interest in them. That's why I flirt with older guys, like you just saw. For me, it's totally safe."

They stared at the sunset, which was now over the fifth hole. Blood red clouds hid the volcanoes. Jen was glad the clouds were there; she could pretend the volcanoes didn't exist. Behind them, to the east, the Sandias glistened in the sunset, and turned as red as granite can turn.

Jen flashed back. She had a similar moment like this with Luna, back when she was the defendant and Luna the lawyer. Now, it was as if the roles were reversed. She was the grown-up and Susie was the child. Susie was the daughter she never had. Oops. She did have a daughter. Jen thought again about Denise, who was locked behind doors less than a mile from here.

"So you want me to give you the birds and the bees talk now?" Jen asked, doing her best imitation of her own mother.

Susie smiled. "Not here. We gotta get us some clothes. It's getting chilly; we probably need overcoats too. I'm from Arizona; my blood can't handle this cooler weather."

"We can go to Walmart."

Susie's face tightened. "I don't think you understand my life, Jen. I can't go to Walmart. Right now, here, I'm just me, but if I go to Walmart, I'm Susie Song."

"Well, I'm always me," Jen said. But was she?

# Queen of the Castle

THEY DECIDED TO GO to Walmart after all. It was after six and most other stores in Albuquerque had already closed for the day. They most certainly couldn't risk the mall. Susie had told her horror stories of being mobbed. Even in the car when she was just thinking about walking inside the store, Susie looked agitated.

After Jean Claude parked the car, Susie handed Jen two crisp hundred-dollar bills. "Just run in and grab two overcoats," She gave Jen her size. "Flasher overcoats. You know what I mean."

Jen laughed.

"And keep the change."

Jen hurried inside, found two trench coats at an amazing Walmart everyday low price.

"So what are we flashing?" Jen asked Susie on the phone. Jen had taken a picture of the coats before purchasing them, sent the photo to Susie, and then called her for approval.

"I don't know yet," Susie replied. "We'll figure it out. You know you are my new best friend."

"BFF," Jen said. "Best friends forever."

"BFF," Susie said. "And I hope forever is a long time."

Jen returned to the Mountain Lyon. The car attracted attention because of its bulk, but people avoided it as if it had a force field. She saw Susie's face through the darkened window, looking like a ghost. Susie ducked when she saw a woman walk by with five kids, four of them girls. Thankfully, the kids didn't notice Susie.

"Where to next?" Jen asked when she got inside.

Susie smiled and pointed to an ad in the *Weekly Alibi*, the local tabloid.

"Are you sure?" Jen asked.

Jean Claude was not so *enchante* to drive them to the Kastle of Love, a gigantic "adult" emporium a few blocks away on Central Avenue. They pulled into the parking lot of a gigantic cinderblock warehouse. The warehouse looked like a smaller version of the downtown prison.

During her waitressing days, Jen had bought a few of her outfits—and all of her shoes—here. The Kastle sat only a few blocks from her mother's house, in a bad neighborhood known as the War Zone.

"Why here?" Jen asked.

"Time to buy clothes for the evening. And I'm betting that there won't be any little girls or golfers coming up to me."

Jean Claude got out first and did a quick recon. Other than a few bums sitting on the corner, the coast was reasonably clear. The three of them walked toward a mechanical door that slid open as they neared it. "This place reminds me of Bangkok when I was in the Legion," Jean Claude said.

Susie panicked when she saw the surveillance camera over the door, its red light on.

"Don't worry," the pimply clerk said. "As long as you got cash and don't shoplift, we don't care who you are, and we destroy the tapes at the end of the day. We're very discrete."

Jen nodded. If the store shared a picture of Susie with the tabloids her career could be ruined.

"Could I see an ID?" the clerk asked. "No one under eighteen can enter."

Susie was only seventeen and Jen realized she was contributing to the delinquency of a minor. A millionaire minor, to be sure.

"She's my daughter," said Jen. The licenses both said "Song," and there was a clear resemblance. "I had her very young."

"She's gotta be eighteen," the pimply clerk said.

Susie stared at the world on the other side of the counter. "Wow!" Susie looked at packages that contained a purported magic powder for "maximum female response."

"Does that stuff really work?" Susie asked. "And what's a maximum female response?"

Jen knew she would have to do something or the girl would die of curiosity.

"Actually, the state law is quite clear," Jen said, doing her best impression of a lawyer's voice. "Young people are allowed to enter adult establishments when accompanied by an adult or guardian. It's law 30-20-17 of the New Mexico Statutes Annotated."

Jen made that up, of course. She had probably given the citation for armed robbery for all she knew, but she sure sounded convincing.

The clerk shrugged. "Whatever. Just make sure you buy something."

"Do you have shoes in my size?" Susie asked.

"Of course. We get a lot of trannics," the clerk explained. "It's good to see *real* women in here for a change." He had a weird grin, as if he'd love to help Susie with her shoes.

"I don't know how real we are," Jen said as Susie ran down the aisle to the clothing section.

"This is like an adult Disney store!" Susie said. She picked up the highest heels they had, nearly twelve inches, and saw the shoes fit her size 11 feet.

"You can give me the talk now," Susie said to Jen.

"What talk?"

"The birds and the bees. I've got a feeling I'm about to get stung."

As Susie tried on the shoes, Jen told her about the "birds and the bees" as best she could. Susie asked surprisingly naïve questions, including, "Will it hurt?"

The pimply clerk came over a few times, but Jen shooed him away. Each time he retreated to the back room. Jen didn't know what—or worse, who—they kept back there.

"Now we have to buy our outfits," Susie said. "I want to make a statement."

Jen recognized a Native American transsexual named Pocahontas, a regular visitor to the UNM Pharmacy and Metropolitan courthouse, spying on them from the other end of the aisle. Navajos used the term "two spirit" for someone like Pocahontas, and she certainly had spirit to spare.

"Susie Song!" Pocahontas said. "I did *you* for my last show!"

Pocahontas frowned when she saw the outfit Susie had her eye on, a severe black outfit that looked appropriate for a minister's wife. It was by far the most boring outfit in the store.

"Girl, you gonna be playing golf the rest of your life if you wear that."

Pocahontas grabbed the black outfit out of Susie's hand. "Let me be your guide, your spirit guide to the dark side. Let me take you from mild child to wild child."

"Is that okay, Jen?" Susie asked.

"Knock yourself out," Jen said. It wasn't like she really was the girl's mother.

Pocahontas decided that Susie was her new personal project. A few short minutes later Susie was too embarrassed to come out of the dressing room and didn't want Jen to come in. Pocahontas entered, though, and made a few adjustments. When Pocahontas left the changing room, she said with a smile. "My work here is done, Sugar."

Hers may be done but my work is just beginning Jen thought when Susie made Jen pick out an exact duplicate of the outfit.

"We really are the Laser Geishas now," Susie said.

"I don't know if that's such a good thing," Jen replied.

Susie kept asking questions as they wandered through the magazine and adult video sections, and the conversation ended up a lot more in depth than Jen had expected.

"What is 'DVD-A?'" asked Susie.

"Hopefully you'll never find out," said Jen.

There was even a "*hentai*" section, erotic Japanese anime.

"That's the kind of stuff I want to draw," said Susie.

Jen looked at Susie with horror, until Susie started to laugh.

"Don't you know when I'm kidding?"

"Not yet."

Jen was hit with *déjà vu*. She had said the same words to Luna so many times, back when Luna was the lawyer, and she was the defendant. But, here in the Kastle of Love, Jen took on the adult role.

"We're the 'Song Sisters,'" Susie said. "And we're ready to rock your world."

The Song Sisters. Jen liked being on the same team as Susie. Eventually the two filled up a shopping cart with various items and made their way up to the pimply clerk.

# Chicken Fried Whale

IT WAS NOW COMPLETELY dark outside. The last of the sun's rays had set over the west, and the garish lights of Route 66 now illuminated the old motels along the street that had been built during the Great Depression. An old jalopy drove by, probably heading to California. Tom Joad from the *Grapes of Wrath* himself could have been driving, happy to be getting the hell out of Albuquerque.

"*Tonight's the night,*" Susie sang. "*It's gonna be all right.*"

"Bob Dylan. 'Lay Lady Lay?'" Jen asked.

"Rod Stewart," Susie said. "'Tonight's the Night,' Jen. I love you and all, but you're a terrible guesser."

"The right answer is always on the tip of my tongue," Jen said. "It just gets lost on the way out."

Jean Claude took a call. "Sir Ian insists that you come to him at once."

"Should we change in the car?" Susie asked.

"Whatever you want," Jean Claude said.

"Ah, that might not be a good idea," Jen said, "and I don't want to go back to the Kastle and deal with Pocahontas again."

"We can change in there," Susie said, pointing to a Long John Silver's. "It looks empty. Well, empty enough. I need to use the bathroom and I don't want to go back into the Kastle either. I think Pocahontas acted a little too happy seeing me in my underwear. Let's just say he's still a man and all, and I don't trust the clerk and those cameras."

"I don't see many cars," Jen said. "It should be fine."

They walked to the restaurant on the other side of the parking lot. It faced a particularly bad stretch of old Route 66, and the greasy food smelled like it came from an ancient, broken down truck. Near the door, a Native American man with a gray ponytail asked if they wanted to purchase some fry bread and fresh mutton.

Jen wondered if an old whaling boat would smell like this. Perhaps, if the crew tried to deep-fry Moby Dick and serve him on the world's largest side order of fries. Inside, the restaurant wasn't quite empty.

A prostitute, well, a probable prostitute, stumbled out of the bathroom, swaying on even higher heels than Susie had just purchased. Jen tried to decide whether the woman was a crack whore or a meth whore. The difference between them was about five dollars a trick, and a tooth or two. This woman had no teeth except for one molar on the back of each side. Jen guessed meth.

"Susie Song!" Ms. Meth said. "I know someone who wants to meet you!"

Ms. Meth ran out of the restaurant before Jean Claude could catch her. The effects of meth could sometimes mimic performance-enhancing steroids.

"Wow, you really can't go anywhere Susie, can you?" Jen said.

Susie shook her head as she went into the bathroom. She really must have had to go, since the bathroom here looked even worse than the one at the Kastle.

Jen stood guard as Susie changed, and Ms. Meth returned just as Susie emerged in her slinky outfit. Thank goodness she was well-covered by her new overcoat. It had only been minutes. The meth whore must have ducked into one of the nearby hourly motels that dotted this stretch of road. Jen was surprised that Ms. Meth dragged with her the cutest twelve-year-old girl. The girl could have been one of the *Cosby* kids. How could this wholesome little girl come from such a mom?

The young girl went to Susie and begged for an autograph. "You're like my idol," the girl said. "You're my role model."

Susie's face brightened. The little girl wore a faded pink Susie Song T-shirt. "Could you sign my shirt?" the child asked. Susie borrowed a pen from Jen and then scribbled, "To Shaniqua. Swing for the stars."

"Thank you," the girl said. "I *will* swing for the stars."

Susie reached into her wallet and gave the girl a hundred-dollar bill. She then pointed to Jean Claude and turned to face the girl's mother.

"You buy this girl something nice. I'll make sure this man comes back to see that you have."

Jean Claude gave his best French Foreign Legion growl.

The girl smiled. "Susie, you're the greatest."

After they left, Jen looked at her. "Susie, you really are the greatest."

"I'm just me," Susie said.

"Well I'm going to take your advice and swing for the stars, too," Jen said, not quite sure, yet, what that meant.

# Playboy on the Bosque

SIR IAN LYON'S PARTY was held at a gigantic spread in the north valley of Albuquerque, right along the Bosque, the endless long grove of trees that ran along the Rio Grande all the way to Mexico. The neighborhood was a rural oasis between the subdivisions in the heights and the subdivisions on the west side. People had ranches out here, but because of the light pollution coming from the rest of Albuquerque, it didn't quite feel rural.

The Mountain Lyon took a turn-off from Rio Grande Boulevard onto a dirt road that was filled with ruts. They entered a deeply wooded area where trees blocked the lights from above.

"Are you sure we're still in Albuquerque?" Susie asked. "This feels like the windy moors of Scotland, where the British Open is. I played there once."

As if on cue, a wind blew some leaves onto the hood of the car.

"Technically we're in Los Ranchos de Albuquerque," Jen said. "But with this moon and this wind, I see what you mean."

The Mountain Lyon eventually came to an electronic gate at the end of the dirt road. An armed guard wearing a Lyon

Aerospace uniform stood there with a high tech gun. Jen felt as if she was crossing into a foreign country.

Jean Claude waved at the man and the gate opened. They drove deeper into the forest before Jean Claude took a few more turns on the narrow road. They heard a coyote growl, or perhaps it was a wild dog.

"The Hound of the Basketballs," Jen said.

"*Baskervilles,*" Susie said. "Sir Arthur Conan Doyle. It was one of the earliest Sherlock Holmes stories."

"I was kidding," Jen said. "I knew that. I'm surprised you knew it. I thought all you did was play golf."

Susie smiled. "I told you, I do have tutors. I even pay attention sometimes when they're talking to me on the plane. I might not golf forever, so I don't want to be a total idiot."

"Did you know that as a nationality, Koreans have the highest scores of all foreign students on American SATs?"

"No thanks to you or me," Susie said.

On the far side of the gate, torches lit the dark dirt roadway, but Jean Claude nearly missed the first sharp turn, and then the next. He swore under his breath when he smashed into a low-lying branch. Once the branch fell away, Jen could see the lights of a mansion in the distance. Jean Claude took the next turns a little too fast, showing off his grand prix skills. If he hadn't been such a skilled driver, they would have ended up face first in the trunk of one of the Aspen trees. Suddenly, they were lined up behind several other vehicles waiting to drop passengers at the door.

"Is Sir Ian here yet?" Jen asked.

Jean Claude pointed to a helicopter that was parked off to the side of the mansion in a small clearing. It would be fun to be in the jet set, Jen thought. So far she had barely made it into the Jeep set.

"It took a lot for him to get a permit to land one of those out here," Jean Claude said as he took them right up to the front of the mansion.

With the line of vehicles, the Tudor inspired mansion could pass for a smaller version of the Playboy Mansion with a fresh coat of stucco. Jen looked at the vehicles. They weren't limos. Several people arrived in balloon chase vehicles that carried the logos of their corporate sponsors. Jen laughed as she scanned the logos. Real estate sponsors she could understand, but why would a pizza delivery company sponsor a balloon? Did the balloon driver deliver the pizza from above? Hopefully no one planned to come to the party by balloon. The darkness could make it quite difficult to land.

A Lyon Rescue ambulance was located off to the side, and a billowing sign made out of a balloon fragment hung on an outer wall of the mansion. It declared: Lyon Aerospace Officially Welcomes Balloonists!

Jen looked at Jean Claude. "Does Sir Ian own this place? Does he live here?"

Jean Claude smiled. "*Je ne sais pas.* I don't know. It's a working vineyard that makes a red wine called Lyon's Blood. It's *merde*. Really shitty stuff."

He was French; he should know wine. Jean Claude added, "Sir Ian only comes here one week a year, for the balloon fiesta. He usually splits his time between his various other houses—two in Colorado, three in England, one in the south of France, places like that. He's got an island, too."

"Must be nice to have a place like this," Jen said.

"You should see my place in Arizona," Susie said.

"I'd like that," Jen said.

"We'll see," Susie said. "If we stay friends."

"What does that mean?"

"I'm kidding," Susie said. "We're BFF."

The "Song Sisters" exited the Hummer and walked toward the door. They wrapped their trench coats tightly around their bodies, so no skin whatsoever was exposed. Jean Claude acted as their escort. From his sick smile, Jen knew he couldn't wait for the big unveiling.

Inside, the home was decorated in the theme of an English hunting lodge, complete with dead animal heads on the wall. One rhino head in particular looked very fresh, as if it had been bagged while it waded in one of the Rio's irrigation ditches. As Jen looked around the joint she decided that if this was Sir Ian's house, he sure had eclectic tastes. Samurai swords were on the walls next to French impressionist paintings. Jen thought of Hearst Castle, and of course Xanadu, the fictional house from *Citizen Kane*. This was Xanadu on acid.

"Is your home this nice?" Jen asked Susie.

Susie glared at the paintings. "Not yet," she said. "My whore of a mom has the world's worst taste in interior design. But when I'm old enough and can kick her out, it will be even nicer than this."

"You're being a brat," Jen said. "You should be nicer to your mom."

"You don't know my mom," Susie said.

Well, that was true. Jen wasn't sure what legal obligation an older cousin had for a seventeen-year-old. She had taken Susie to an adult emporium. That was bad enough. Now a waiter with red wine approached.

"Sir Ian insists," the waiter said.

Jen reluctantly took a glass and almost took one for Susie, but then stopped. If she let Susie drink, that would be contributing to the delinquency of a minor, right?

"You can't drink," Jen said. "If I get you a drink, it's a felony."

"Okay, *mother*."

"But, I'm an adult. I can drink all I want." Jen chugged her glass. Eew. Lyon's Blood was indeed *merde*. Even so, she took another glass. Jean Claude would drive her home, right? She was also off probation and officially a lawyer, so she could do what she wanted. Still, she did have to be responsible. "Sir, make sure this underage girl doesn't drink."

The waiter shrugged and turned away.

"Are you sure you're a responsible adult?" Susie asked.

They went into the bathroom and adjusted their makeup in the mirror. "I'm sorry I snapped at you, Jen, but I'm really nervous. This is like my debut. I was supposed to be a debutant in Arizona last year, but I had to miss the season, for golf of course."

"*Your debutant knows what you need, but I know what you want*." Jen sang. "I think that's Bob Dylan."

"I don't know what I want." Susie actually shook. "Suppose he doesn't like me?"

Jen gave her a hung. "It's impossible for someone not to like you, Susie."

Susie hugged her back. "Thank you for being my friend."

"Swing for the stars, Susie."

When the cousins emerged from the bathroom, they saw Claus with a gaggle of lawyers on the fringes of the party. He wore a blue polyester jacket over a red shirt that was buttoned all the way to the top without a tie. If he was trying to be cool, he had failed miserably.

"I did a will for a balloonist a few weeks ago," Claus said. "He never paid me, but said I could come to the party instead."

Jen noticed that he carried a brown supermarket bag that was filled with little sandwiches.

He shrugged. "I've got to bring home the bacon anyway I can. Hungry mouths at home."

"I thought you won a million dollar verdict."

"It was overturned on appeal."

Jen may have had lousy math skills, but she attempted to calculate the cost of raising seven children in a down economy. She gave up when the DJ started playing and people hit the dance floor with a vengeance.

"What's under the overcoat?" Claus asked.

"It's a surprise."

The beat got louder and Jen began to move in time with the music.

Claus smiled at her. "Do you want to dance?"

Before she could respond, Jean Claude strained to hear something in his earpiece. He then nodded to Jen and Susie. "It's time." He escorted the women down a hallway into a main living room. Only a few partygoers were here.

Jean Claude waited until Sir Ian and Hal appeared by the fireplace and sat down in matching chairs made out of some kind of animal skin. The two Lyons wore matching smoking jackets with LYON AEROSPACE OFFICIAL BALLOON PAJAMA PARTY patches on their pajamas. The patch showed Aslan, the lion with wings from the Narnia books, standing on top of a balloon.

Sir Ian poured a glass of Lyon's Blood for himself and for his son. Then he made a toast. "To our sweethearts and wives," Sir Ian said. "May they never meet. It's the traditional Royal Navy toast, of course."

He took another look at the bottle of Lyon's Blood and shook his head. A waiter brought him a bottle labeled LYON'S SCOTCH, then poured a shot for himself and the boy. "May the wind always be at your back."

The balloonists laughed and all downed a shot.

There was still some whiskey left, so Sir Ian emptied the bottle amongst the people around him and poured one last toast for himself and Hal.

"May the road rise up to meet you." They both downed their drinks, but the balloonists hesitated; a road rising up to meet you wasn't always a good thing.

Another bottle was brought to him. Sir Ian poured two more rounds, but this time didn't bother to toast to anything. Jen did the math. That was at least five drinks for his son, clearly over the legal limit. Since the swearing in, Jen was surprised that she had started thinking like a lawyer.

Wobbling just a bit, Sir Ian then nodded at Jean Claude. Jean Claude smiled and turned to the crowd. "There will be no photography. Anyone who violates that policy will be, as we say in the Legion, terminated with extreme prejudice."

One look at Jean Claude and the balloonists knew that he meant business. Susie looked at Jen, and Jen could sense that she was nervous. Jen remembered the book *Memoirs of a Geisha*.

Why did she feel this was some kind of an auction—for both of them? When it came down to it, Jen felt self-conscious, too. The Song girls were fully clothed in their trench coats, yet she never had felt so naked in her life.

Susie whispered something to Jean Claude.

"*Mesdames* and *Messieurs*," he announced to the crowd, as if he was a DJ in a Paris strip club on the seedier of the two banks of the Seine. "For the first time ever, may I present *Les Mademoiselles Song*, also known as *Les Geishas de Laser!*"

Jen and Susie went to the center of the dance floor, which were actually some wooden tiles in the middle of the room. Jean Claude hit a remote control and a throbbing remix of the Laser Geisha theme song came on. It still had echoes of The Beatles "I Wanna Hold Your Hand" sung by Yoko, but today it sounded like a drunken Yoko was doing a strip tease.

Jen followed Susie's lead and they both threw off their trench coats. There was a loud gasp from the room. Most of the men knew that Susie had an athlete's body, but they were shocked when they saw her in her sexy Laser Geisha outfit. Susie Song, the cute little tomboy with the big golf swing, was all grown up.

Jen was quite self-conscious. She had shown far more than this as a waitress in a club, but this was different. Then Jen realized that she was invisible. All eyes were on Susie.

Susie busted a move and Jen aped her movements. Susie strutted in her muscular glory, as if she was on a catwalk. Jen followed. Then she stared at Sir Ian. She practically shouted, "Take me, if you dare."

Susie went over to Hal's chair, and pretended to do a lap dance. Jen felt the alcohol go to her head, and then down to her hips. Jen stumbled onto Sir Ian's lap. He smelled amazing. Did he also have a fragrance called Lyon's Sweat? It must have had some hormones mixed in at the lab. She started grinding. She was surprised that she enjoyed the feeling of being next to someone so powerful. He grabbed her and she had a bit of a Janet Jackson moment when her Geisha outfit had a wardrobe malfunction. It was only a moment before she covered herself. She noticed Claus, still holding his grocery bag of food, staring at her with amazement. The music ended abruptly, and Jen hurriedly covered herself with the trench coat.

Suddenly, two sets of hands began clapping. Sir Ian and his son. Sir Ian looked down at his son and jokingly put the ice bucket over his son's crotch.

Jen felt terrible. She had contributed to the delinquency of a minor. Or, perhaps it was that the minor had contributed to *her* delinquency.

Hal rushed over to joined Susie. He had two glasses of champagne in his hands and Jen did more math regarding his alcohol consumption. Aggravated DWI, mandatory two days in jail, was a point one six and he was probably getting close to that.

Susie, still in her Geisha outfit, disappeared with him. Jen hoped they weren't driving anywhere. Jen stayed wrapped inside her trench coat. She worried about Susie, but Susie was a big girl, right? And, what had she just done, dancing like that? She tried to reassure herself by looking around. In addition to the balloonists, there were a lot of aerospace engineers, and worse, there were adventure capitalists—or whatever those people who did big deals were called.

Jen left the room for a quieter place. Was this an English sitting room? The room contained plush couches made out of a beautifully grained leather that she did not recognize. In one corner, a drunken Japanese industrialist bent Sir Ian's ear in slurred Japanese. They occasionally switched to English when they used technical terms such as "launch windows" and "avionics."

The man then pointed to Jen.

Sir Ian held up his hand, indicating that Jen should wait there by the couch.

Presently, Sir Ian came over. "That gentleman, Mr. Wagatsuma from Kobe, saw you dance and apparently thinks you are for sale."

"For sale?"

It took Jen a moment to realize what he was talking about. That was a line she had never crossed, not even as a waitress at a seedy club.

Before she could say anything Sir Ian continued. "I have told him quite firmly that you are not for sale."

"Well, thank you," Jen said.

"You're already *mine*."

Before Jen could ponder the exact meaning of that statement, Hal approached his father. The boy now held a half-empty bottle of Lyon's Blood. Was there something worse than aggravated DWI, because Hal was way over that line. His father had to steady the boy from falling into the Japanese industrialist's lap. After a heated discussion, Sir Ian reluctantly threw a pair of car keys to his son.

"Have fun, boy," he said. "Don't do anything I wouldn't."

Susie now emerged. She had her trench coat back on, and looked as if she was ready to leave. Hal stumbled back over to her and pretended to glance down the overcoat. Susie pushed his hand away, but then grasped it for support.

"Tonight's the night," Susie yelled to Jen, blowing her a kiss.

"Are you sure you want to go with him?" Jen asked. "Sir Ian, are you sure you want your son to drive?"

No one heard her. "Susie, I don't think—"

Susie was already leaving the room.

Sir Ian had already resumed his business discussions, this time with an emir. They were talking about financing, but Jen didn't care. Agitated, she approached Sir Ian when Snape, the English bodyguard, physically blocked her way.

"Let it go," he said.

Jen turned and saw Susie walk toward the garage with Hal. On the way, he grabbed a final drink off the waiter's tray. She thought about yelling to Jean Claude. He could do the driving, at least, but the Frenchmen had vanished.

"I'm not my cousin's keeper," Jen said to herself. But she was, wasn't she?

It would all be all right, Jen reassured herself. Susie would be fine. Jen hadn't seen Susie drink anything. Susie was just horny. Breathe. Deep breaths. Okay. Tonight was going to be Hal's lucky night indeed.

Despite her reassurances to herself, Jen shuddered. She had been arrested for a DWI when she was in high school. Luckily, that lawyer author dude had got her charges dismissed when the cop didn't show for the third time. Still, the entire ordeal terrified her. Her mother hadn't talked to her for months. Jen knew from her old cop boyfriend that the balloon fiesta was one of the peak times for drunk driving, right up there with Halloween, New Year's Eve, and *Cinco de Mayo*.

One of the few things Jen could pride herself on is that she didn't drink and drive. Hopefully Hal would get one of the goons to be the designated driver. But, Jen wanted to make sure. Tonight she was her cousin's keeper, so she moved through another room to avoid Snape. She eventually found her way to the garage door, but it was locked.

"Susie!" Jen yelled at the door. She didn't know if she liked being the grown up, always chasing after her cousin. "Susie!"

Someone grabbed her shoulder. "Sir Ian needs to see you," Snape said. "Forthwith." He had a freshly broken nose, as if he had earlier been in a fight. Jen followed Snape back to the sitting room, where most of the guests had begun their exodus. They were balloonists after all, and had early flights the next morning.

Jen found Sir Ian in a small office next to the sitting room. Unlike the rest of the house, this office was very modern, decorated with aerospace paraphernalia and pictures of Sir Ian posing with airplanes and rockets. His biggest trophy stood directly above him, the cone of a rocket poking through a side door, as if Sir Ian had shot the rocket down on his last safari.

In the office, he chatted up several Arab industrialists who were dressed in traditional clothes. Sir Ian apparently didn't push the pajama requirement on them. One of them, a man she recognized as international investor Ahmad Assed, was an emir, a prince, who invested in anything that caught his fancy, from films to football teams.

"Are you sure that your son and Susie are okay?" Jen asked Sir Ian. "He looked kinda drunk."

Sir Ian frowned. "Snape," he said to the hooligan. "I think Hal has had too much to drink. Find Jean Claude and have him drive them wherever they need to go. Then tell him to wait outside and drive them back."

Snape nodded. He was nasty, but at least he was sober. Well, mostly sober.

Sir Ian shook hands with the emir. "You will come down to the spaceport and see my launch next week."

"Wouldn't miss it," the emir said. "We'll talk, then."

Sir Ian smiled. He kissed the emir on both cheeks, and the emir left through a side door.

Sir Ian positively glowed. He patted the rocket cone on its tip, as if it was a ritual, and then poured himself glasses of Lyon's Blood from an already opened bottle. "I may have lost a billion dollar deal with Wagatsuma."

"Was that my fault?"

Sir Ian laughed. "Don't worry, I'd do it again. You're worth a billion dollars to me. But I'm not finished. I may have lost one billion dollar deal, but I gained another."

Jen smiled.

Sir Ian smiled back, the one Englishman in the world with good teeth. "I think I just closed a two billion dollar deal with the emir!"

He hugged her. Even to a man like Sir Ian, two billion dollars was still real money.

Jen didn't know what to say besides "Congratulations!"

She stared at the rocket cone. Was it inching forward?

Sir Ian got another glass. "You're not driving, so drink up."

"Cheers," she said. "To you, Sir Ian."

"Cheers," he replied. "You must come down to my launch next week, the new prototype for my space tourism venture."

"Do you launch in Florida?"

"Haven't you been paying attention to the news?" Sir Ian asked incredulously. "I'm part owner of the new spaceport to the south."

"Spaceport?"

"Space tourism. It's a stretch now, since we can barely get people into orbit. But we have to consider new profit streams now that the helicopter business has gone bottom up. I don't suggest the wine business, or the balloon business either, for that matter. What did the guy tell Dustin Hoffman in the *The Graduate*?

"Plastics?"

"Rockets are the new plastics." He pointed to the cone. "My first prototype."

On his desk, he showed her a plastic replica of a rocket that was maybe twelve inches tall. He threw it to her. "Catch."

She fumbled it for a moment, the rocket felt surprisingly heavy. Finally, she caught it in both hands.

Sir Ian smiled. "If you drop the rocket it's bad luck."

"I've never been to a launch before," she said. "Your rocket will really go all the way into outer space?"

"Well, at least into orbit someday."

Maybe living in the world of Sir Ian wasn't so bad. She stared at him. He wasn't young, more of a lion in winter. Even drunk, he was beyond distinguished and beyond rich. Having a rocket in your pocket wasn't such a bad thing either. Was the alcohol affecting her? She felt a strange attraction to this dashing man. He was a gentleman who had given up a billion dollar deal just for her. That was cool.

"Let's celebrate privately," he said. He took another gulp of wine. Jen couldn't even calculate Sir Ian's intoxication.

Maybe she should catch up. But, she wasn't sure how alcohol would affect all her meds, so she just sipped a glass.

"Hand me that rocket," he said. He unscrewed the nose cone and poured some white powder onto his shiny desktop. He arranged it into lines.

"Ladies first," he said.

"Cocaine?"

"Something even better," he said. "Cocaine, Viagra, ecstasy and testosterone all rolled into one, mixed with other sundry chemicals developed in my lab by my rocket scientists. I call it rocket fuel. Try it. You'll like it."

"I don't know," she said. "That doesn't sound totally kosher. I'm an attorney now."

"Well then, consider this attorney client privileged."

He snorted a few lines, back to back. "Smashing!" He smiled with exhilaration. "Just because you're a lawyer doesn't mean you can't have fun."

"I can have fun," Jen said. "I just want to do it without drugs. I'm on a lot of prescriptions right now, and I don't know how I'll react."

Sir Ian wiped his nose; it was bleeding now. He then reached for her hand before cleaning his own hand off. She hesitated. She hadn't been with anyone since her engagement to Dan Shepard. Before that, her one fling had resulted in Denise. Talk about taking a mulligan on that one. Why did sex have to be so complicated? She stared at the Lion in Winter. She had certainly been with worse. She certainly had never been with anyone better.

She then took his hand in hers, even though she could still feel bloody rocket fuel snot on his hands. His hand was rough, kind of like the rhino he had killed. It wasn't a bad thing.

"Follow me," he said. "This is my office and I don't mix business with pleasure."

As they walked down the dark hallway, Jen felt a sudden chill go down her back. The chill went so deep into her core that she stopped and asked, "Where's Susie?"

"She's a big girl," Sir Ian said. "She can take care of herself, and you can trust my son."

"You're probably right," Jen said.

"Have I told you I have a thing for Asian women?"

"We're hard to resist," Jen said. "Just ask my last boyfriend. He called me yellow kryptonite."

She instantly regretted saying that. Sir Ian walked faster, grabbed her hand and pulled just a little too hard.

# Seppukku Suite

JEN AND SIR IAN walked down a long hallway, past more bagged animals. This man did love a good trophy. The ranch house was only one story, yet it extended forever. The remaining sounds of the party faded in the distance. What would a one night stand with Sir Ian be like? What would it be like to be a mistress to a billionaire? To be a concubine? To be a geisha? She stared at a portrait of Sir Ian with his first wife. The woman could be a Thai version of herself. What would it be like to be Sir Ian's wife? Jen thought it would be like living Cinderella's dream—with a balloon and a helicopter. Except this prince also owned a rocket that would never turn into a pumpkin.

Jen tried to read Sir Ian. It looked to her as if the drugs pumped him up far more than what was healthy. She could hear his heart beat, and it was even faster than the Laser Geisha theme song. His bloodshot eyes stared at her. It wasn't quite lust, more like greed. She was an acquisition, a hostile takeover, something else to snort up. Jen wasn't sure she liked that.

They finally came to a metal door that looked like the door of one of Sir Ian's rockets. Sir Ian punched a few buttons on a keyboard, and the door slid open just like the door on *Star Trek*. They walked outside into the cool night air, and the door clicked closed behind them, automatically.

Where had she heard that sound before?

There was a sudden gust of hot air and Jen saw a fire in the distance, probably a bonfire for the guests.

Sir Ian took her into a guest house on the far side of a breeze way. The building looked like a modified barn and also had a metal rocket door. He punched a few more buttons and the rocket door slid open.

Jen remembered where she'd heard that clicking door sound. It was the same sound she heard when she visited the jail and the door closed behind her. She had never liked that sound; it made her feel trapped.

"When I'm in Albuquerque I live here in my own guest house," he said. "As you can see, it used to be a barn."

"This isn't like any barn I've ever been to," Jen said. His private bedroom could be a super-villain's lair, filled with the latest high tech. It had a modified Asian theme, sort of sci-fi samurai. The rear of the barn was glass, and looked out into the trees beyond. People in glass houses shouldn't throw stones, right?

"It's a company place, but I come here once a year for Balloon Fiesta," he said. "Do you like it?"

"I love it," Jen said, even though she was nervous. "I'd have a place like this if I was a billionaire. I love the swords."

It was hot, so what the hell, she took off her trench coat. "Do you like my outfit?"

Before answering, Sir Ian grabbed her hard from behind. He had more than a rocket in his pocket. He spun her neck around and started to kiss her, wildly, on the lips.

She kissed back. He had alcohol on his breath and that powder had made its way into his lungs. She couldn't calculate his blood alcohol, but it was way beyond impaired. That would make it Aggravated DWI if he drove, not counting whatever a Drug Recognition Expert would find. This was aggravated criminal sexual contact.

And then it got even more aggravated.

Sir Ian liked it far rougher than she wanted. He even called her several racist names. Then he slapped her, hard.

Jen didn't like being called names, even if he was just talking in the throes of passion. She was a lawyer now, after all. Lawyers weren't supposed to get slapped.

He bit her on the shoulder, and then on the neck, like a vampire. He sucked blood out of her neck, and licked it up. For one brief moment, Jen felt that she would turn into one of the undead. She pushed him away, gently. "I don't know," she said.

He pushed her back, and she fell against a mirror, which broke into several pieces. One piece pierced her skin. It hurt.

"It's only a mirror," he said. "You must have a really hard ass."

She definitely didn't like the way he mentioned her ass. Not tonight. What would she tell Susie? Was this happening to Susie, too?

Sir Ian approached her like a horny zombie on meth, but lost his balance. The alcohol and drugs waged a battle with his equilibrium.

No, she didn't want to be this man's concubine, or even his geisha. She looked for an exit. She had been in this position so many times before. But she had been younger then. She wasn't going to let it happen again.

"Stop!" she said. "I mean it."

"What?" He was amazed that someone had actually said no to him.

"I said 'stop!'" She stared at him. "No means no!"

Sir Ian stopped. He was on his knees and then started crawling toward her again. "I know about you. All about you. I know you like it hard. Real hard."

He knew about her? No one knew about her. She put her high heel against his head and pushed him down. He let loose a string of obscenities as if he was from a Cockney gutter rather than the playing fields of Eton.

She was a killer, right? She could just take one of the swords and behead him right there. She actually touched one of the samurai swords. It wasn't bolted down. She could take it and make him do *seppuku,* a form of Japanese ritual suicide by disembowelment.

No, she was no killer, despite what Dr. Romero had said. The doctor said she turned into "Pink" when there was imminent danger. Well, she wished she would turn right now. Maybe she was too close to the ground to kill. Heights set her off, right? She was under too much medication and the alcohol didn't help. Still, there was no need for Pink; she could handle this just fine.

No, on second thought, she was in real trouble. Big trouble. Sir Ian reached for her again, but she backed off and he fell flat on his face. She put her high heel on top of his temple. She could kill him with just one jab. She touched the wound on her neck. No, she wouldn't turn into a vampire after all. She would handle this with logic, not emotion, and certainly not with magic powers.

"I'm leaving, Sir Ian," she said. "Please don't follow me or I'll call the police and press charges."

He stared at her as if calculating a poker hand. This was just another deal to him. He frowned. "You're not worth it anyway." Then he laughed. "You're too old."

"Too old?" Jen looked at him. He looked like death itself. She wiped the blood off her neck. "What, you want Susie?"

Speaking of her cousin, she'd better find her and get them both hell out of here. Hopefully, Hal wasn't as bad a guy as his father was.

# Geisha Down

JEN FEARED THE BARN door wouldn't open, but she pressed a button few times and it finally slid to the left. She exited briskly, and as she felt the night air she realized she had left her trench coat back inside. She hoped she didn't have another wardrobe malfunction. She sure didn't need something like that her first weekend as a lawyer.

Who would people believe, the gazillionaire or the geisha? On the outside, they would believe her of course. Luna was a judge after all. She'd stick up for her. And as a lawyer, her own word was her bond or something like that. Nice New Mexican lawyer versus evil English lord.

But, here she was in Sir Ian's moors, not in her own New Mexico. On Sir Ian's estate, she was little more than chattel. She might not make it out alive, if he said the word. His minions— Jean Claude and Snape—could easily tear her apart, and Sir Ian's wife had died under mysterious circumstances.

Jen headed toward the bonfire. She sped up to a brisk walk, which was difficult in heels. The bonfire was down the road, next to a tree. When did bonfires have vehicles so close to them?

It took a moment for Jen to recognize that this was no bonfire. It was a car accident. Worse, she recognized the vehicle; even though the front half of it was gone. It was the Mountain Lyon. The vehicle had gone head first into a tree and had smashed like an accordion. She had never trusted that vehicle. It took her another second to realize what that meant. Her mind was still a little slow from the alcohol. "Oh God! Susie!" she shouted. She didn't care if Sir Ian was out to get her. Susie was probably in that car. She needed to save Susie, her cousin, her friend.

"Call an ambulance!" she shouted.

"Stay away from there, missy!" Snape's cockney accent.

"Damn it! Call an ambulance!"

Snape took a call. "Right, mate. She's here right in front of us. I'll bring her back."

Bring her back? That couldn't be good.

Snape walked toward her with deliberate intent. Jen looked into her heart. Snape did not seem friendly any more. She had some training in martial arts. If she couldn't become Pink because of the booze, maybe she could take these guys, just like her idol, Ziyi Zhang, in those period martial arts films. For one brief moment, she expected to turn into a super heroine. Maybe that's what I've been repressing.

No. It was time for her to be real. She was terrified and a little drunk from two glasses of bad wine, and whatever pills lingered from the morning. She had no tolerance any more. Could she call 911 on her phone? No, she would be tackled before she dialed the second digit. She would have to make a run for it. She kicked off her heels and turned toward the Bosque.

His deliberate intent suddenly became far more deliberate.

"*Arrete!*" Jean Claude shouted. "Stop, you bitch."

Where had he come from?

Jen could barely see, even in the full moon. She ran smack into a fence and fell. The two men got closer and Jen said a silent prayer. If there was any time she could transform into that killer, now would be the time. She shook her head. Shit. Nothing.

Jen did feel something magical inside her, though. Maybe she was a vampire after all. She tried to jump. Suddenly there were thick arms around her. She didn't know whether it was Jean Claude or the other hooligan.

"Got her!" a voice shouted.

Somehow he grabbed only fabric. She might not be a superhero, but she was pretty quick in the moonlight. Jen hurried deeper into the woods and tried to get her bearings. She heard the Rio flowing to her left. That meant civilization lay to her right.

Jean Claude and Snape hurried after her and Jen picked up her pace. Unfortunately, she fell into a muddy ditch. She cursed the mud. She tried to turn on her phone, but couldn't find the right button. The firelight revealed a gap in the fence, where a tree had fallen down. Sir Ian only came here once a year, so his security wasn't perfect after all. She darted to the gap and squeezed through it, jumping onto the tree trunk.

A deer wandered by, then another. Then the deer started running, stepping on one tree branch after the other. The noise threw off her pursuers, who headed in the wrong direction, giving her valuable time.

"Get the bitch!" Snape shouted. "Where'd she go?"

Jen stayed still and tried not to make any noise. She couldn't abandon Susie. Should she go back and rescue her? No. Those dudes had guns. She needed to get help from people with guns of their own. They were going to kill her. What was going on here?

She saw a passing car in the distance, on the other side of a row of trees. The road must be that way. Confident she could outrun her pursuers she hurried to the road and squeezed through the barbed wire. She looked at the two lanes of rural Rio Grande Boulevard, the road that paralleled the Bosque. If memory served, a coffee shop lay down the road.

She didn't have much time. She also didn't hear any sirens. Why hadn't anyone called an ambulance? She found a quiet place behind a rock and dialed 911.

Her memory of the last few minutes was hazy. Jen hoped she wasn't somehow responsible for Susie's death. If only she could have turned into a real Laser Geisha. "Why couldn't I become Pink?" she asked herself.

*"Be careful what you wish for,"* a voice inside her said.

Then Jen fainted. The earth rushed forward toward her, but somehow she saw the mosaic floor of the District Courthouse. But this time she didn't see any glowing light as her head hit the ground. That couldn't be good.

# ACT II
## Reluctant Witness

AFTER SHE REGAINED CONSCIOUSNESS and made it to the parking lot of a gas station, Jen felt safe enough to call Luna. Luna didn't sound pleased when she answered on the tenth ring.

"I thought we'd outgrown this," she said.

"Please Luna, this could be serious."

"I'm on my way," Luna said, and hung up. Luna might complain, but she usually came through.

Minutes later Luna arrived. Jen ran to Luna's car and hopped in before Luna came to a complete stop. She yearned to see Luna's familiar face, the only face she could trust.

"What happened?" Luna asked after an uncomfortable pause. "Why are you dressed like that?"

"I don't know yet," Jen said. "I mean I don't know what to tell you."

Luna stared at her while she drove, and she noticed the blood. "Should I take you to the hospital?"

Jen took time to think. She could report Sir Ian for attempted rape, but it was hardly a slam dunk. She had gone to the room willingly in front of witnesses after giving the man a drunken lap dance, complete with a wardrobe malfunction that had revealed her left boob to dozens of people. She heard the clicking sound of a million cell phone cameras. The entire scenario looked bad. She was a good lawyer, but she wasn't *that* good. She didn't want to mess with a guy like Sir Ian. He was a billionaire and way smarter than her.

"I'm fine," Jen said.

"Are you sure?"

Jen paused. "I'm afraid of him," Jen said. "Sir Ian."

For one brief moment, Jen expected Luna to insist on taking her to the hospital, or insist on taking her to the police, but Luna shivered slightly and drove faster, away from the valley.

"You should be afraid of him," Luna said. "Guys like that don't mess around. He could throw you off his balloon and no one would care."

"That's harsh," Jen said.

"I'm sorry. I'm not myself these days."

"I don't know if I'm ever myself," Jen said.

As they took the exit for Lomas Boulevard and passed University Hospital, Luna looked at her. "Last chance."

Jen felt a tinge of nervousness. No, she didn't want to mess with Sir Ian. She insisted that her cuts were minor, and asked Luna to take her home. It would only take a band-aid to fix her neck wound and some disinfectant to clean up her cuts.

"What about Susie?" Luna asked.

"I've got to find out," Jen said. "I don't know where they're taking her—or if they're taking her."

Luna turned north off Lomas, and passed the huge hospital complex. After a roundabout, she drove Jen the few blocks to the Caddy Shack.

Jen hurried inside and immediately pulled the Internet up on her phone so she could see any news stories about the accident. She glanced at a video of an ambulance emerging from the property. Jen shuddered. It was Sir Ian's private ambulance from Lyon Rescue.

Those bastards! If they did anything else to her. . . .

According to the story, Susie's condition was critical, but stable. Her whereabouts were unknown. Sir Ian had vanished. Jen figured he'd lifted off in his big helicopter and was already outside of jurisdiction.

Prince Hal hadn't been so lucky. He had died upon impact.

Jen nearly broke the screen of her phone as she frantically pushed the screen harder. She wanted her fingers to grab the information right off the web. There was a lot out there, and yet there was nothing. Susie was the biggest athlete in the world, so every site had an opinion.

One site reported Susie was drunk and driving, another speculated that Hal had been the one to lose control at the wheel. On another site, an attractive blond woman drawled in a southern accent about how New Mexico statutes limited insurance recovery against a parent for the intentional acts of a child to five *thousand* dollars.

The blond host rolled her eyes. "That wouldn't even pay for Susie's caddy for a day on the LPGA tour."

Jen knew one thing. If Susie survived, her life would never be the same.

# Malpractice Makes Perfect

SUSIE WASN'T THAT FAR away after all. Jen spent her first Monday as a lawyer sitting in the main waiting room of University Hospital. Susie's condition remained critical, but stable, although no one would reveal the extent of her injuries. Jen did find out from a news broadcast that the hospital had flown in specialists from Arizona, along with Susie's personal physicians. Susie was apparently too important to trust to New Mexico's finest.

The waiting room usually held families of gunshot victims, but today the room bulged with dozens of Susie's fans, including young Shaniqua from Long John Silver's. The hospital's private waiting room was closed. The nurse said VIPs were in from out of town, but offered no other explanation.

Next to Jen, another family waited patiently. Jen heard a discussion about uninsured motorists, and how no lawyer in town wanted to take their case. Jen shuddered. Hal wasn't from America, and had lived all over the world. Did he even have a driver's license? Or insurance?

A man muttered something about that "damn five thousand dollar cap" when it came to parents. The five thousand dollar cap, again? Jen swore under her breath. A five thousand dollar cap sounded like something Susie wore on her head, rather than a point in a lawsuit.

Finally, long after the last of the little girls had gone home in tears, Cherry, a nurse summoned Jen to the desk. "Susie can see you now."

"Is she going to be all right?" Jen asked.

"She wants to see you now," Cherry said again. Jen realized that the nurse hadn't answered the question.

Susie had been moved to a special wing of the hospital on the top floor. The entire floor was silent. Had they cleared everyone out just for Susie? A nurse's aide, whose nametag read ARIANA, guarded Susie's door. At this hospital, nurses apparently were allowed to wear any color of scrubs they wanted. Some favored cartoon characters such as Mickey Mouse or Betty Boop to lighten the mood.

Ariana's scrubs did nothing to lighten anything. They were blood red, the exact color worn by high risk inmates in jail. Indeed, Ariana's right side neck tattoos pledged allegiance to the Maximum Bitch Unit, a pod in the woman's prison. Her left arm tattoo showed a cross, and the right showed a praying Virgin Mary. That should count for something, right?

"Have you been here all night?" Jen asked.

"Yes. I work for Susie," Ariana said. "I will always be here."

"You work for Susie?" Jen asked.

"Susie's people have me on contract for the duration."

"Susie's people?"

The woman offered no further explanation. She could have

been hired by Susie's management team in Arizona. Maybe Susie had insurance that paid for an aide like Ariana. Jen figured a rich patient like Susie could hire her own staff at her own expense. Still, Jen felt something wasn't right about the woman.

A uniformed police officer now came to the door. "I need to ask your patient some questions for my report."

Ariana shook her head. "No one can see her unless they're family. Doctor's orders."

The officer turned and walked away.

Ariana clearly relished her role as bouncer. "Now," she said as she turned to Jen, "what's your name?"

"Jen Song, I'm her first cousin."

"Jen Song? You can come in. You're on the list." Then she patted Jen down, looking for contraband.

Inside the hospital room, Jen gasped when she saw the crumpled heap on the bed that once been the greatest female golfer in the world. Susie's eyes were bloodshot, as if she had been crying blood rather than tears, and she wore a neck brace. Jen wanted to hold her cousin's hand, but Susie looked so fragile that she feared the hand would accidentally break off.

Jen's eyes scanned the room. There was a nurse, also wearing blood red scrubs, finishing up her rounds. The nurse shook her head, checked her phone, cursed, and scurried out of the room. Ariana now entered, as if to stand guard.

A tall, handsome Indian doctor hovered over Susie, nodding. "Susie, remember what we discussed." He had an English accent and sounded like a war correspondent. The doctor introduced himself but Jen couldn't pronounce all the syllables in his name. She decided to nickname him Dr. Ghandi. Under a lab coat, he wore a blue double-breasted suit with a red tie that matched Ariana's blood red scrubs. On the coat, there was embroidery with his hard to pronounce name, as well as various initials. Jen lost track after the letters "M" and "D."

Dr. Ghandi had a plastic mock-up of the spine with him, as if he used it to demonstrate spinal injuries all the time. "I can keep the police out for a while, but this one's family, correct?" he asked Susie in a crisp English accent.

Susie blinked.

The doctor turned to Jen. "As I was just telling Susie, her MRI was inconclusive, but we believe the trauma from the vehicle hitting the tree has caused an injury to the spine above the tenth thoracic vertebrae."

"Do you have the x-rays?" Jen asked. She figured that was something a lawyer would ask.

"System's down right now."

He pointed to Susie's mid-section. "She eventually will be fine above the umbilicus, but it is difficult to say if she will regain full, if any, use of her legs, or much sensation."

He indicated a spot in the plastic spinal cord about halfway down. He then touched his back, a few inches above where his belt would be.

Jen touched that spot on her own back and then dragged the finger around to the front. "So she basically has no feeling below the belly button."

"I'm afraid not. But we can always hope."

He stayed in the room, and pretended to read something on his iPad, but Jen knew he was really watching them out of the corner of his eye.

"Can I go over to her?" she asked the doctor.

"Don't touch anything," Dr. Ghandi said.

Jen walked carefully to Susie's bed, but did not touch her.

"I'll never play golf again," Susie said groggily. "What do I do now?"

Jen did not know how to answer.

"Can't feel below my waist. I'll never. . . ."

Jen still didn't know what to say. She had heard of amazing medical advances, but she didn't want to get the poor girl's hopes up.

"You are my only friend. My mother, the whore, didn't even come."

"I'll do anything for you, Susie. You know that."

"Anything?"

"Yes."

"Be my lawyer," Susie said. "Make them pay. Sir Ian. His company. All of them. I wrote a note. I can use my hands at least."

Jen took the note from Susie's hand. The note stated, "Jen Song is my lawyer." Susie had signed it in block letters. It had been notarized by Ariana.

"I got my notary," Ariana said, "after I got my pardon from the governor. It's something I do on the side."

Jen wanted to ask Susie why she hired Ariana, but one glance from the woman in red indicated that she should let the matter be, at least for the time being. Jen turned her focus back to Susie.

"I don't know how much I can help," Jen said. "There's a five thousand dollar limit when a child takes his parent's car."

Susie thought for a moment. "Hal doesn't have a license here. England either. So where is Hal?"

"She doesn't know?" Jen whispered to the doctor.

Dr. Ghandi looked up from his iPad. "You need to go. She's very weak but there's something I need to tell her."

As Jen walked down the hallway she heard a wail from Susie's room. She must have been told the news about Hal. Jen ran back to check on her cousin, but Ariana had resumed her post at the door.

"There's nothing you can do for her right now," Ariana said. "Go. Go and let her rest,"

# Billion Dollar Baby

JEN COULDN'T SLEEP THAT night, of course. She eventually gave up and kept the light on while she stared at Susie's "Jen Song is my lawyer" note.

Then she actually knelt and prayed. "I will do whatever it takes to help Susie," she said over and over again.

"I'll keep that in mind," a voice said.

Did the voice have a *Japanese* accent?

Claus called the next day. "My sons are having their birthday party; you're welcome to come by. They got a write up in today's *Journal* for their big game."

"I have to pass," she said. "You heard about Susie?"

"No. What happened?"

Jen quickly explained.

"That's terrible," he said. "I better let you go. Call me if you need any assistance. I'll help any way I can."

"I'd like that."

Jen tried to call Susie's room at the hospital, but there was no answer. After breakfast, Jen visited Luna at the courthouse in her seventh floor office. After the previous day and night, Jen felt like an aging Geisha after entertaining a troop of horny samurai.

When she got out of the elevator, a force seemed to pull her over to the balcony, like a bad magnet. She held on for dear life at the railing and looked down at the mosaic tile floor three stories below. The fall would be enough to kill her, especially if she impacted head first. She felt that premonition again, that vertigo, that wind washing up from the ground. For one instant, the light changed, and everything shimmered, as if an artist was covering the entire world in transparent ink. She tried to look for the source of the golden light, but could find nothing. When an elevator door opened behind her, Jen jumped and hurried away from the railing.

Jen's swipe card no longer worked on the door that protected the judge's offices. She pressed the buzzer and Mia opened the door.

"Are you okay?" Luna asked from her inner office down the hall. Luna had gone with the Hollywood producer look for her office. Her office was decorated with signed posters of movies such as *Crater County*, and the one about the prosecutor in the small town who fell in love with the defense attorney. Luna had sworn she would sue the author, but apparently he bought her off with a signed poster. Luna never seemed comfortable being a judge. In fact, Luna didn't seem comfortable being Luna most days.

On one wall, there was a picture of Luna with her friend, Diana Crater, the current governor. Although appointed by Diana, New Mexico district court judges face a retention election their first time out and had to win fifty-seven percent of the vote to retain their seat. No district court judge in Albuquerque had ever been voted out. Yet. Luna was unopposed, but she hadn't bothered to campaign. She had made some unpopular rulings and had earned the nickname Judge Looney Tunes. Word on the street was that she might be the first judge to lose.

"I was with Susie," Jen said.

"I didn't know you two were so close all of a sudden."

"We are," Jen frowned. "Like you and I used to be."

Luna shook her head. "Sorry. We've both moved on. People change."

"I guess," said Jen. "Why didn't you tell me you fired me?"

Luna shrugged. "Well, you're overqualified to be my law clerk. Mia can work for free while she's in school. And she had an amazing resume."

"You don't know the half of it," Jen said with a smirk.

"You should be happy you're not a clerk anymore. You're a grown up now."

Jen was surprised to find a tear in her eye. "Well, Susie wants me to be her lawyer. I don't know if I'm up for it."

"Her lawyer? Is there a criminal case against her? I heard she was drunk and she was driving."

Jen was surprised. "The paper said that? No, it wasn't that at all. She was at Sir Ian's party. She left with Sir Ian's son; he was the drunk one."

Luna's eyes opened wide. "Sir Ian's son?"

"Hal Lyon. Prince Hal himself. He was totally drunk. His dad even served him alcohol. That's still legal, right? Dads are allowed to serve their kids alcohol at home, I think."

"Sir Ian let his son drive, knowing he was drunk?"

"He definitely knew about it," Jen said. "He probably also knew that Hal didn't have a license, but he still gave him the keys right in front of me. I even told Sir Ian that his kid was totally shit-faced. He then had one of his goons go look for Hal, but it was too late."

"The do-do rule," Luna said.

"The what rule?"

"If you *do* know about something, you *do* have liability."

Jen thought about Sir Ian's attack, but hesitated to tell Luna. She would let that one go—just as she'd let the other attacks on her life go. Things were complicated enough already.

"Has she talked to the cops yet?"

"No. Her doctor is keeping them away."

Luna stared at Jen. Jen had never seen Luna look like this before. It reminded her of the look on Sir Ian's face, that hostile takeover look.

"Whose car was it?" Luna asked.

"The Mountain Lyon," Jen said. Suddenly things were making sense. "The official balloon chase vehicle. It was Sir Ian's *corporate* vehicle."

Luna's eyes grew wider with every second. "This party was a business party?"

"It was a company party for the balloonists and some aerospace dudes. Now that I think of it, it was sponsored by Lyon Aerospace. There was this big banner on the house that said 'Lyon Aerospace welcomes balloonists.'"

"Where did the accident take place?"

"It was on the property. They crashed into a tree a short way from the house."

"Who owns the property?"

"I think Lyon Aerospace does. It's a vineyard."

"You are aware that Lyon Aerospace is a multi-national corporation worth tens of *billions* of dollars."

"So?"

"And you say you're Susie Song's lawyer?"

Jen showed Luna the piece of paper. Then it started to sink in. "So I could sue Lyon Aerospace on Susie's behalf?"

"You can also sue Sir Ian personally. You can sue him here in New Mexico, in State court. Or you could sue the company in Federal court. I think his company might be based in Colorado. He gave something big to the law school back when I was at CU. I was a semi-finalist in the Lyon Aerospace Moot Court competition."

Jen frowned. "Suing Sir Ian or his company sounds like a lot of work for only a few thousand dollars. A third share would barely pay for the filing fees."

Luna laughed. "Jen, don't you get it? Susie is a paraplegic. Susie Song, the greatest golfer in the world, will never golf again just as her career is poised to take off. That's like at least ten million a year, not counting advertising and sponsorship, for twenty, maybe *thirty* years. Do the math."

"What's the going rate for an injury like this?" Jen had never done civil law, and rarely did math. "I'm sure I can recover a million dollars for someone like Susie."

Luna looked at her. "We're talking Susie freaking Song here. I'll do the math right now." Luna played with her phone for a minute before she found the calculator feature. Like Jen,

Luna was hardly the mathematician. Luna even pounded on the phone when it took some extra moments. Jen had never seen Luna with this look in her eyes before.

"Okay. Susie is seventeen, at the very start of her career," Luna said once the calculator was up and running. "Assuming a twenty-five year career, assuming inflation, assuming loss of consortium—"

"She was still a virgin," Jen said. "She wanted kids, too."

"A virgin? Even better," Luna continued without irony. "Assuming Susie has no sensation below her waist, that's another factor we can put in. Did she like kids?"

Jen thought of the time, she saw Susie with the little girl at Long John Silver's. Susie loved kids. Jen might be bad at math, but even she got the picture now.

"Susie's case is worth about a *billion* dollars. That's chump change to Lyon Aerospace. Sir Ian's worth like twenty billion, even with his helicopter business tanking. I'm sure with his rocket business he can pretty much write a check."

Jen remembered Justin Timberlake's line in *The Social Network*. "A million dollars isn't cool. You know what's cool? A billion dollars."

"So if I take the case on contingency and get Susie a billion; what would that be worth to me?"

"Three hundred thirty-three million and change."

Jen shrugged. Even the "change" would be worth more than her salary now.

Luna frowned. "Jesus Jen, you've been a lawyer for less than a week. You're over your head. Way over your head. Sir Ian is ruthless."

The two women stared at each other. Finally Jen said, "I'm going to need your help, but you're a judge."

"I'd quit being a judge for three hundred million dollars. Still, I can't get involved. You have to pretend you didn't tell me about this. Appearance of impropriety and all that."

Jen felt the vertigo welling up, as if she was going to fall through the floor right there in Luna's office. "I can't do this alone, Luna. You're my only friend who knows what to do. I need someone I can trust. I've got to be there for Susie."

Luna walked to the door and made sure it was locked.

"I'm not supposed to be involved in any case while I'm a judge, especially not a case that will be filed in my building. I can't get a dime from this, not one. I'm totally serious. If I get involved, it's out of love."

Jen laughed. "I never knew anyone who would turn down a couple of million dollars."

"It's not the money. It's my job. It's my license. It's my soul."

"There's got to be a way you can help me."

Luna gave Jen a hug. "I'm risking everything, but yes, Jen, I will find a way to help you and Susie."

Jen thought some more. "Maybe we should get my friend Claus involved. It sounds like he needs the money worse than we do."

"I'll put a team together," Luna said. "I'll help you with the dirty work, but as I said, I can't take a single piece of this, even though a case could be worth hundreds of millions."

# The Lawyers of Sierra Madre

STILL IN LUNA'S OFFICE, Jen tried to call Susie again, but there was still no answer.

"Are you really sure you're her lawyer?" Luna asked.

"I have her note."

Luna had Mia bring in a file with a sample letter of representation. With a billion dollar case, Susie's handwritten letter just wouldn't cut it. Mia quickly typed up something more official. Jen felt a tinge of jealousy. That used to be her job. For a moment Jen wished she was just a law clerk, or a waitress in a strip club. Mia had a lot less stress—that was for sure. Sting had once sung, *"Wish I never woke up this morning. Life was so easy when it was boring."*

As Jen left the building, she realized something was bothering her. She stared at the piece of paper Mia had typed. She knew something was missing, but couldn't quite place what it was.

✝

Still bothered, Jen hurried back to the hospital. First, she could not find a single parking space in the massive garage. Then she nearly got in an accident waiting for another car to back out. Why was she so anxious? She tried to make it about Susie and not about the money. But, three hundred thirty-three million dollars was a lot of money.

Jen wasn't sure if Susie was still in the same room, so she ran to the reception station at the front of the hospital.

"I'm looking for Susie Song. She is recovering from a spinal injury. I'm her cousin."

An elderly volunteer stared at the screen. "You're family? Good. That girl needs family now. She should be in the NSI, the neurosurgical ICU."

As Jen walked toward the elevator bay, she noticed an unkempt teenager talking on a cell phone.

"She's here," the teen said into the phone, obviously talking about Jen. Then Jen blinked and by the time she opened her eyes, he had disappeared.

"Please tell me you're not another lawyer." The floor's receptionist could pass for a vampire with her pale white skin and black outfit.

"I'm family," Jen said. "I'm Susie's cousin. Jen Song for Susie Song."

"That's cool," Vampire Girl said. "I'm sick of these ambulance chasers. You better hurry up and save her."

Jen knew she was headed in the right direction. Every warm body with a bar card and a calculator stood in line. Technically it was against the canons of ethics to solicit clients, but the possibility of one *billion* dollars made a lot of lawyers bend their ethical lines.

Security had long given up hope of blocking this many lawyers.

Jen recognized a few faces from billboards and TV ads. One man who wore a Hawaiian shirt was the guy famous for ripping up checks and shouting "Don't take a check until you check with me!"

Jen overheard another lawyer saying, "Pretend we'll cook her free kim-chee every day, free of charge. Or is it *pho?* Which country eats dog? I get all these wogs confused."

"Shut the hell up," Jen said to the man, surprised by her anger. "She's Korean, like me, and we don't eat dogs. And, I can guarantee she won't hire your sorry racist ass."

Others in line weren't even personal injury lawyers, but somehow hoped against hope to cash in. As she passed by, one lawyer revealed to another that he specialized in name changes. "Your first vowel is free; consonants are assessed according to law."

She wasn't the least bit surprised to see the guy who had represented her on her DWI, that weird author guy.

"What are you doing here?" she asked.

"Research," he said with a smile. "Tell Luna not to sue me."

"What's going to happen next?" Jen asked.

"I don't know," he said. "I haven't figured out who the bad guy is yet."

In fact, it looked to Jen as if the only lawyer in town who didn't make it today was the late Paul Dellagio, father of little Denise. But, there was some rattling in the pipes above her head, as if Dellagio's poltergeist was trying to get a piece of the action.

Jen reached into her purse, grabbed a pill, and downed it without water.

Jen finally made it to the front of the line, stepping on the toes of two other lawyers in the process. She half expected one to sue her for intentional infliction of emotional distress.

"I'm *family!*" she shouted several times in the same voice she'd used to announce she was a lawyer back at district court. She wasn't a part of the personal injury fraternity, so no one recognized her as a member of the bar.

At the front, Ariana stood guard in her blood red outfit. Did it now have blood stains on it? It was impossible to tell.

"Thank God!" Ariana said. "These guys are driving me nuts. I'm so glad you're not a real lawyer."

Jen held her tongue.

Dr. Ghandi walked out just as Jen walked in. The doctor gave her a dirty look. "If she didn't keep asking for you, I wouldn't let you in."

"Jen's cool," Susie croaked. "She's the only one I trust."

The doctor gestured that she could pass.

Inside, Susie's bed was now elevated about thirty degrees. There now was a picture of Hal on the window sill with a flower next to it.

Today Susie looked a little less puffy, but as tired as if she'd just finished a million hole course on a windy day. She still had the neck brace. Is that where they did spinal surgery? At the sight of Susie, Jen was reminded that this wasn't about money. She cursed her own moment of greed. Susie was a real person, not a paycheck.

There was a flush from the toilet and a middle-aged Asian woman came out of the bathroom. She wore a tight leopard-skin mini-skirt, which exposed her long legs—and her pink underpants. She also wore the highest heels Jen had ever seen.

At fifty, the woman had bleached blond hair with jet-black roots, but her colorist had missed a streak of gray. She looked like a Korean Cruella de Ville. She wore blue contacts that made her eyes looked like they were stolen from a Navajo fetish necklace. Her boob job, under a tight black shirt, must have sucked all the saline out of the Great Salt Lake.

"Who are you?" Jen asked. "You have no right to be here!"

The woman laughed, but did not offer her hand. "I have more of a right than you do. I'm Jae Lee Song. I'm Susie's mother, and by the looks of it, your aunt."

Jen knew little of the family history on her mother's side, other than her mother's maiden name was Song and she had married another Song, a distant cousin. Jae Lee Song was her mom's only sister, the only two daughters from her crazy grandmother, the late Un Chong Song.

Before they could exchange either niceties or threats, a very small man entered the room. Despite his tiny stature, he was stocky and had a thick beard, as if he was trying to hide his face.

Jae Lee smiled at Jen. "And this is my lawyer," she said. "Tommy Taranto. I guess that makes him Susie's lawyer, too."

Jen had a sinking feeling when she suddenly remembered what the agreement was missing.

# Mommie Dearest

SUSIE FORCED HERSELF INTO consciousness as she heard the commotion. "You're not my mother," Susie said. "You're a whore." The effort of denying her mother was almost too much for her.

Jae Lee approached her daughter, her hand outstretched.

"Screw you," Susie said to her mother. "You ripped off my trust account, you witch. I don't think that's even your lawyer. I bet that's your pimp."

Taranto said nothing, but gave a knowing smirk. Being a pimp and being a lawyer were not always mutually exclusive.

"Show her the letter, Jen."

Jen showed them the letter.

"That won't hold up in court," Taranto said. "You know that."

Susie looked at Jen. "Work something out. I'm counting on you. Make them go away."

Jen was taken aback. She saw the pain and need in Susie's eyes.

"I think we'd better go outside," Jen said to Jae Lee and Taranto.

✛

Jae Lee, Taranto, and Jen went to the balcony lounge. Through the massive windows, Jen could see all of Albuquerque beneath her. Thankfully, they did not have to look west toward the Bosque, the scene of the crime. Instead they stared off to the east, at the Sandia Crest. Jen could barely make out the Sandia Tram on its descent from the crest. She shuddered again as she thought about the time she nearly had a fainting spell going up the tram.

Premonition?

Jen turned her attention away from the window and toward her new companions. How had Susie sprung from such a trashy woman? Jae Lee must have hung out in the bar while her sister, Jen's mom, had gone to nursing school. Her eyes were almost as bloodshot as her daughter's.

Jen then experienced a sinking realization in the pit of her stomach. Jen could have turned out just like Jae Lee, if she had not met Luna and saved herself. Jen recalled various urban myths surrounding Jae Lee that had been posted on the Internet. She'd been a stripper, or perhaps an escort at a legal brothel near Vegas when she got herself knocked up by a pro golfer on tour. Still, Jae Lee always had money from somewhere. There was no such thing as a free boob job. Did it really come from Susie's trust account?

In another myth, one of Jae Lee's summer boyfriends was a golf pro at a local resort in Tucson, or perhaps a caddy. This mystery man supposedly taught nine-year-old Susie how to play golf, in exchange for the favors of Jae Lee.

That Jen had never met her aunt was not surprising. Jae Lee and Chan Wol never spoke, and the rest of the family had shunned Jen and her mother since the murder charges a few years back.

They shunned *us*? Jen shook her head.

The only reason Jen knew Susie was because Susie did that stretch with her mom at the old group home for troubled girls. Jen didn't even know she had an aunt until a few years ago. She realized now that she hadn't missed much.

Jen took another look at Tommy Taranto. He was a walking gangster cliché, except for his size. He had Al Pacino's suit from *Scarface*, with Robert DeNiro's yellow metallic tie from *Casino*. He must have stolen his lounge shirt from Tony Soprano. It was not a coincidence that the FBI relocated mob criminals to Arizona. Taranto must have spilled the beans on some pretty big guys in order to keep his law license.

"I don't think there's much to talk about," Taranto said. "Actually, case closed. I'm her lawyer, despite what your little scribble might say. Susie has not reached the age of majority. She can't sign a binding contract without her mother, who is her legal guardian, signing off on it."

"But—"

Jae Lee flashed a smile; a few of her teeth were gold.

Time to suck it up. Jen didn't smile back. "I understand Susie has considered becoming emancipated, especially if she stays here in New Mexico, which it seems she will have to do for the foreseeable future. Susie also wants a complete review of her trust account, and have it reviewed by a New Mexico judge."

"Yeah?" Jae Lee asked.

"Susie told me you use her trust account like your ATM."

Jae Lee said nothing. She was taller than Jen, even without heels, and could probably suffocate Jen in her boobs alone.

"What do boob jobs go for, ten grand?" Jen asked. She now looked at Taranto. The sheer size of Jae Lee's breasts suggested that she had gone top dollar. Either that or had a volume discount. "That would make it felony embezzlement in Arizona. Maybe a Federal crime if you crossed state lines. You won't be able to spend the money while you're in prison."

Taranto frowned. "It will take a court order for a complete accounting."

"I'm a lawyer," Jen said, feeling good. Shooting Jae Lee was like shooting fish in a barrel. "By the way, my sister is a judge. I can get a court order in an hour."

"Then we're at an impasse," Taranto said.

Just then Jen's phone rang. She picked it up, even though her phone displayed an unknown number. She recognized Sir Ian's voice immediately.

"I understand you're considering litigation," he said.

"This is not a good time. I'm at the hospital right now."

"So I've been informed," he said ominously. Informed? Who informed him? Jen looked at Taranto. She didn't trust him as far as she could throw him.

"Hmmm. Perhaps we should talk," Jen said.

"That might be in our mutual interest," he said.

"Could you hold on for a sec?" Jen asked. She looked at Jae Lee and Taranto. "It's Sir Ian."

Part of Jen thought she should take this call privately, but she wanted to relish the power she had at the moment.

"What is he saying?" Taranto asked. "We could end this impasse right now."

Jen nodded. "Sir Ian, you said you wanted to talk?"

"I'll be back in New Mexico tomorrow morning. I'll be at the launch down at the spaceport for the Star Prize contest.

Why don't you come down? By yourself. Hopefully we can resolve this issue. We have a launch set for two o'clock in honor
of my son. You might want to stay for that."

Jen looked Taranto in the eye as she covered the phone.

Taranto smiled. "If we could resolve the issue tomorrow that
might be best for all concerned," he said.

"Sounds good," said Jen. "What kind of a launch?"

"A special launch in honor of my son. It will be quite emotional. Please be here noonish," Sir Ian said.

"Of course. I'll see you *noonish*."

Jen hung up, and then stared down Taranto.

"Mr. Taranto," Jen said. "Sir Ian wants to talk with *me*, not
you. By myself. I do have the signed paper saying I am Jen's
lawyer. What's that old saying? A bird in the hand and all that?
I have some leverage over him that you don't have."

Jae Lee laughed. "But I'm Susie's mother."

Jen ignored her. "If I am Susie's lawyer right now, I can ne-
gotiate with Sir Ian directly, as soon as tomorrow. This contingency agreement gives me one third. You will get an equitable
share to be determined by a court. We can fight over those issues at a later time, and can put the settlement money into escrow until then. Aunt Jae Lee, you need to sign off as her
guardian, just so we can get the ball rolling."

If she didn't insist on an escrow account, Taranto would
move the money somewhere. But, Jen had enough confidence
that if they could get a signed agreement quickly, that everything would work out by launch, well, by *lunch*, tomorrow.

They all traipsed back into Susie's room.

"I want Jen to be my lawyer!" she said.

"If that's what you want baby," Jae Lee said. "But mommy dearest has to sign, too."

Jen first handed the agreement to Susie. She had to bring the agreement up to Susie's face, and Susie nodded. Jen brought it really close to Susie.

"I told you I can move my arms. Other than being stiff from the crash, I'm totally fine *above* the waist."

Susie signed the agreement with a flourish.

"Do I have to date it?" Susie asked.

"I can do that," Ariana said. "As I said, I'm a notary."

"My turn," Jae Lee said.

Jen then handed the retainer agreement to Jae Lee. In her years of martial arts training, Jen had learned that when you bow to your opponent, you never take your eye off them. Jen kept her eye trained intently on Jae Lee.

Jae Lee looked at Taranto, who nodded. She signed next to Susie Song as "Jae Lee Song, legal guardian of Susie Song."

"Once we get the money it will go into an escrow account immediately," Jen repeated. "We can fight over it then."

Taranto smiled. "Of course," he said. "And at that time, we'll resolve all our differences.

"I guess we're all in bed together. For now."

Taranto and Jae Lee left. They didn't even bother to say good-bye to Susie on their way out.

Jen squeezed Susie gently on the shoulder, as far away from the neck brace as possible. "I'll try to get this over quickly. I'll try to get you some real money."

Susie then whispered in Jen's ear, "Help me, Jen. You're my only hope."

# Buttes Like White Elephants

JEN STARTED SOUTH ON I-25 before dawn in the Saturn she had inherited from Luna. Since Saturns were extinct, the car was made up of replacement parts from other brands—a bionic Frankenstein on wheels. The vehicle now had over one hundred sixty thousand miles on it. When her phone rang, Jen was surprised to see it was Susie. Through the speaker, her voice sounded weak.

"Where are you?" Susie asked.

"Los Lunas."

"Is there a Starbucks in Los Lunas?"

Jen looked to her right, off the freeway. "Yes. I think it's the last Starbucks until Las Cruces. Why do you want to know?"

"So you can keep me posted about your adventures. Let me know about every Starbucks. I was supposed to have a sponsorship deal with them. The Susie Song thermos to keep your coffee warm for early morning golfing."

Jen wished she had a Susie Song thermos right now, filled with coffee.

"Okay. I just hope Sir Ian will resolve this thing quickly."

"Me too. Make sure you stay for the memorial service, either way. I really could have loved Hal."

Jen sensed a rush of emotion coming from Susie's end. "Was he the one?"

"I don't know. He was the first boy who wasn't afraid of me. Maybe once we got serious I could have learned to love him. Maybe we could have even had children. Just think about what those kids would have looked like. . . ."

Jen formed a picture of the most beautiful mixed race children in the world.

"Now we'll never know," Susie said before she hung up.

On the other side of Los Lunas, the village of the Lunas, Luna herself called. "I've talked to a forensic accountant slash investigator," she said.

Jen had a vision of a CSI crime scene with a man in a white coat holding a calculator. "What's that?"

"It's someone who can look at financial records and find out what's stolen or not."

"That sounds like a good idea."

"His name is Cowboy Begay. Used to be a cop on the rez."

Jen nodded with recognition. A few years back Cowboy Begay had helped her fake her own death on the Indian reservation. He was a good man and a good cop.

"He's now a private investigator," Luna continued. "Apparently he got his CPA while on the force to investigate fraud at the casino. Jen, this is going to get sticky, especially with Taranto and Jae Lee. They may seem to be on our side, but they're not."

"Duh," Jen said.

"Once we get the money, the real fight could begin."

Jen thought back to Taranto, the mobster dwarf. That man did not scare easily. "Well, hopefully, right now Sir Ian is going to write me such a big check that it won't matter."

"Do you really think that's going to happen?"

Jen didn't know what to think.

Before she knew it Jen had passed Belen, the next town. Then she passed Socorro and headed for Truth or Consequences. This stretch of the interstate, past Socorro, was pretty bad for her. She had ADD, and there was nothing to look at in either direction. That made her feel agitated.

Lonely, she called Susie back. Ariana answered, and then put Susie on speaker. "I'm heading toward Truth or Consequences."

"Is that a real town?"

By the sound of her voice, Jen knew Susie had been crying.

"I don't know. They named it after a game show."

"So what will you find, truth or consequences?"

"I like truth *without* consequences, but we'll see about that, won't we?"

This stretch of desert was barren to the point of existentialism. If you squinted you could see the brown waters of Elephant Butte Lake way off to the southeast, but usually it looked like a mirage in the dusty desert air, and that somehow made it worse.

Hills like white elephants? That was Hemingway, right? Here the elephants looked a little tanner, the hills fatter. Did that make them hills like white hippopotamuses?

The road became a roller coaster as it ascended and descended the great arroyos. As she sped down arroyo La Canada

Alamosa getting the car up to ninety-five, she felt another bit of vertigo. For one brief moment she could almost glimpse her past, but as she went up the other side, the glimpse faded away.

Why couldn't she remember?

As the car descended into the next valley, Nogal Canyon, the feeling came back. She could remember remembering. In addition to Ed Hobbs, there had been two more deaths—her boyfriends Paul Dellagio and Adam Marin. She couldn't have killed them both in cold blood, could she?

Now, the highway straightened and her depression lifted. She saw the border patrol station north of Exit 150. It had to be the most interior border patrol station in the nation.

She remembered that Ed Hobbs had been detained there and busted for drugs. If he had never been busted, she'd still be his legal secretary. Jen didn't want to think about her past, so she forced herself to concentrate on the rest of the road.

Jen was nervous about the meeting with Sir Ian. She sure hoped he would give her a suitcase filled with cash and she could keep driving south. She'd heard that Brazil was lovely this time of year.

Susie called again and they talked more about the desert. "You're my eyes now, Jen."

"Your eyes?"

"My doctors are being jerks right now. I want to move to a rehab center, but they're worried about an infection after the surgery. I so do not want to be here!"

"Then I have to bring back enough money to get you out of there."

# Tatooine

A FEW MILES SOUTH of Truth or Consequences the traffic increased. Every car seemed to be headed in the same direction, toward the spaceport. When Jen finally reached the exit, near Upham, she felt she might as well be in line for the balloon fiesta, except she wasn't a VIP. She waited semi-patiently behind a million recreational vehicles from all over New Mexico—and even Texas and Arizona.

The spaceport was the location of the Star Prize Rocket Tournament that occurred a few weeks after the balloon fiesta. Many of the players were the same. Often, people who designed rockets also dabbled in balloons. Many retirees also took in the fiesta one weekend, toured around New Mexico, and then went to the Star Prize.

As she drove slowly east on the access road, Jen saw all sorts of mock-ups of rockets and spacecraft. Workmen constructed massive buildings whose purposes she could not even imagine. The cylindrical spaceport terminal building itself was still half finished. The highest part of the cylinder looked like a two-story rattlesnake's head about to bite its own tail.

Jen called Susie. "I'm at the spaceport."

"Jen, do me a favor, keep it light. I'm going through a lot right now with the pain. Cheer me up."

Jen thought for a moment. "Well, the spaceport reminds me of Tatooine, the home planet of Luke Skywalker in *Star Wars*." Jen could hear a giggle on the Susie's end. "Do you see any sand-people?"

"I see some *Jawas*," Jen said. "I really do see some little people in hoods. Some of the big guards could be Imperial storm troopers."

"If they bust you, just say 'I'm not the droid you're looking for,'" Susie quoted.

"They might turn you into a droid," Jen said. "A bionic woman."

"I don't want to be a droid," Susie said. "Not yet at least."

"There's a band here, they look like a cantina band."

"What does that make Sir Ian, Jabba the Hutt?" Susie asked. "And what does that make me, Princess Leia in a slave outfit?"

"You're nobody's slave, Susie."

"Damn right, keep doing this Jen. You're cheering me up. Ariana is changing my ummm . . . *bag* right now, so it smells pretty bad."

Ariana must have hung up the line.

Jen's Saturn crawled forward. Suddenly, someone tapped on her window. Jen jumped. She almost expected to see a mutated lizard. It was only Jean Claude.

"*Mademoiselle*, park over there and come with me."

She liked being called mademoiselle, rather than what he had called her when he was chasing her. After parking in a private lot, next to Sir Ian's gigantic private helicopter, Jean Claude escorted Jen to a silver trailer that looked like it had landed there, like a flying saucer. Jen wondered if the helicopter had dropped the trailer down with Sir Ian in it. The silver trailer had antennas everywhere, and some cable connections going into the ground made it look like Han Solo's smuggling ship, *Millennium Falcon*, in a desert dry dock.

Jean Claude punched in a code, and the metal door slid open.

"*Mademoiselle*," he said again, indicating that she should enter. He remained outside and guarded the door.

Jen gulped before she walked up the stair and entered the trailer.

Inside, the saucer brimmed with the latest high tech, and was far more cramped than expected. It looked more like a geek's basement than a command center. Jen imagined that Sir Ian could launch a rocket attack anywhere in the world if he wanted, or else he could just use the TV screens to watch the latest porn from Bangkok. Sir Ian hastily turned one screen off before she could check it out.

He made eye-contact briefly. Sir Ian looked hung-over and wore black, Darth Vader with the helmet off. His bloodshot eyes looked even redder this early in the morning. However, his blonde hair, even his beard, looked blonder. Had he dyed it? She scanned his arms; he still had some bruises from their encounter. Had she really scratched him that hard?

He broke eye contact and stared at a countdown screen on a monitor. Then he fingered an urn on the counter.

"Shite," he said under his breath.

Sir Ian was not alone. A nattily dressed South Asian man introduced himself as Mr. Gupta. Gupta's suit with its sideways Gordon Gekko pinstripes probably cost more than a rocket.

Jen noticed that Gupta held a briefcase.

This is it!

"What's in the case?" she asked, far too eagerly.

"Sir Ian is prepared to offer you one hundred *thousand* dollars," Gupta said with a plastic smile. "If you don't press charges for the alleged assault."

"What?" Jen was confused. "He assaulted Susie, too?"

Gupta was surprised. He pressed the briefcase closer to her. "For his alleged assault on *you*."

"Huh?"

"Of course, we'd like to see your medical records from the hospital. Do you have them with you?"

"My medical records?" She was confused. "I'm not here about that."

"You're not?" Gupta asked. "Then what?"

Jen took a deep breath. She pushed the briefcase away. "I'm representing Susie Song."

"You're here for Susie? You?" Sir Ian started laughing.

Gupta started laughing as well. He looked at her. "You're representing Susie Song? As a lawyer?"

Jen suddenly felt two inches tall. "She's my cousin."

Sir Ian laughed even harder. "I mean, didn't you used to be a stripper?"

"I was a waitress. I never stripped."

"What was your waitress name? Pink, right?" he still laughing. "What do you think, Pink, you're going to show me your tits and I'll give you a billion dollars for a private dance?"

Jen didn't know how to respond. She now felt one inch tall.

"You went to UNM and were in the bottom half of your class." Gupta said. "You went to the University of Nothing Much. They didn't even admit you to the bar for a year after that. You were on probation. Technically, you're still on probation."

"I did all the clinical programs." Jen said. "And, I passed my probation year just fine."

"How much for a VIP dance, Pink?" Sir Ian said. "I mean, why do you think we invited you to the party?'

"I keep telling you, I was just a waitress."

"You're being disingenuous."

So that's what he meant when he said her reputation preceded her. Jen now wished that she was completely invisible.

Gupta tried to return the conversation back to a measure of civility. "So you were at the hospital visiting Susie? You weren't there for yourself?"

Jen nodded. She didn't know if she could talk at this point.

"You never got a medical examination, did you?" Gupta asked, as if scoring a major point before the jury.

They could check her medical records with a court order. She felt her neck. The bite was barely more than a mosquito bite. "Uhh . . . no."

Gupta smiled . "It would look very suspicious if you had a medical examination *after* you met with me, don't you think?"

Jen didn't know how to respond.

"Then it looks like we'll see you in court with Susie, then," Gupta said. "Wear something pink."

"Are you sure we can't work out something for Susie?"

"Miss Pink," Gupta said. "We will be litigating Sir Ian's defense with the utmost vigor. There will be no settlement."

"No settlement?"

He smiled. "Unless of course you wish to take the hundred thousand dollars that we have right now. Considerable evidence will come out concerning your client that makes this offer a most generous one."

Jen almost took it. Her share would be more than she made in a year. Maybe it wasn't in her best interest to tilt at the world biggest windmill.

"Let me talk to my client."

Gupta laughed. "You do that, Miss Pink."

Jen walked out into the desert with Jean Claude trailing behind her. After a few attempts, where her phone's signals failed to launch, Jen finally got through to Susie. Ariana picked up and put her on speaker.

"Hold on," Ariana said. Ominous creaking noises emerged from the speaker.

"What's going on?"

"My bed is going up," Susie said.

Susie was panting. Just being moved a few feet was exhausting to her body.

Jen took a deep breath of her own. "Sir Ian is offering a hundred thousand dollars."

There was a long pause. Jen could hear the sound of machines whirring on the other side of the speaker. "That's a lot of money isn't it?"

"No, it's not. That won't last me for the rest of my life. That won't even replace what my mom took from my trust account. But you said they would offer more."

Luna had once told her that the worst words a client could say to a lawyer were "but," "you," and "said." Now Susie had just said those words to her.

Jen thought of Gupta and his smirk. She wanted to get this over with. "The money isn't that important, is it? It's the principle. You'd be able to put this behind you and go on with your life."

"What life?" Susie asked.

"So what should I tell him?"

Jen hoped Susie would take the money and this whole thing would be over. She would still get thirty three thousand or so. That was something.

There was a moment of silence on the other end. Then Susie said, "Tell him to fuck off."

Jen was embarrassed to go back inside, but gathered her courage and did so anyway. "She's not going to take your offer."

Sir Ian sneered. "That's your final answer?"

"I guess so." She looked at the briefcase and imagined the money inside. It was more than she could make in a year.

Sir Ian looked at the urn. "Well, Pink, it wouldn't be right to send you away after your long journey. Feel free to stay for the launch. It's the least I can do, the very least. You did meet my son after all. I'm sure he would want you here. You can be here as Susie's, how should we call it . . . as Susie's *liaison*."

Jen wanted to protest, but couldn't think of anything to say.

# No Such Thing as a Free Launch

JEN LEFT THE CRAMPED trailer and walked into the dusty Tatooine air as she pondered something Gupta had said: "All the evidence against your client." What did that mean? Had Susie been the driver? Could Sir Ian sue *Susie* for the death of his son? Then she noticed Jean Claude was right behind her. They obviously didn't trust her. At all.

"*Mademoiselle,* if you'll accompany me."

Most of the RV crowd waited behind a barricade. It was a NASCAR kind of crowd, more Talladega than Tatooine. The crowd mostly consisted of families that had coolers filled with various beverages. Other than a slightly higher preponderance of nerdy boys—and nerdy men—this could be an afternoon at an Alabama football game. The children looked quite enthusiastic. Some fathers looked like they wanted to see a crash.

The spaceport had one of the longest runways Jen had ever seen. She could not see the end of it. But, she could see a few missile silos off in the distance.

Jen felt part of the elite as Jean Claude escorted her past the main crowd and toward the grandstand, a temporary structure that was in surprisingly bad shape. As she walked up each step, Jen worried that she might fall through the gaps in the stands and do a face plant in the sand below.

Jean Claude escorted her to a seat at the very top, next to a few engineers who were jabbering in a foreign language. Jen looked below her seat in the stands. Were those rattlesnakes wiggling in the shadows? No, she definitely didn't want to fall down there.

A sign warned the crowd to WATCH FOR RATTLESNAKES, but snakes were the least of her worries right now. The grandstand began shaking under the weight of several heavy-set men in suits who were climbing up the stairs. One actually tripped, but someone picked him up before he could fall on anyone.

Jen looked around at the nearby crowd. This wasn't rabble. She recognized people from the party, including Wagatsuma and the sheiks. Their long white *thobes* seemed the most sensible outfit here in the desert. Albuquerque was in the high desert, but here, a few thousand feet lower in elevation would be the lower desert, right? A few wild palms swayed in the wind.

In the front row, Jen saw several college girls wearing little black dresses, and a rugby team wearing their black dress uniforms. Jen also recognized Claus sitting a few rows lower down. He had brought his family with him for a day in the country, and they all sat together quietly. Claus was a heavy-set man and the Samoan triplets, or whatever they were, probably weighed close to half a ton combined. The bench sagged under their weight. She waved to him and he waved back, as did the entire bunch. They were all so cute. Why couldn't her family be like that?

Claus hurried to her. "How is your cousin?"

"It changes from day to day," Jen said, purposefully vague.

"As I said, if there's anything I can do to help," he said. "I would even do it *pro bono*."

"I'll keep that in mind."

After an interminable wait, Sir Ian finally emerged from the little trailer. He now wore a black blazer over a black shirt and slacks. The blazer had the same lion's crest with gold and red trim as the rugby team. The gold perfectly matched his hair and beard, and the red matched his ruddy face. Jen wondered if that was a coincidence.

Snape followed Sir Ian, eyes darting everywhere as he carried the urn.

Jen's phone rang. It was Ariana. "Susie wants to hear the memorial service. Hal meant a lot to her. I'll put her on speaker."

Sir Ian went to the podium and began to address the crowd in the stands, but Jen sensed something wasn't right as Sir Ian mumbled that his son was "a fine young chap."

Even Susie noticed it through the phone. "I've been crying my eyes out and I'm not even there. For someone who just lost a son, he doesn't sound too hurt," she said.

Jen shivered, then sweated, then shivered once again. Damn wind.

By the time Sir Ian finally finished talking about his son even the rattlesnakes had gone to sleep. He then introduced a burly Navajo woman who came up to speak.

"Who's that?" Susie asked.

"I know her," Jen said. "She's Heidi Hawk, a friend of Luna's. She was a former clerk at district court who became a female boxer. My ex boyfriend, Dan Shepard, knew her from way back, too. Apparently she's now a shaman, or a skinwalker, or whatever they're called. I guess she's going to do a Native American blessings."

"A boxer turned skinwalker, how cool is that?" Susie asked, her breathing becoming labored. "I think a skinwalker is the spirit itself, not the person who calls it. Maybe someone will write a novel about her some day."

On the makeshift stage, Heidi nodded to Sir Ian and spoke a few words in Diné, the Navajo language. She then chanted some blessings. Despite Jen's skepticism, the beauty of Heidi's chants penetrated her defenses. Heidi could take generations of sadness and turn it into music, and as her voice steadily rose, she somehow put in an undeniable dollop of hope.

Heidi's chants ended abruptly, as if to symbolize a young life cut short. Her words echoed throughout the canyon. Then the desert grew silent, except for distant mechanical sounds and the rattling of people in the stands.

"That was like so beautiful," Susie said. Jen could now hear tears on Susie's end. "Give me a minute."

Jen cried, too.

When Susie had composed herself she said, "It has, what do the Native Americans call it, *medicine.* I actually feel better over here."

Heidi took in her surroundings, then frowned as if she sensed something wasn't right. The elements were out of balance and she began chanting anew. This time, it sounded more like a curse than a blessing. She again stopped abruptly but this time she glared at Sir Ian. If that was medicine, it was bad medicine. Jen felt something odd stirring in the earth as the wind picked up.

"Well, all right then," Sir Ian said dismissively. He nodded at Snape, who boarded a pimped-out black golf cart with the Lyon Aerospace logo and drove to the rocket in the distance. Snape showed off as he maneuvered the golf cart through the brush like the Mars rover.

Jen took a good look at the rocket but couldn't judge its size from this far away. She thought the rocket was a small one, maybe six feet high. It looked more like a World War II relic than a modern missile, but she supposed it still cost a lot of money.

Snape placed Hal's urn into a compartment on the old rocket's body, and then returned quickly. Perhaps he didn't trust Sir Ian's trigger finger.

Right behind Sir Ian, an electronic clock began a countdown. Two minutes to go.

Those two minutes took ten. The ancient rocket's guidance system wasn't synching with modern electronics. Several times the electronic clock reached thirty seconds before it jumped back up to five minutes.

Jen noticed that a man the size of the Hurley, the fat guy on *Lost*, grew quite impatient. Claus moved his heavy-set family up another row, to distance themselves. Could the stands handle the stress of all the weight?

Jen also noticed that many of the investors were squirming, as if watching their sons on the losing end of a junior high football game.

"How can he expect me to invest in manned spaceflight, if he can't launch one tiny urn?" one asked.

Jen wanted to leave the spaceport, get back to civilization, and get away from Sir Ian, but when was she ever going to see another rocket launch in person?

"I don't care what happens," one teen said. "I just want it to blow big time."

"Boom, boom," said another. "Just like the Death Star."

Jen had given up hope of ever seeing the rocket launch when smoke finally emerged from its base. This really was it. The rugby players began doing the "We will rock you," double-stomp and single clap.

Jen joined in. She really wanted to be rocked, although she wasn't quite sure what that meant under these circumstances.

The boys chanted, "We will *rocket* you!"

Susie said something through the phone, but the noise surrounding Jen was too loud for her to hear.

Heat came from the direction of the rocket, a blistering desert heat. A few seconds before she expected, the rocket began a slow ascent into the New Mexico desert air. The rocket lifted slower than a balloon and was buffeted by the quickly changing winds. Something wasn't right. The ancient rocket vibrated as if the air itself was shaking it. The fins shook more and more with every foot of altitude. The rocket strained for more one moment and then abruptly exploded.

The flash of the explosion was so strong that Jen momentarily lost her vision. When she regained her eyesight, the rocket had shattered into a million pieces, and flaming debris rained down over the desert, like hell during monsoon season.

People screamed and raced from the shaking stands. A few jumped, which made the stands shake even more. Hurley started bounding down, before tripping and falling hard on his left side. Then everyone else began an avalanche of humanity.

Jen thought about soccer riots where the stands came down on top of everyone.

Behind the barricades, the NASCAR crowd ran in all directions. Thank God she sat in the stands above them or she could be trampled to death. Even the snakes had scurried away.

But, perhaps she wasn't that lucky after all. Suddenly, the rickety stands beneath her feet disappeared. Jen felt herself flying in the air and for one moment she was like a cartoon character who hadn't realized she was falling. But then she looked down.

"Jen!' Susie yelled through the speaker. "Jen! Are you there?"

# Unstuck

JEN FELL DEEPER AND deeper into the darkness; the earth came closer in the light of the golden sun below. Golden sun below? That was impossible. The sun should be in the sky not below. Was she at district court, falling? But that hadn't happened yet, had it? Time rolled around like a figure eight, like the infinity symbol, like a rattlesnake biting its own tail.

The golden sun lurked below her, rotating like crazy, right there in the courthouse, about to go supernova. The sun was in the courthouse? And it was below her? That didn't make sense. She knew the little sun below her, that rotating disk of light on the fifth floor was somehow vitally important. That light could save her life, yet she could not figure out why or how.

The light was the passageway to the next world. It was the light. Go to the light?

But didn't the light mean death?

Time felt like a bungee cord as she lost consciousness and her memories flung her backward.

✝

Jen looked around. For one brief moment she thought she was in hell; there were fires up above her and also rumbling down below. It took Jen a moment to realize that she was back on the volcano the night of the 4th of July fireworks, the night Ed Hobbs died. As before, the light felt flat, the colors as intense as if they had weight. She had returned to the *anime*.

Jen floated above the earth like an angel. She saw herself, below, as Laser Geisha Pink and Pink was not alone. Jen tried to place the time. It must be a year after she had killed Hobbs. Pink sat with Jen's old boyfriend Adam Marin. Adam smiled at her. Pink smiled back. He had undressed down to his bare chest and was approaching her. There was lust in his eyes. He was going to hurt her again.

"He's going to rape her." In that one instant, all the violence in their relationship flashed through Jen's brain. "She's going to kill him," Jen said out loud.

"Hold on a second, baby," Pink said, down below. "I got something for you that'll help improve the mood."

Pink slowly slipped pills into his drink.

From above, Jen tightened. How could this woman be so casual, so evil?

Adam smiled at her as he gulped the drink down. He stumbled for a moment, and then fell into a deep sleep right in front of her. He did not wake up.

That was what she had wanted, right?

Jen's soul kept floating above Pink. She was shocked to see there was no remorse on Pink's face.

"Was that really me?" Jen's soul asked. "Am I that cold blooded killer down there?"

Pink said nothing. She stared at Adam's dead body for a moment before she poured a gallon of gasoline over the corpse and lit a match.

Up above, Jen's soul cried.

"That isn't me," Jen said. "Please, dear God, let that woman down below not be me!"

# Lunar Landing

JEN AWOKE IN WHITENESS. For one brief moment she thought she had indeed crossed over, but there was no way she could end up in heaven after all she had done. Just no way. She looked at the face of a woman, an angel. The woman sang to her softly in Korean, a lullaby, the sweetest song she'd ever heard. It took a few moments to recognize her own mother.

"Where am I?" Jen asked. "Am I alive?"

"Duh," Luna said, imitating Jen's old catch phrase. She stood next to Nurse Song. "You're in the hospital in Albuquerque," Luna said.

Nurse Song tried to play nurse. "You had a minor concussion, but you're all right now."

"How did I get here?"

"Medics transported you," Claus said, emerging from the bathroom. "All the beds in Las Cruces were full so they brought you here. I followed them up." He took her hand and nodded. "Now that you're awake, I'll leave you with your family."

Jen frowned. "Do you have to go?"

He was already out the door.

"I am so glad you are awake," Nurse Song said. "We were so worried. What happened?"

"I don't know. I was taken up in a big tornado and taken to this magical land. And you were there," she said, pointing to Luna. "You were there, too," she said pointing to her mother. "After getting up in that tornado, now I realize that there's—"

"No place like home," Jen and Luna said together.

"Jinx!" They shouted.

No one said anything after that for a long while.

Jen knew she was supposed to say something. "Where's Denise?" she finally asked.

Nurse Song gestured to a nurse who brought the little girl in. Nurse Song nodded at Denise and the little girl gave Jen a dutiful kiss on the forehead. It was as if Denise was fulfilling a contractual obligation. Denise then looked at Nurse Song. She didn't say anything, but it was clear that she wanted to go.

"Denise, why don't you go out and play with Nurse Ratchet," Nurse Song said.

Denise took the nurse's hand and walked out of the room without a second glance at her mother.

"Why does she hate me?" Jen asked. "Does she ever talk when I'm not around?"

"No," Nurse Song said. "She's waiting for the right time."

Jen wondered if the time would ever be right.

# Check Up From the Neck Up

As Luna and Nurse Song went out the door a doctor came in to check on Jen. It wasn't Dr. Ghandi, but another Indian doctor named Patel.

"When can I get out of here?" Jen asked.

"We're going to give you a psych consult first," Dr. Patel said. "Standard procedure."

Jen had some anxiety about that. What should she say to the doctor? I'm a recovering serial killer? An hour after the psych interview ended, Dr. Romero entered the cramped room.

"I need to be alone with my patient," she said, sending a nurse scurrying for the door.

Dr. Romero squeezed Jen's hand. "How are you doing?"

"I had a flashback," Jen said. "I know how I killed Adam Marin. I slipped some pills into his drink on the volcano. That sounds pretty deliberate. It wasn't a temporary bouts of insanity. Pink took over for a long time and was totally calm."

Dr. Romero took her hand. "Jen, you were in a psychotic state. It's a symptom of your illness. You couldn't tell right from wrong. Don't worry about it."

Jen wasn't convinced. "I've got demons."

"Everyone has demons. You acted out under extreme conditions toward people who had harmed you. Through counseling and medication you've learned to control yourself."

Jen still wasn't sure. Then she noticed that Dr. Romero kept holding her hand long after it was professional to do so.

"What is this really about?" Jen asked. "Why are you trying so hard to convince me that I'm sane?"

Dr. Romero checked to make sure the door was still closed. "Jen, I first met you when Luna wanted me to give you an evaluation for sentencing."

"I *do* remember that," Jen said. "It took forever. You kept asking me all kinds of questions, personal questions; I wondered if you knew what you were doing."

"Do you remember when I said that occasionally there are patients I actually like as people?"

Jen paused. It didn't sound right when the doctor said that.

"Uh . . . yeah," she said at last.

Dr. Romero cleared her throat. "Jen, I'm over forty in Albuquerque. It's like being over forty in Siberia. I'm very single. Everyone my age is in a committed relationship. In Albuquerque, being over forty and single is like being seventy everywhere else."

Jen didn't feel comfortable with the direction of the conversation.

Dr. Romero continued. "You are so beautiful. I was always impressed by how hard you tried to cure yourself. How you struggled so hard to be a good person. How you wanted everyone to like you. I found that so charming."

Now it sunk in. Dr. Romero squeezed her arm, and then caressed it. Jen pulled her arm away. "I'm your patient, *doctor*."

"I've never violated the doctor-patient relationship. After I sign the forms today and you are released, I can write a letter of discharge. In about two months—"

"I don't know," Jen said. "It just doesn't feel right. I'm not like that."

"I love you, Jen," Dr. Romero said, her professionalism long since gone.

Jen tried to imagine them as a couple. Dr. Romero was strong, very tall; there was something almost masculine about her. She did love Dr. Romero, but as a doctor, not a woman. No. This was a line she did not want to cross.

Jen didn't want to hurt the doctor's feelings. "Let me think about it, okay?"

Dr. Romero filled out the discharge form.

Jen suddenly felt a nauseous feeling in her stomach. "So you've been in love with me the entire time?"

"I guess so."

Then Jen had a revelation. "So does that mean I'm not really cured?"

A nurse came in before Dr. Romero could answer.

# World's Shortest Deposition

JEN SIGNED SOME PAPERWORK from the nurse and she was officially discharged. She didn't know how to process what Dr. Romero had told her. As if on cue, her brain recited the beginning of the Cypress Hill song "Insane in the Brain." A rapper asked *"Who you trying to get crazy with,* ese, *don't you know I'm* loco?"

She was *loco* all right. She now felt like she had nothing left to lose any more. Besides she was going to die anyway when she hit the floor of district court, right?

Instead of leaving the complex she wandered through the hospital until she finally found Susie's wing. No one tried to "get crazy" with her. Maybe it was her eyes.

Jen entered Susie's room without knocking.

"I need to talk to her alone," Jen said.

"Is this going to take long?" Ariana looked at Jen with daggers in her eyes. She had already scared off a cop, and maybe a half dozen lawyers.

"One question. It will be the world's shortest deposition." Ariana looked at Susie.

"I'm safe with her," Susie said.

"You've got two minutes," Ariana replied as she closed the door. "I'm going to get in trouble if anybody finds out."

"This isn't about you," Jen said. "And besides you work for Susie, right?"

Susie forced a smile. She waited until Ariana shut the door, and her footsteps made it a safe distance down the hall. "Go ahead, Jen."

Jen took another deep breath even though it made her head hurt. "What really happened that night?"

"That's a big question."

"It's a billion dollar question," Jen said.

Susie was quiet, thinking. "I left with Hal," she said at last. "I knew he had been drinking, but I thought he was cool to drive. He said he'd take me to the Rio to watch the moon set over the water. He knew the perfect spot for—"

Jen didn't want to know too much information. She herself had once had a dangerous rendezvous by the Rio. There was something about the sound of flowing water in the desert, the moonlight reflecting off the shimmering water—she quickly changed the subject. "Were you driving?"

"That's two questions."

"No, that's a follow-up."

"No, I was *not* driving."

"Are you sure?"

"Yeah, I'm sure I wasn't driving. Isn't 'are you sure' a new question?"

"It's another follow up. Were you drinking that night?"

"I had one sip of that terrible red wine."

"So here's my final follow up. Sir Ian's lawyer said the accident might be your fault. Why would he say that?"

Susie blushed. Much of her body might have been frozen but her face turned a vivid pink.

Jen didn't know how to read Susie. The girl was a seventeen-year-old superstar who now looked as if she was four and had peed her pants at pre-school. Jen suddenly had a horrible vision. It all made sense. Susie bent over Hal as they drove down the road. Jen wondered if she had ever done that herself. Thank God she hadn't. Then again, who knows?

"Were you being . . . ah . . . inappropriate?"

Susie blushed. "No, of course not. What kind of person do you think I am?"

Susie was genuinely offended. Jen wondered if she had offended her cousin to the point of ruining their blossoming friendship.

"I'm sorry, Susie." Jen said.

Jen tried to think of other explanations for the crash. "Were you changing the radio station, or something like that, and accidentally knocked his shoulder and bumped the wheel?"

Susie said nothing, but there was a tear in her eye.

"Were you taking off your overcoat when you distracted him? Accidentally playing footsie with him and kicked the accelerator?"

"Kinda," Susie said, still red from embarassment. "I leaned over to kiss him. On the mouth."

"That could be contributory negligence," said Jen. "That could ruin the whole case."

"When did you start talking like a lawyer?"

# Fellowship of the Song

ONCE SHE WAS OUTSIDE the hospital Jen called Luna. "We've got to talk."

"I kept my end of the bargain," Luna said. "I've put together a meeting tomorrow."

"Where?"

"You'll see."

Jen didn't have any immediate plans upon her discharge from the hospital. She knew she should take care of herself—eat, drink fluids, and relax, but she felt out of sorts. Thankfully, Luna gave her a purpose by asking her to retrieve the police records on Susie's accident before the big meeting. Claus had dropped her car at the hospital, so Jen could drive downtown to the combined Albuquerque Police Station and Bernalillo County Sheriff's Office.

The clerk at the records department took down the information and then went back to the computer. Her name badge read TINA. Tina was an attractive Asian woman and looked similar to what Jen imagined herself looking like if she had married young and had four kids.

"It should be filed by now," Tina said with a smile. Then the smile turned to a frown as she stared at the screen. "Are you sure about the information?"

Jen gave it to her again.

Tina went back to the screen, frowned some more, then returned.

"There's no record," she said.

"I just saw Susie in the hospital," Jen said. "Are you saying it didn't happen? Like if a tree falls in the forest, but no one's around?"

"Not at all," Tina said. "I'm just saying there's no record of this particular tree falling in my computer. Are you sure about the spelling?"

Jen frowned. This didn't sound good. Was it possible for a billionaire to have the records removed? Jen thought briefly about the command center. Sir Ian could check on stuff up in orbit from that stupid trailer. Deleting police records would be easy.

"Shite!" Jen said under her breath.

"Why are we having the meeting out here?" Jen asked Luna the next day as they rode through a lush northern stretch of the Bosque, right along the Rio Grande, on an Indian reservation north of town. The forest looked primeval, unspoiled.

Jen didn't really like horses. She couldn't help but think of Christopher Reeve, the former Superman in the movies. He had been thrown from his horse and had never walked again. Then he died. Her mind then quickly raced to Susie.

Her horse slowed for a moment, and then started back up again. She had put her faith, as well as her spine, into the control of this large animal. Luna rode ahead, as if her horse knew the final destination; as if Luna was just along for the ride.

Jen took another look at her horse, and then a dizzying look down below at the ground.

"Don't throw me, okay?" she said to her horse, whose name was Shadowfax.

Shadowfax snorted.

After a bit Jen realized that Shadowfax was not Secretariat, but a placid horse meant for tourists. She could relax. A bit.

"Should I call Susie?" Jen asked.

"Not yet," Luna said.

Jen frowned. This entire scenario reminded her of Middle Earth from the Lord of the Rings books—or its earthly equivalent, New Zealand. Even her horse had the same name as Gandalf's horse. Some of the trees here retained the last of their leaves, although the elves in this forest might have left a few beer bottles lying around. The trees had gnarled features on their trunks; some of the markings even reminded her of faces. She remembered the name of one of the trees in Tolkien's trilogy, Treebeard. She swore that Treebeard's twin deliberately swung a branch down to hit her. Shadowfax calmly moved out of the way.

"Good horse," she said.

+

Luna turned from her horse and smiled at Jen. Luna's horse was jet black.

Jen remembered one of her first experiences with Luna. They were waiting for the grand jury to come back on Jen's case. The two had sat in the woods a few miles down river, in a Bosque much like this. Luna was great at making stressful experiences less stressful.

"Thanks Luna," Jen said. "I needed this. I haven't slept at all or eaten much of anything since I was discharged. I feel so vulnerable.

"We're here for a purpose," Luna replied, somewhat mysteriously. As they rode deeper into the forest, Shadowfax snorted again as if to say, "Relax."

It was like old times when they came to the Rio. The Rio Grande actually flowed with clear water here, just a few miles north of Albuquerque. It was like a real river, rather than a mud bank. Jen wished she could take Susie riding with them. She'd heard that equine therapy was excellent for paraplegics.

They finally came to a small pagoda in the center of a clearing at the edge of the Rio. The pagoda was quaint, but hardly Rivendell, the place of the meeting in Tolkien's book.

After Luna hitched Shadowfax to a tree, Jen nearly fell to the ground when she tried to dismount. After a brief moment of vertigo, she managed to land on her feet. Jen walked over to the pagoda, a little stiff from the ride. She recognized two people who were sitting at a table, Taranto and Cowboy Begay, the Navajo cop. Claus rode in, moments after she did. He hurried over to join the table.

"Who invited you?" Taranto asked.

"I did, "Luna said. "Jen recommended him."

"Thanks for your faith," Claus said.

Jen didn't know the two others at the table. Luna made the introductions. "This is Mr. Black and this is Mr. White."

"Are those your real names?" she asked. "I feel like this is a scene out of *Reservoir Dogs*."

"I'm Joe Black," the first man said. "I'm a plaintiff's lawyer in Santa Fe."

"I'm Winston White," the second man said. "I do tax and corporate work in Los Angeles."

"Then I guess you can call me Mrs. Pink," Jen said with a smile. She frowned when she remembered that Mr. Pink in *Reservoir Dogs* was the weasel-like Steve Buscemi.

They all exchanged pleasantries and Jen felt like a hobbit amongst the big guys.

Luna then called the meeting to order. "I hope you don't mind the out of the way location. We need to discuss things privately. Sir Ian is famous for his resources and I was afraid that any room we used would be bugged. Technically, I'm not even supposed to be here, since I'm still a sitting judge, so I want to go out of my way to say that I don't want one dime of any settlement. Not one."

"Couldn't you get disbarred just for being here?" Jen asked.

"I'm not here for the money," Luna said. "I'm here for you Jen, because I'm afraid that you're in way over your head."

The others nodded.

✛

Luna took control, as if banging a gavel with her eyes. "Let's get started."

Jen tried to be pro-active. "I went to the records department yesterday. I think Sir Ian had the records expunged."

Mumbling came from the table. White talked about getting a private accident re-constructionist. Black feared that Sir Ian had destroyed all the evidence, or worse, had manipulated the medical records. It was also unclear which insurance company, or companies, would be involved.

The topic switched to the potential bankruptcy of Sir Ian and his corporation.

"Of course," White said. "Sir Ian has that right, but we might be deemed a super-priority creditor."

"That would be great," Jen said.

"Yes, but it means time is of the essence. We had better be first in line, and we need to file our lawsuit before anyone else sues for any other debts. I believe there are some paternity suits out there as well."

"Can't we just write a demand letter?" Jen asked.

Everyone laughed.

"Do you really think Sir Ian Lyon is going to roll over and play dead because of a letter?" White asked. He checked his calculator. "My gut instinct is that we had better file by the end of the November. I've also heard one of his Vietnamese manufacturers will file a breach of contract suit."

More groaning came from the table. "We can't get a brief out in a month," Taranto said. "We can't even get the medicals. We don't even know where the vehicle is."

"Was there auto insurance for Hal?" Jen asked.

"Obviously that's the first thing we looked at," Begay said, rolling his eyes. "Prince Hal had no auto insurance. He didn't even have a driver's license, and would not be covered under the car's insurance through the corporation either. Susie has insurance that covers her medical care only, not loss of income. It says so specifically. Her advisor must have been retarded."

Begay shot a look at Taranto, who shrugged. "That was the only way we could get coverage."

Jen wondered if she had screwed up already and her career as a plaintiff's attorney was over before it began. Black winked at her.

"Well, can we just file something without really knowing what we're doing?" Jen said.

Luna smiled. "That's why I called Claus in."

Claus then took control, and indeed, he did sound like Santa Claus. "I have an idea. We can speed this up by going with *res ipsa loquitur.*"

Jen tried to remember back to her first year torts class. *Res Ipsa Loquitur.* The thing speaks for itself. Drunk driving. Accident. Paraplegic. They could file the lawsuit without the accident report.

"I'm the king of *res ipsa,*" Claus said. "I won a two million dollar case in Salt Lake once on a motion for summary judgment."

They all smiled, as if counting on getting the money in time for Christmas.

"Too bad the Utah Supreme Court overturned it on appeal," he said. "But I wasn't the lawyer for that part. I say we file first, ask questions later."

The legal team, this new Fellowship, talked amongst themselves. If Claus could write a good brief and force a settlement quickly, before Sir Ian completed a merger or filed for bankruptcy, they would be first on the list of creditors. They'd have their money and it would be spent long before the higher courts could get involved.

Begay then rose. Even in his plainclothes, with his long ponytail, barbed wire tattoo, and blue sweatshirt, he still looked every inch the cop.

"Sir Ian is in the process of selling his corporation," Begay said, as if talking about a dead body rather than a legal entity. "The negotiations had broken down with a Japanese consortium, the Wagatsuma Conglomerate, and it looked like he was selling to Ahmad Assed, an emir of some oil kingdom turned high tech hub. Still, I hear that Wagatsuma remains interested. This is one more reason we need to get this thing filed fast, so we can attach his assets quickly before the ownership situation gets complicated."

Jen thought back to the party and remembered the Japanese man and the Arab sheik.

Black jumped in. "The Lyon Corporation has one major asset in New Mexico, a partial ownership interest in the spaceport. That's worth billions, even if the State and the Federal government also have shares."

"You *can* win," Luna said. "But collecting could be a bitch."

"I can be a bitch, too," Jen said.

"Jen, there are grown-ups here," Luna warned.

Taranto interrupted. "If we have to fight to get a billion, I say we settle quickly for a hundred million. Sir Ian wants to pay to make this go away."

"Why do you want to settle so quickly?" Black asked suspiciously.

"I represent Susie's mother, Jae Lee, and she expressed a desire for a quick settlement."

"I don't know if that's a good thing." White talked about tax liability and the discussion continued for nearly an hour about piercing the corporate veil and spreading out the settlements.

Some Fellowship. Everyone was at each other's throats already.

Jen stared at the trees. Why did they keep talking? She was Susie's lawyer and no one seemed to realize it. She felt like an invisible person. White argued with Taranto about setting up a trust. Jen had no idea what the other lawyers talked about. It was all about corporations and taxes and whether to sue in State or Federal court, or both, and let God sort it out.

Jen looked at the horses. Susie would have loved to be out here riding with them, she thought just as Luna noticed her discomfort.

"Are you all right, Jen?" Luna asked.

Jen wasn't all right, not with the fatigue and the stress, but that wasn't it. "I think we're forgetting someone." Jen said.

"Who?" White asked. "I don't think we need to bring in a UK lawyer. There's enough to go around without suing the corporation in a UK court and subjecting the winnings to English taxes."

"This isn't about us," she said at last. "This isn't about money."

The other lawyers, even Luna, looked her as if she was from Mars.

"This is about Susie," Jen said. "Remember her? The poor girl will never walk again. She will never play golf and won't have much of a life. And, she's only seventeen."

"Then that's what your duty is," Luna said, "You have to remind us about Susie."

That didn't sound like much of a duty. But, after another hour or so of argument, they achieved consensus—a law suit in New Mexico State Court against Sir Ian personally and a law suit in Denver Federal Court against the corporation. The Federal suit would make it easier to attach Lyon Aerospace's corporate assets in Colorado.

Despite the consensus, the conversation continued. Bored, Jen went back to Shadowfax.

"Where are you going, Jen?" Luna asked.

"I'm going to do my job," Jen replied. "I'm going to see Susie."

# I Know What You Did Last Summer

SUSIE DIDN'T PICK UP when Jen punched in her number, so Jen hurried to the hospital. No time for water, no time for food. It was all about Susie. She raced up to Susie's floor, but the room was empty.

Jen asked a nurse, one wearing those blood red scrubs, about Susie's location. The nurse pointed to a room on the far end. This end of the hospital wasn't as well lit. Were they having budget cuts over here?

Ariana blocked her path at the door. "Susie's in treatment in another part of the hospital with her physical therapist."

"What kind of treatment?"

"Experimental stuff," Ariana said. "Real high tech."

Jen had a vision of the bionic woman, or worse, some kind of human-robot hybrid. Jen's mind raced through the various science fiction clichés. But, despite all the experimental treatment, chances were that Susie would remain stuck in a wheelchair for the rest of her life.

Ariana's phone rang. "Excuse me," she said as she walked down the hallway.

Jen swore she heard something inside the room. She peered inside. The bed was empty and the room smelled of too much disinfectant. This room was more cramped. Susie was becoming less of a priority to the hospital.

A sound came from outside, down below. Was it an accident victim arriving? Were they transporting Susie to another hospital?

Jen hoped in this new therapy that Susie would improve. She walked away from the room to the lounge, the same place she had confronted Jae Lee. She noticed a balcony and the desert wind seemed to pull her outward into the open air. Against her better judgment, something made Jen look down, toward the parking lot. Damn, she was high up. Jen realized that her defenses were down; she hadn't slept in days. She had not eaten much since the incident at the party, and had not drunk much water since her discharge from the hospital. She kept staring at the ground, as if staring at a hypnotist's watch. The ground seemed to come up to meet her and she felt Pink taking over again.

Jen became unstuck in time, felt herself falling in the district courthouse once again. This wasn't animated, like the other flashbacks. This was *real*!

She knew in her heart that this was reality, and the rest of her memories were the flashback. Somehow she could glide in slow motion, closer and closer to the disk that kept shining in the light. It wasn't the disk of the scales of justice. No, this disk sat on one of the floors below and was maybe a few feet wide. It vibrated, as if it was the portal to another world, or another kind of life.

The gold disk was important, very important, but Jen didn't know why. She heard voices that tried to tell her—tried to warn her—about something, but she couldn't make them out. And then the colors shifted to the anime world. She felt her own consciousness shift away.

She then heard Dr. Romero's voice call, "Jen, stop!"

Jen awoke to the sound of sirens. It took a moment for her eyes to adjust to the darkness. She couldn't tell how much time had passed but she knew she was no longer in the hospital. Instead, she was in front of the mental health clinic a few blocks away. How did she get here? Where was Dr. Romero?

A very short officer got out of a squad car and hurried to her.

"Are you Jen Song?" a female voice shouted over the sound of her beating heart. "Stay right there!"

Jen read the APD officer's badge. Bebe Tran. Bebe was a Vietnamese woman who wore way too much make-up. Today she looked as if she had just come from an undercover prostitution sting, and only had time to change the outfit. Jen nearly gagged from the officer's perfume.

Officer Tran touched her on the arm indicating that she was not to go anywhere. "You're Dr. Romero's patient, right?"

Jen's heart now beat faster. "Yes. Why?"

Officer Tran's eyes scanned Jen as if Jen herself was evidence. "Come with me," she said at last, as if taking Jen in to dust for fingerprints.

"Am I a suspect?'

"I don't know," Officer Tran said. "Do you need a lawyer?"

"I am a lawyer," Jen said. "I guess."

They entered the clinic and took the dark stairs up to Dr. Romero's office. Jen had never taken the stairs; she had always taken the elevator.

Or had she?

Jen's insides shook wildly. Had she come here in her sleep? She had no recollection of leaving the hospital. She must have driven in a trance. Or someone drove her. Or she walked. She looked at the mud on her clothes. Horseback riding, right?

Dr. Romero's office had been ransacked. Even the frame of the New Mexico Highlands diploma had been smashed. How could anyone hate New Mexico Highlands? Jen nearly cut herself on some glass. The last thing she needed was to leave DNA evidence at a crime site. She spied a lump under some papers, a lump about the size of a dead body, but it was only textbooks.

"Look over there," Tran said.

Jen noticed that one file cabinet was open and picked clean. She already knew it was her file, her drawer."

"What happened?" Jen asked.

"That's what I want to ask you about."

Jen and Officer Tran went into an office down the hall. This office was identical to the Doctor Romero's, sans the trashing. Jen sat on the couch, but could not make herself comfortable. Tran sat in the doctor's chair, as if she was playing shrink. Tran had big soft brown eyes. Perhaps she had been a therapist in another life. Jen desperately wanted to open up and spill her guts out.

"Shouldn't you read me my rights?" Jen remembered that the New Mexico Supreme Court had recently ruled on "custodial interrogation."

Tran read Jen her rights in a soft voice, as if starting a therapy session. "Do you understand?"

"I hope so," Jen said. "I did graduate from law school."

"Then we're both overqualified to be here," Tran said. "I have a master's degree in forensic psychology, and I'm about to start a dual degree in law and medicine."

Tran went through a standard list of questions from memory. They weren't that much different from those of a real therapist. Police work could be a type of therapy after all.

Jen answered the best she could. She said she'd gone horseback riding and then to the hospital to visit her cousin at the hospital.

"How did you get here?"

"I don't know."

"Do you remember anything?"

"I remember slipping into a trance when I was on Susie's floor at the hospital."

They talked a bit about visions. Tran really would have been a good therapist "So what are you feeling right now?"

"I've been real anxious lately," Jen said.

"Any trouble sleeping?"

"Yeah."

"So why did you come here in the middle of the night? For meds?"

Jen stopped herself. She wasn't a patient. She was a suspect in a burglary, possibly a kidnapping, and even a murder.

Tran now glared at her with a cop's cold eye, as opposed to a therapist's warm one.

"I'm not sure I did. I do blank out sometimes, and I guess once in a while I walk in my sleep. If I had done this, I'd been on video, wouldn't I?"

Tran smiled an evil smile. "Someone broke in through a back door, so it's not on camera. There aren't many cameras in here, due to issues of confidentiality. So it could have been a patient, or someone else who had access and knew where the files were."

"I don't know about any back doors," Jen said.

"Maybe you don't know what you know."

"Could you please tell me what happened to Dr. Romero?" Jen asked. "Is she okay?"

Tran frowned. "We don't know," she said at last. "Her home was burglarized as well. The doctor is missing. Again, all the files that were stolen relate to you."

"I don't even know where she lives," Jen said.

Jen didn't know, but did Pink?

Jen now switched out of patient mode. Time to lawyer up, even though she was both lawyer and client. "I don't really have anything more to say," she said.

Tran gave Jen her card. "Call me if you remember anything."

Jen almost told Tran about hearing Dr. Romero's voice in her dream, but thought better of it.

"I can take you home," Tran said. "I don't want you walking in your current mental state."

Her current mental state? Jen wanted to say no, because she knew that Tran would keep her under a microscope. Jen wanted to prove her innocence to Tran, prove her innocence to herself.

"Sure," Jen said.

The two got into a white squad car. Tran took the long way, driving around the entire golf course before taking her to Coronado's Caddy Shack. Jen feared that Tran would get on the freeway and book Jen into the Maximum Bitch Unit at the Metropolitan Detention Center. On top of her fear of heights, Jen also had claustrophobia.

No, Tran knew exactly where Jen lived and came to a stop outside her front yard.

Jen was happy to see her Saturn right where it was supposed to be. She fiddled around; her keys were in her pocket.

"One last thing," Tran said as Jen opened her door. "You said Dr. Romero was treating you for anxiety. What are you so anxious about?"

Jen felt Tran had lulled her into a false sense of security.

"That would be confidential. Lawyer-client."

Tran stared at her as if that was an admission of a crime.

"I mean doctor-patient."

"I see," Tran said. "Have a safe night."

Jen walked slowly to her front door. Tran kept the car idling, perhaps to make sure that Jen arrived safely, but more likely to observe her suspect a little longer. Before she opened the door, Jen noticed footprints. She hadn't left footprints running out, had she? No these footprints headed toward the door.

Should she tell Tran?

No, Tran would just call her in for more questioning. That was the last thing she needed in her fragile state. She followed the footprints. A small plastic square sat on her front door. Tran probably wouldn't be able to see it from her car. Good. It was just an ancient DVD case.

For some reason, Jen relaxed. If someone wanted to kill her they would have dropped off a dead dog or something, right?

Tran waited in the squad car as Jen bent down and pretended she was looking for a key under the mat. She picked up the DVD and hid it under her sweatshirt, then opened the door. She waved at Tran. Tran stared back at her and Jen hesitated. Should she call the cop inside to help her? No, she didn't like being under a microscope.

Tran finally waved back, and then drove away.

Safely inside, Jen looked around. Her house was a sty, but it was always a sty. Someone might have come to the door, but no one had come inside, no one had violated her inner space.

She relaxed and checked the DVD again. *I Know What You Did Last Summer.*

What did she do last summer? She had never seen the movie. She used her phone to check the Internet movie database. Apparently the characters murdered someone and thought they had gotten away with it. Unfortunately, during the rest of the movie they start dying one by one.

Ouch.

She couldn't tell a cop that someone was blackmailing her over murders she committed while she was insane. To make things worse, her therapist indicated that she was *not* cured, and both her therapist and her records were missing. Jen took a deep breath and headed toward the medicine cabinet. Too much was never enough.

Jen walked away from the medicine cabinet carrying all of her pill bottles. She then dropped the lot of them into her bathroom sink and stared at the huge pile. She picked up one bottle, opened it and took one. Thorazine. She now knew Thorazine was *not* a thyroid medication. "To be or not to be," she asked herself. She decided to go with "be," for now, although she was keeping her options open.

She put the bottles in a gym bag and stuffed it under her bed. She then piled everything she could fit under the bed to block her access. Later tonight, if she decided to choose the "not to be" option, it would take considerable effort to get to the pills. She had learned that trick from Dr. Romero, who always told her to count to twenty backward and take ten deep breaths before acting rashly.

Where was Dr. Romero?

Jen really wanted to remove all the debris and reach for the pills, but she forced herself to stand still and count to twenty. Backward. Jen had only reached thirteen when she heard rustling outside her door. Was someone out there?

She waited by the phone like a baby sitter in a horror movie who didn't know the killer was already in the house. Jen grabbed every possible thing she could use as a weapon and locked every door, double-checked every window. She heard more rustling. Until now, Jen didn't believe in guns. She always worried that she would use it on herself. Suddenly, she wished she owned one—maybe an Uzi—just in case. She almost laughed when she realized the most dangerous item in her house was a golf club she'd found on the course. She hoped she could swing as hard as Susie.

With one hand on the nine-iron, she stood by the door. Her phone rang. Unknown number. Not good. She denied the call. The phone rang again. Jen looked at the nine-iron, and then turned the phone off.

Just in case she was the killer, she left a little origami shape propped up against the door. She burned the exact location into her memory. If the shape had moved between now and in the morning, then *she* was the killer.

The rustling outside stopped and Jen went to bed. Unfortunately, she tossed and turned so much that she nearly fell off the bed. Perhaps the exertion of trying to fall asleep tired her out. Right before she hit unconsciousness, Jen had one reassuring thought. She figured she would probably die falling in the atrium in district court the moment her head hit the ground. So until then she was immortal, right?

Jen awoke as the morning light hit her house and immediately went to the origami sculpture. It had not been moved. All that meant was that she hadn't killed anybody, *after* she went to sleep. She turned her phone back on and checked her voice mail. In the first message, she heard her own voice under hypnosis talking about Hobbs's death on top of the volcano.

"Holy crap." she said.

Sir Ian must be trying to scare her, to get Jen to drop the lawsuit. Jen considered her bed and thought about reaching under it for the pills. Time for her to choose "not to be."

She tried to pray.

"My thoughts above, my words remain below," she said out loud. Was that from *Hamlet*? "Words without thoughts never to heaven go."

She couldn't talk to her mother, couldn't talk to Luna, certainly not Susie. There was only one person in the world she could talk to right now.

# Inevitable Inmost Cave

WHEN THE GUARDS BROUGHT him down to the cramped jail interview room at the downtown jail her father did not look well. Sick, greenish, he could pass for Yoda in a blue jump suit. The downtown jail held Federal prisoners and Jen wondered who had been in the room right before them. Had someone already vomited in here?

This man, a Mexican doctor, had fathered at least three diverse women with three different mothers—Luna, Jen, and Selena. Unfortunately, he also had fathered a prescription drug smuggling cartel in Mexico, and would spend the next few years here as his various appeals went up and down the Federal judicial food chain.

This interview room was like a converted closet, and the ammonia smell was at war with the septic odor. Jen didn't know which to root for. The cell had only one exit, and her father insisted that he face the door so she could be closer to the open air.

This visit was bitter sweet. Jen didn't like to advertise that her father was a convicted drug dealer. She took one last gasp of the relatively fresh air of the sally port then reluctantly shut the door behind them.

"How are you?" she asked.

He shrugged. "I'm still sick," he said. "This is the one place I can get my medication, though, so it's okay."

Jen already felt like she was in a coffin. She certainly didn't want to spend her last days here."

"Why are you here?" he asked. "You look even worse than I feel. And I'm dying."

She looked around the converted closet and maybe understood why her father wanted to be here. It was safe. The outside world couldn't touch him inside his cell.

"I'm a bad person," Jen said, "and I think a lot of bad things, really bad things, are going to come out about me. I thought everything was fine, but now I'm finding out that my past is not going to go away. I—"

Jen stopped. She found herself crying, at first a few whimpers, then sobs. The sobs echoed through the little room. A guard even opened the door to check on them.

"I'm fine," she said, nodding.

"She's fine," her father agreed. "Just give us a moment. Don't tell anyone. There's no crying in prison."

The guard laughed. "Usually it's the inmates who do the crying."

Once the door closed and the tears resumed, Jen told her story to her father, told him everything. Her father became her priest at that moment. After nearly an hour, Jen dried her eyes, looked at her father, and expected him to have some great words of wisdom, some kind of absolution.

"I certainly can't judge you," her father said at last. "There's a tattoo I see a lot in here, 'Only God Can Judge Me.'"

"That's it? All you can give me after all this time is something from a prison tattoo?"

Her father wasn't finished. "From what you've told me, Jen, you're not a good person. You've never been a good person. It's probably too late for you to be a good person at this stage of the game." He smiled. "However, you *want* to be a good person. Your heart isn't a good heart, but it *wants* to be good. That's something. That's a start."

She frowned. He was doing his best, trying to make up for lost time. He didn't give her a "win one for the Gipper" speech. It was way too late for that, for both of them. She half expected him to imitate Yoda and say, "There is no try."

He didn't do that either.

Instead, he did what could only be reality therapy. If what she said was true, he told her the truth would come out and she would eventually be disbarred. She had no duty to tell anybody what she had done, but she couldn't lie about it either.

"These things take years," he explained.

"So what are you saying?"

"You've got to make your life count," her father said. "Lawyer or no lawyer."

Jen nodded. She would only get this one case, this one chance. She had one chance at redemption, to get justice for her client. That would be something.

"You could end up in here with me," he said at last. "But I can now look myself in the mirror. Because of you, because of what happened down at the border, I got my soul back. Even as I sit here, I would do it again when I stayed behind to save you while you gave birth to little Denise. I call it my 'Get out of jail free card.'"

"But you're still in jail," she said.

"Not in here," he said as he pointed to his heart. "Not in here."

The guard came and Jen moved to hug her father.

"No physical contact," the guard said. "Unless it's a family member."

"My daughter, the lawyer," he said to the guard.

# Stained Briefs

JEN TOUCHED BASE WITH Claus later that day, and soon joined him in his home office to draft the initial complaint. He worked in a converted Victorian home east of downtown, in the "Edo" neighborhood. Edo was the original name of Tokyo and the home had a Zen quality to it. The crisply painted interior white walls and the nice pine trees in the yard formed an oasis of calm in a changing neighborhood.

Claus's home could have been a peaceful missionary's retreat, except for the construction within. Jen wanted to call the house Santa's workshop, because Claus obviously made continual improvements on the home; he was an avid do-it-yourselfer.

On his walls, Claus had posted lots of photos from his missionary days. He had started on the Navajo reservation where he met his wife, an EMT with the Navajo Fire Department. They then worked in the Pacific islands, where they adopted the triplets after a typhoon. He also had another wall that detailed his exploits with a major international relief agency in Rwanda, Iraq, and Afghanistan.

Claus told Jen about his wife, who had worked as a helicopter pilot flying in medical supplies. There were pictures of her posing with children in front of a black helicopter. She had apparently gained a lot of weight since the photos. Instead of taking scalps, Claus had adopted a child from just about every place he'd been. He and his wife certainly had a houseful.

There was a newly framed clipping of his Samoan sons. ACADEMY TRIPLETS LEAD THE CHARGE, the paper announced in a glowing review about their athletic prowess. Technically the boys weren't really Samoan. Claus met them *in* Samoa, but their ancestry was a mélange of various island peoples and military personnel.

The article also explained that the boys weren't really triplets; rather, they were cousins from an extended family. The triplets had adopted the names of Samoan stars. Their nicknames were Troy, Junior, and Rock. They had let their curly black hair grow since Jen had first seen them, and each sported locks that would stick way out of a football helmet. As she stared at the wall, Claus came closer to her.

He laughed. "If I wasn't happily married," he touched her arm and then took it away.

"I'm flattered. Now let's get this brief done."

The brief took days to draft. During that time Jen learned that Claus was all about his family. No matter how far along they were on a point of law, they stopped abruptly a minute before six, so he could go next door for family dinner at six o'clock sharp. Jen joined them as Claus's wife made hearty indigenous dishes from around the world.

One day, one of the triplets made a joke about "eating Sartan" next week, apparently a reference to the upcoming big game against St. Pius, the local Catholic High School.

Jen wasn't exactly sure what a Sartan was.

Claus smiled at his son. "Next year if you're at Stanford, you'll be eating Trojan, Beaver, Bruin and Duck.

"Claus means the USC, Oregon, Oregon State, and UCLA mascots," his wife said.

"Assuming we can get three full ride athletic scholarships," Rock said.

"Well, hopefully we'll get a nice Christmas present," Claus said, "and we won't have to worry about those scholarships."

"We don't want to work again next summer," Rock said. "I'm sick of cleaning toilets after the tourists."

Jen didn't have time to ask them about their summer job before Claus nodded at them all.

"Let's say grace."

They all bowed their head, Jen included. This was wonderful, a real family. This homey setting made her feel so distant from her own. As the meal was served, Claus played a video of last week's big game against Bernalillo High on the big screen, and they all demolished Navajo tacos stuffed with something from Indonesia.

Jen could see why this family had gained weight, even though the portions were small. Claus pointed out their exploits on the defensive line—Rock knocking out the lineman, Junior sacking the quarterback, and Troy scooping up the fumble and running it back for the touchdown

He looked at Jen. "Why are you smiling?"

"I've never seen someone so proud of his kids," Jen said. "I'm not used to families that *aren't* dysfunctional."

"Don't be so sure," Claus said. It was hard to tell if he was kidding.

When they got to dessert, something from the islands, Claus took time for his youngest son, the one who looked like Pocahontas. After a few more minutes of family time, Claus took Jen across to his office and they returned to work.

"Families are such a blessing," he said.

"I wouldn't know," Jen said. "My daughter doesn't talk to me. My dad is in prison. I have two half-sisters and we all hate each other."

"Well, maybe you can be part of my family," Claus said.

"I'd like that."

One evening Claus's wife combined Ethiopian cuisine with Korean spices, apparently for her benefit. It was an unlikely combination, but somehow it worked. Jen gained a few pounds along the way, but it felt great.

"Don't worry about the extra pounds," Claus said. "I'd rather be loved than thin."

After the rustling the other night, Jen was too afraid to stay at the Caddy Shack. But Claus had a spare bedroom in Santa's workshop, and she felt somewhat safe there. The family soon treated her like their slightly older, but slightly less mature sibling—their crazy single cousin from Korea.

The triplets were constantly rough housing. Their bodies pulsed with an unhealthy mix of hormones, steroids, and their mother's fry bread. Jen spent a lot of time with the youngest, child, the seventh son, and bonded with him.

"You're like the son I never had," she told him.

As for the brief, the other attorneys contributed lines here and there, but Claus did the heavy lifting. The man was smart. Jen showed Susie their work, but she and Claus had done such a good job that Susie didn't have much to add on her end.

"I trust you Jen," Susie said. "I'm taking some pretty hard core meds right now and undergoing some brutal physical therapy, so I'm in your hands."

Life wasn't perfect, though. Jen had an awkward moment with Claus when they were buried under the weight of researching jurisdictional issues under the electronic research system. She recognized the "Ends Zone" in a reported case involving a personal injury claim.

"I used to work there," she told him.

"Isn't that a strip club?'

"I was a waitress."

They sat silently. Claus covered his lap with a heavy book. What was he hiding down there? Jen realized Claus probably had a crush on her. He never seemed to exhibit any visible passion for his heavy-set wife. Perhaps that was why he had adopted so many kids. Claus also revealed that more than one of their biological children was conceived through artificial insemination.

Jen smiled at Claus. "Let's just get the brief done."

Once Claus sent the Fellowship the first draft, all hell broke loose. The Fellowship called and e-mailed each other regularly with spirited debates over the various State and Federal claims. Everyone had an opinion about how to proceed.

There were also issues with the medical records. Many seemed to be missing. Had someone hacked into the university computers to ruin the case? The hospital was required to release the records, but claimed it was having difficulty retrieving them. That didn't make sense. Even worse, the Mountain Lyon still could not be located in any of Albuquerque's storage lots.

Someone wanted to make this case impossible to win.

Jen now had new rituals after her daily meetings with Claus. First she visited Denise at her mother's place. The girl had discovered the Laser Geisha comic books, so every day Jen read a comic book to her daughter. The girl showed only the slightest engagement, but still said nothing.

At least Denise had started wearing a pink bow that Jen had given her.

"She's *almost* bonding with you," her mother said, seeing the bow.

"Almost is a start," Jen replied.

"According to the court order," her mother said, "it's my decision whether you get an unsupervised visitation, and I think you're ready for a short visit on your own."

Jen's heart beat faster. "You mean I can take her out, just the two of us?"

"We'll see."

"I don't know if I'm ready for that."

Giddy, Jen walked around the golf course and, upon arrival at the hospital, updated Susie in her new, smaller, hospital room. Susie was still under the watchful eye of Ariana, but today was working with a petite, but tightly muscled, physical therapist named Yesenia. Yesenia wore a UNM gymnastics sweatsuit under a blood red lab coat. She was showing Susie how to do curls with small weights.

"I've done curls before," said Susie as a protest. "I can hit a golf ball three hundred yards."

Yesenia smiled. "I just want you to be able to push your wheelchair around by yourself. Now do five more."

Susie grimaced, but kept pushing. She did a few sets more than the therapist wanted. "I told you, I'm fine above the waist."

"Then we'll increase the weight."

Jen waited until Susie was done with her next set of five.

After Yesenia departed, Susie stuck her tongue out. "That chick was treating me like a child."

"I'll never do that," Jen promised. Then she proceeded to update Susie on the law suit.

"Whatever, Jen. You're my lawyer. Whatever you think is best."

Jen frowned. "You don't seem yourself lately,"

Susie shook her head, or at least tried to. The effort was painful. "I don't know if I will ever be myself. I don't know who I am any more."

"I'm doing my best to help you get back to being you."

Jen didn't want to tell Susie how heated it had become during the most recent Fellowship phone conference. Jen sat with Claus at his computer for that one, munching a Navajo Taco—fry bread filled with mutton. Apparently they had a connection to mutton back on the rez and got it cheap. She now understood how Claus's wife had put on the pounds.

They still weren't able to get Susie's medical records. The hospital was stonewalling. Black was the one with the medical malpractice background and he said he would handle it. Jen was grateful; she didn't want to know too much about Susie's insides. Meanwhile, everyday they read financial records that indicated Lyon Aerospace was on the edge of liquidation.

"Can we file without the records?" Jen had asked. "Time is kinda of the essence here."

"Yes. Remember, we file first and ask questions later." Claus had said. "Once we file we can get the judge to give us the discovery."

After all the haggling, and back-stabbing, the Fellowship came to a new consensus: they would first file a personal claim against Sir Ian in State court in New Mexico, and then they would see what other claims they had once the State court judge ruled on their discovery motions. New Mexico juries were considered more generous.

Jen called Susie, who wanted New Mexico as the venue. "I want them to wheel me into court so I can see him write me a check."

"I'll wheel you in personally."

Because her personal life remained unsettled, Jen enjoyed staying with Claus and his family. But every night Jen received phone calls from a mysterious caller. The messages were always the same: a recording of her own voice under hypnosis. Jen changed phone numbers, but the calls kept coming. She decided that maybe she didn't need a phone after all.

Dr. Romero still had not surfaced.

Jen began reading books to Susie after her stints reading to Denise. Susie liked the *Twilight* books, but was eclectic in her other tastes.

"I have ADD," she said. "So just read me a chapter or two out of different books."

Through the magic of the Kindle app on her smart phone, Jen downloaded different chapters from various books, ranging from *Laser Geisha mangas* to one of the legal thrillers from that marginally famous Albuquerque lawyer turned writer. That book was the only one Susie didn't like. "I don't think he gets female characters," she said with a frown.

"He's trying," Jen said. "Lord knows, he's trying."

Once the flowers stopped coming, fans began sending Susie other things, including stuffed Laser Geisha dolls. A Laser Geisha Pink doll sat on Susie's bed. "So, I can think of you, Jen."

Jen managed to hide a tear.

When the brief was in a near final draft, Jen arrived in the cramped hospital room as Ariana was changing Susie's waste. Susie winced a few times from the pain of being moved, but insisted Jen stay. Jen wanted to look away. Susie Freaking Song should not be reduced to this.

After Ariana had finished, she gave them a rare moment alone. Jen went through the brief line by line. "What's a consort?" Susie asked as they hit one line about "loss of consortium." "Isn't that like being a whore?"

Jen slowly explained "loss of consortium" as the fact that Susie might never be able to have a normal sexual relationship. Susie cried for a full ten minutes. "When I grow up, *if* I grow up, I want to be a lawyer just like you,"

"Me?" asked Jen. "I'm stupid. I'm dyslexic. I have attention-deficit disorder. I don't even know the law." She paused. She was about to say that she was a murderer as well, but thought better of it.

Susie giggled, and wiped away the last of her tears. "That's not important. You're a lawyer I would trust with my bedpan. That's pretty rare."

"Time for you to go," Ariana said to Jen.

As October raced to a close, the Fellowship grew even less friendly in their daily Skype video chats. Black joked that if a camel was a horse designed by a committee, then they had created a forty page, double spaced, fourteen point type camel. Everyone contributed a line or two, but Claus did most of the editing of their drafts. They also wrote motions for extending the page limits as well. That, of course, led to more bickering.

They achieved consensus at midnight on October 29 with their final draft for the lawsuit in New Mexico State Court in the Second Judicial District. They all sat at their various computer screens, Jen at her usual place next to Claus in his home office in Edo.

"We're good to go," Claus said. "We e-mailed the finished draft to Taranto in Phoenix, and he had Jae Lee sign off."

Jen looked at Claus with amazement. "Jae Lee isn't the client," she said, angrily.

"What do you mean?"

"I don't know about you, but I'm doing this for Susie. If she doesn't want to do it, I'm out."

Jen didn't know whether Susie's signature had any legal merit. She didn't care.

The next morning, October 30th, Jen took the final draft to Susie. Susie was covered head to toe in blankets. Ariana was doing some basic housekeeping.

Jen used the same voice she had used to read, but Susie had trouble following the several hundred paragraphs. Jen carefully explained the issues, the best she could. Susie frowned. She looked nervous, scared.

"Should I really go forward with this?" she asked. "I don't know if I'm up for it."

Jen didn't tell her that since her mother had already signed off, this was all legal fiction.

After re-reading the pleading, Susie looked at Jen. "Could you give me a minute, alone? I have to make a call."

Jen frowned and headed out the door. Who was Susie calling? Jen put her ear to Susie's door and could hear Ariana moving around. Was she changing a bedpan? Scratching an itch? Jen thought she heard Susie whisper into a phone. Then there was silence.

Jen could see district court's flat blue roof from the lounge at the top floor of the hospital. She forced herself not to look at the ground. Maybe this whole thing *was* a bad idea. She felt that familiar vertigo. It would all end right over there. She just knew it.

Jen knew instinctively that helping Susie would bring her to the atrium, to her fall from the top. This law suit would be the death of her, somehow. She looked at the building again.

Before Jen could turn around, Ariana returned and indicated that Jen could come back in.

Inside, the room, Susie forced a smile. "I'm ready."

"Do we need a witness?"

Ariana smiled "I keep telling you, I'm a notary."

"I didn't know felons could be notaries," Jen said.

"Remember that I got a pardon from the governor. I have friends in high places."

Once the paperwork was signed, and notarized, Jen felt very good for the first time in many days—until she realized that the next day was Halloween. All kinds of evil came out on Halloween.

# File High

ON HALLOWEEN, AT DAWN, Jen and Claus took the papers down-town to Albuquerque's Second Judicial District Court on the corner of Lomas and Fourth. There were three courtrooms at the intersection: the majestic Federal courthouse, the lean and modern Metropolitan court and this building, the ugliest of the three. If Susie was Metro court, and Luna was Federal, the Second Judicial court would be me, Jen thought.

Jen didn't make any jokes as she passed through court-house security; she had the equivalent of a billion dollars in her briefcase. She and Claus had arrived at the clerk's door right at eight. Unfortunately, due to budget cuts, the office did not open until ten. Plus, there was already a line of people who were waiting to file everything from assault to paternity.

For the next two hours, Jen and Claus waited impatiently outside the office door, as crowds of criminals and their lawyers hustled into the lobby elevators. It felt like being stuck at an airport watching other people flying off to exotic destinations. Claus indicated that Jen should sit in one of the uncomfortable plastic chairs so she would stop fidgeting.

Finally, a heavy-set gentleman in a tie opened the double doors to let the crowd into the cramped clerk's office. Jen and Claus fell in line behind a smiling gray haired woman who could pass for a Leprechaun's mother. Jen noticed that the woman carried an entire box of pleadings; must do the filing for half the lawyers in town. There wasn't a clerk on the civil side, so they had to wait even longer.

Jen looked around, still nervous. The lobby could pass for a ghetto pharmacy, but here the clerks scrutinized pleadings instead of scribbled prescriptions. Some of the pleadings were edited by people in line, and consisted of crossed out words and sloppy insertions. Other pleadings were completely handwritten.

In these troubled times, some lawyers couldn't even afford printers.

The clerks were as courteous as possible, considering that they stood behind bulletproof glass and had a hard time hearing the agitated folk on the other side. On the criminal side, one lawyer had failed to properly write in the caption of his notice of appeal, and now feared his client would die in prison. At another window, a crying mother tried to convince a new clerk to use the computer to make her son's murder case go away.

"Just press a button," the mother said. "Delete his case. I beg of you."

"I'm sorry, ma'am," the clerk kept repeating. "That's not our policy."

Another clerk convinced a man that he didn't exist because he didn't have the right date of birth. They finally realized that the computer had switched digits and 1990 had become 1909. "I exist, damn it!" the man yelled.

"Not to the computer, you don't," the clerk replied.

"This is like something out of Kafka," Claus said.

"Is that a band?" Jen asked. "I think I liked their earlier stuff."

Claus looked at her. "Don't you know when, I'm kidding?" Jen asked. "Why does everyone think I'm stupid?"

Jen sighed with relief when a civil clerk finally appeared on the north side of the lobby.

"Next!" she shouted. This clerk looked like one of Marge Simpson's sisters from *The Simpsons*. She scanned the pleading for errors, going line-by-line to make sure the pages were in the correct order and that each of the hundred of numbered paragraphs followed the proper guidelines.

"Make very sure you get a 'return of service,'" the clerk said after taking the money order for the filing fee. "That's our policy."

Claus talked to the clerk about mailing the document to Sir Ian's "registered agent" in New Mexico, but no one wanted to risk anything on a billion dollar lawsuit. Without proper service of process in New Mexico, a judge could throw the lawsuit out.

Jen was so nervous that she was already out the door by the time the clerk stamped the final copy. Claus stayed behind to pick up the papers.

"Next!"

On her way out, Jen felt compelled to check out the fourth floor of the courthouse. It was as if something sucked her into the elevator and then pushed her out on the fourth level.

The lobby of the fourth floor stood at the bottom of a three-story atrium. Jen looked up at the seventh floor balcony. There was an almost three-foot barrier that separated the floor from the open air. Jen had a brief flash of seeing her own body falling from the top. Could she have fallen off? No the barrier was just high enough to prevent an accident, but not so high that someone couldn't throw her off without too much exertion.

Who would throw her off, and why?

It wasn't a dream; she knew in her heart that this really was going to happen someday. She even looked at the floor to check for her own bloodstains.

To make sure this wasn't a dream, she touched the glass statute of Lady Justice in the middle of the floor. There were no bloodstains on it either, but she *knew* her fall was destined to happen in the future. The unseen force pushed her back into the elevator. She then rode up to the seventh floor. She expected to feel something, but whatever psychic ability she had was gone. She looked over the little barrier to the floor down below, but the sun-like disk that she had seen in her vision didn't exist—at least not yet.

What was it, anyway?

"You coming, Jen?" Claus called to her from the elevator bay on the seventh floor. "Why did you just disappear?"

"I, ah, had to check something."

Jen sensed that Claus was somehow connected to her visions. She hoped so. It would be good to have a man like him at her side when things got rough.

# You Got Nerved

THE SUIT HAD BEEN filed, but they still needed to serve Sir Ian personally. The next day, Black texted them that Sir Ian's registered agent in New Mexico had refused service. White speculated that Sir Ian might file a countersuit.

The next morning, Ariana said Susie had a tough time during her physical therapy so the cousins weren't able to visit. On the plus side, Nurse Song let Jen stay with Denise unsupervised in the family room. For the first time, Jen noticed an autographed picture of Susie on the wall. Jen read an entire *Laser Geisha manga* to her daughter and for the first time, Denise actually smiled a full smile.

That smile took Jen away from the stresses of the rest of her life, but only for an instant.

Luna called Jen later that night.

"Sir Ian will be here in person tomorrow," she said breathlessly. "At the party for Diana Crater at the Parq Central Hotel."

"Why would he come here for that?"

"Diana is up for another term as governor and she's got control over state funding for the spaceport. Word on the street is that he's coming in to give her a check, and jetting right out."

"So you can just serve him yourself?"

"Jen dear, I'm a judge. I don't serve anyone."

"Can I do it?"

"You're a lawyer in the case. You can't serve anyone either. But, I can get you into the party if you want to see the action."

"I'm going to that party," Jen said. "I want to see the look in Sir Ian's eyes when we serve him. But who's going to serve Sir Ian for us?"

"I have a date. Maybe he can do it."

"Who's your date?"

"I hate to say. You might not like him."

"Do I know him?"

"You might say that."

Late on Saturday afternoon, Jen and Luna met at Milton's, a greasy spoon across Central from the hotel. Jen hated Milton's because half the people in the joint seemed to be packing heat. Tommy Lee Jones had actually shot a scene here in an obscure film, *In the Valley of Elah*. The diner had a craggy façade, just like the actor.

Jen was amazed to see that Luna's date was Dan Shepard, her ex-fiancé. Dan Shepard, the Rattlesnake Lawyer.

Dan looked great, despite the passing of time. He was a little grayer perhaps, maybe a pound or two heavier, but Dan still looked handsome in a Clark Kent sort of way. He had new glasses and she could tell that they were bifocals. He wore blue jeans and his famous rattlesnake boots.

Damn, she loved those boots.

Their life could have filled a book back when he had a "conflict contract" with the State public defender and she had faked her own death and posed as Nastia, a femme fatale to help him find Luna's daughter. They had reconciled when she had "come back to life," but it was clear that he had his heart set on another.

Unfortunately, she had no idea it was Luna, who finally had dumped Gabriel Rose, an entertainment lawyer, when he was indicted for tax fraud. Jen wondered if Dan was really an improvement.

"Why didn't you tell me you two were dating?" Jen demanded angrily.

"It's complicated," Dan said. "I didn't want to hurt you."

Jen was about to slap Dan right there. How could he date her own sister? But she caught herself. "I'm a professional," she said. "This is about Susie." She handed him the papers.

They all walked across the four lanes of Central Avenue to the gleaming hotel. In the process, they dodged a few cars that were going way too fast down old Route 66. Dan nearly lost the papers while crossing.

The hotel was four stories high and had once been the asylum for the wealthy un-well of New Mexico. The outside now had a fresh coat of stucco, or was it terra cotta? Spanish tiles accented the pale walls. Jen wondered if any former patients had been cured and if they had recently spent the several hundred bucks it took to book one of the suites.

The three of them showed their IDs to one of Diana's staffers. They then passed through a metal detector and took the elevator to the roof. The elevator opened into a small bar area, the "apothecary bar" that had been the room where patients could relax and take in the view after a bad dose of electroshock therapy. The bar was empty except for a tuxedoed bartender who was stacking glasses.

Jen didn't drink any more, not since the night at Sir Ian's, but something alcoholic sure sounded good. "I'd sell my soul for a drink," she said to the bartender.

"You'll have to go outside then, I'm not ready for you yet." He pointed to the party outside on the rooftop deck. It was filled with political big wigs who were making the rounds. Sir Ian wasn't there yet and Jen's stomach fluttered more with each nervous step.

Luna immediately went to work shaking hands with the high rollers, but Jen felt out of place. Plus, it was so windy outside that Jen was afraid she would blow right off the roof.

The Parq Central had a perfect view of Albuquerque and to the west mesa beyond. It was barely a mile east from downtown, and with a little squinting one could probably see conventioneers having affairs within the Hyatt or the Doubletree hotels. After the lushness of the Rio Grande valley, where the Bosque's trees were starting to turn a muted yellow, Jen got a sense of the isolation of being stuck here in the high desert. Past the black volcano cliffs, the mesa extended all the way to Arizona.

Jen recognized Susie's doctor, the out-of-state specialist Dr. Ghandi. Since the hotel was close to the hospital, it often became an extended stay place for medical staff. Dr. Ghandi had apparently come all the way from Bangalore, India.

Jen wondered if the doctors were at the party because they were guests of the hotel, or, more likely, if it was because these doctors were big donors with vested interests in the governor's health care legislation.

Jen didn't feel like being sociable. The heights were getting to her, and the wind made it worse. Dan was standing next to the edge, holding Luna's hand. For a moment, Jen felt Pink rising up in her. She had a sudden urge to push Dan over the ledge for breaking her heart. Even the wind seemed to be pushing her toward them.

"Do you need a drink, ma'am?" a waitress asked. "The bartender said you'd sell your soul for one."

Before she could reply, the elevator opened up and Sir Ian entered the room. When he emerged onto the rooftop, Snape and Jean Claude trailed behind him, packing heat. Were those Uzis or AKs? Jen didn't know her guns. All eyes turned toward the British billionaire.

Jen gave Dan a look that said he'd better "man up." Or was it Pink who gave him that look? Dan gulped and released his grip on Luna.

Snape and Jean Claude saw Jen and headed toward her. They had blood in their eyes. If Jen had become Pink, she reverted to her old self once she saw the two big men come toward her, with guns at their side. She looked back at the governor. Diana wasn't going to stop her biggest donor from getting what he wanted.

Dan waited for an opening and when the bodyguards had taken their third steps toward Jen, he casually walked over to Sir Ian. The bodyguards would have ignored Dan anyway; he was still Clark Kent, even with his rattlesnake boots.

"Sir Ian Lyon," Dan said, trying to sound tough as he handed Sir Ian the paperwork. He had become Superman again. He echoed the words of an old movie. "You got served!"

# Zoo Boo

On Sunday, her mother came through. "I talked with the lawyer for Denise's father's family," she said by phone. "Now that you're a lawyer, they're going to give you some leeway. You can take Denise out for a few hours, unattended.

"That's amazing!"

"You should take her to the Zoo Boo," her mother said. "Kids get in free at the zoo this week because of their Halloween celebration."

When Jen arrived to pick Denise up, she wore a pink bow.

"Do you want to go to the zoo?" Jen asked

Denise shook her head. She mouthed a word. At first Jen thought she was mouthing the word "zoo," and then realized that it was "Susie."

"Susie?"

Denise nodded. Jen recalled that Denise knew Susie through Nurse Song and had last met at her swearing in. Jen remembered Susie's magical effect on the little girl at Long John Silver's. Hopefully Susie, even in her diminished capacity, could sill work her magic on Denise.

"Okay then. First, we're going to see your Aunt Susie," Jen said. Technically, Susie was a cousin once removed to Denise, but the girl wouldn't understand that.

Denise again nodded and mouthed the syllables for "Susie."

Jen smiled and ruffled her daughter's pink bow. Hopefully she wouldn't get it trouble for this.

They walked around the golf course, which was still green even though it was now early November. Jen felt ecstatic that there was no wind, and even more so when her daughter grasped her hand.

In Susie's cramped hospital suite, Jen and Denise found their cousin in good cheer. "My meds are finally working," she said. "And the weights are keeping me sane."

She flexed a muscle.

"Could I borrow a few?" Jen asked. "The meds not the weights."

Susie smiled. "Who do we have here?"

"Your biggest fan. After me of course."

Denise hurried to Susie and gave her a hug. Susie hugged her back.

Denise pantomimed swinging a golf club, and Susie forced a smile. Jen was jealous for a moment, but seeing Denise happy was worth it. She was also glad to see that Susie could now wheel herself around without an attendant.

"My physical therapist nearly killed me, but I have more strength in my arms," Susie said. "Almost like what I had before the accident. It's just below the waist where I'm paralyzed."

After recounting the service of process story, Jen changed the subject to Susie's progress. Susie related that the doctors said she was doing well. "Enough about me, what are you two doing the rest of the day."

"We're going to the zoo," Jen said.

"Can I come?" Susie asked.

"Can you travel?"

"Let me make sure," she said. Susie had Ariana page Dr. Ghandi.

"We've been talking about this for a few days now, and I already got approval to use my van," Ariana said.

Jen looked at Dr. Ghandi. "How did you know Denise and I would be going to the zoo?"

"This was all a set up," he said.

Jen looked at him. "A set up?"

"Your mother, Nurse Song, coordinated this. She figured the three of you need a girls' day out."

"The four of us," Ariana corrected.

They all looked at Ariana. They were stuck with her.

"You can take Susie out until dusk," Dr. Ghandi said. "After that she turns into a pumpkin."

After a few minutes, Dr. Ghandi finished signing the paperwork, which Susie initialed and then signed. "You're free to go," he said.

"Ladies, let's start our engines," Susie said.

"We can hit the zoo *and* the aquarium if we're lucky," Jen said.

Denise was positively giddy and was clapping her hands with excitement. She almost looked like she wanted to say something, but her smile was enough. For now.

Ariana draped Susie in blankets and pulled her hair back. She had disguised the neck brace with a native-made blue scarf. Susie wore turquoise jewelry that could have been a gift from one of her young Navajo fans.

"Someone told me I look like a Navajo," Susie said. "You know the whole land bridge story of the Native Americans coming from Asia? Ariana said that Song could be a Native American name."

Jen noticed that Susie had an envelope with her, hidden in a basket in her chair. What was in the envelope? Jen tried to force all such thoughts out of her head. She needed to be there for Susie—and Denise. Going out into the real world for the first time since the accident was a big deal. Nurse Song must have pulled a lot of strings for this to happen.

Ariana wheeled Susie out the door to the parking lot. "I'll go get my van," she said. She left the three cousins at the entrance and soon pulled up in an unmarked white van with a disability lift. Jen didn't want to know where she got the van, and Ariana didn't volunteer.

It was another unusually warm day for this late in fall—not just an Indian summer, more like a Navajo summer, as if Heidi Hawk had done another blessing. When they arrived at the zoo, they left their jackets in the van, and Susie went with one Navajo blanket, a blue one. There were some female couples there with their children, and Jen wondered if people thought that she and Susie were just another couple taking their daughter to zoo. That impression was confirmed when a heavy-set woman said, "You all look like such a happy family."

Jen didn't know what to say. The happiness didn't last long. Denise was getting agitated, and began pulling on her mother's arm. Jen wondered if this whole zoo thing was a mistake. But, once inside, Denise smiled when she saw her first giraffe. She then pointed up to the top of the neck and nodded.

"Which animal would you be?" Jen asked.

Denise pointed toward the tigers in the distance. As if on cue, one roared.

"That's nice. I don't like anything that sounds like lions," Jen said.

Susie smiled. "Hal was nice."

They walked past more exhibits, and Denise ate some cotton candy.

"So how about you, Jen," Susie asked. "If you could be any animal, which one would you be?"

Jen was stumped. She took the cotton candy away from Denise, as the girl was had started to shake from the influx of sugar.

"I don't think I would be a mammal, because I'm not good with kids. And, I most definitely would not be a good kangaroo."

Jen thought some more as they came to the exhibit of birds. "I wish I was an ostrich and could keep my head in the sand."

Susie laughed. "Then your ass would make a big target."

Denise laughed, too.

"She knows what's going on," Susie said. "She's probably smarter than you."

"That wouldn't be hard."

They made it through the zoo more quickly than expected, as much of the facility was closed due to renovation. They had seen the lions, but the bears were hibernating. They were also feeding the tigers fresh meat and no one in the group wanted to see that. With time to spare, Ariana loaded Susie back into the van. She had apparently done this before for her last client.

"He was in the witness protection program," Ariana said. "So don't ask me about it."

Who was this woman?

They drove the short mile to the aquarium. In the van, Jen pantomimed a fish swimming and Denise nodded. Inside the small facility Jen expected Susie to remark on how pathetic Albuquerque's aquarium was compared to nearly all others, but the girl truly appreciated escaping the confines of her hospital room.

There was a "touch pond," and Denise pulled a starfish out of the two inches of water and handed it to Susie. Susie smiled and waved the starfish off as best she could.

Mortified, Jen took the starfish away from Denise and put it back in the pond before the guards even noticed.

Susie smiled. "I am not nearly as tired as I thought I'd be." Susie had so much pride that she could now accomplish the most basic things herself.

"That is so cool," Jen said.

"It's all because of you, Jen."

"I doubt it."

"You daughter is going to say something soon," Susie said. "I can just feel it."

They went into the next room, past the jellyfish, and across to the shark tank. Jen noticed that no one recognized Susie in her wheelchair. All the little girls who once crowded her now gave this woman, covered in blankets in her wheelchair, a respectful distance.

"I like being invisible," Susie whispered.

"I guess I would have to be a shark," Jen said, going back to their earlier conversation. "It's a cliché. I'm a lawyer after all. And I feel as if everyone's trying to kill me. Not a great white shark because I'm kinda stupid these days, so I guess a hammerhead."

Susie laughed. "Okay, Hammerhead. I guess your mother would be a nurse shark."

Denise pointed at the slowest shark. It took a moment for them to realize that the shark was pregnant. Jen had broken up with Dan once in this very aquarium, but seeing her daughter engaged took away that sting.

Susie thought for a second. "I guess I would be a turtle. They're trapped, but they keep moving."

"I like that," Jen said. "You're a turtle. They live forever, too."

"I don't know if I want to live forever," Susie said.

They next watched a turtle flap furiously through the water on top of the tank. For one brief moment, it looked like the turtle would fly out of his enclosure. Denise's eyes grew wide and Susie, Ariana, and Jen looked at her expectantly. The turtle stopped, turned, and dove back down to the depths of the tank. Denise had a tear in her eye as she shook her little head.

The turtle tried again, but Denise had already turned her attention toward a blank wall.

"Maybe next time," Jen said.

The turtle tried once more, but fell downward, exhausted. It was turning around for one more run when they left.

"Turtles never give up," Susie said, "so don't give up on Denise."

"I won't."

"Don't give up on me."

"You know I won't."

Denise turned around. She was paying attention again. Denise pointed to the turtle, and smiled.

They dropped Denise off with Nurse Song. Jen gave her daughter a hug, and for the first time her daughter hugged her back.

Nurse Song checked the clock. "Just in time. Do you want to do it again?"

"Definitely," Jen said. She hugged her mother.

They were a few minutes late getting back to the hospital, but Dr. Ghandi was nowhere around.

"What's he going to do, ground me?" Susie asked, as Ariana wheeled her in.

"You know what," Jen said, following, "you're making me a better mother."

"You were really good already," Susie said. "You just didn't know it."

# Complaint My Wagon

JEN HAD A GOOD night's sleep. Perhaps everything was working out because Monday didn't start badly. Luna took her out to lunch, thankfully without Dan. They ate at Sumo Sushi, a small sushi joint on the south side of Federal court. It was run by Koreans, like most of the other sushi joints in Albuquerque, and they gave her a warm welcome.

The two sisters caught up for hours. "It's getting serious with Dan and me," Luna said. "I've got a feeling that this could lead to something. I can see us getting married."

"That sounds like a book," Jen said.

Luna was going to do a jog around the golf course and then run home, so she asked Jen to drive her to the Caddy Shack. Jen could see from the road that there was something odd about her home—there were footprints in the dirt front yard, and a large envelope sat on the front doorstep.

"Do you think it's all right?" Jen asked. "Could it be a bomb?"

Jen stayed in the front yard while Luna walked over to the envelope and shook it. Jen tightened.

"It's not a bomb. It's something worse. I think you'd better take a look."

She stayed in Luna's footprints as she crossed the yard, as if afraid that her yard was a minefield. Jen felt so vulnerable. The respite with Susie and Denise had lowered her defenses. She had put down her guard and now she felt as if she had entered a boxing ring with her hands tied behind her back.

"You read it," Jen said.

Luna scrunched up her face as she glanced over the letter that had been inside the envelope. She wasn't very good at giving bad news. "It's from the disciplinary board," she said.

Jen reluctantly took the document and read it. Shite! Shite! Shite!

"Is any of it true?" Luna asked. "You don't have to tell me the particulars."

Jen glanced over the five-page complaint. "Enough to get me disbarred," Jen said.

The complaint alleged that Jen Song was a mentally ill murdering liar who manipulated her client through undue influence. Based on Jen's past, she should be taken off Susie's case immediately.

Everything was accurate, but none of it was true, was it? The complainant must be the one who obtained the tapes of Jen's visits to Doctor Romero. The doctor had obviously taped everything Jen said under hypnosis. Jen winced. She looked for clues that indicated the name of the complainant, but didn't find anything. She didn't know whether to feel better or worse.

So, whoever broke into Dr. Romero's files used that information to file the complaint. That was kosher; the D-board could rely on inadmissible evidence to disbar someone. Worse, she could technically be innocent of everything, but still go down on the "appearance of impropriety." One lawyer had represented himself on eighteen counts of tax evasion, won all eighteen, and still lost his license.

Jen sighed. She positively reeked of the appearance of impropriety.

"Are you sure you're okay?" Luna asked.

"I'm fine."

"I can stay as long as you want."

"I think I want to be alone," Jen said.

"Laser Geisha Blue," Luna said, forcing a smile.

"You were right, Luna," Jen said. "It's time to move on."

After Luna left, Jen went under her bed to search for her pills. She once had boxes of them that Dr. Romero had prescribed during experimental phases of her therapy. Time to do some more experimenting.

Unfortunately, the boxes were filled with empty bottles. Her prescription for Thorazine had run out the day before. She was starting to get the shakes. Probably psychosomatic, but like a cartoon character who realized she was running in mid-air, her body now realized that there would be no more support from the pills. She could call in an order, but without Dr. Romero, it would be impossible to get a refill. If she tried to use another doctor, it would arouse suspicions, and she certainly didn't want that. She wished she had booze in the house.

That evening, Jen went to see Claus. She felt sluggish when she arrived at his workshop, as if the disciplinary complaint was an anchor around her neck. Going off her meds wasn't helping either.

Should she tell him? Part of her didn't want to fight the complaint. She hoped she could just leave it with Claus and he would magically make it go away. Inside the compound, he wore a red sweater, which barely contained his gut. He certainly acted like a father figure. Claus maintained his composure as he read the complaint.

"Aren't you going to ask me whether it's true?" she asked.

"If you were my child, of course I would," he said. He pointed to a family picture of his rainbow family. "But you're not. You're my client. Thus, truth doesn't matter one way or another. It's what they can prove."

"Truth doesn't matter?" How could the fact that she was a psychopathic serial killer just off her meds, not matter?

He laughed his Santa laugh. "I'm a lawyer. We think like that. You'll learn to think like that, too."

Jen didn't know if that was a good thing. "I don't know if I want to."

"Normally we'd have thirty days to respond. I've noticed that since it's around the holidays, they've given extra time. We'll take it. Hopefully we'll find out the identity of Dr. Romero's burglar by that time. The fact that the complaint is anonymous is a good thing. Anyone who is afraid to sign a complaint must have some serious issues."

"If you say so."

"Don't worry," he said. "Everything will work out just fine. I'll take care of it." Jen left all her documents with Claus, and a weight lifted off her shoulders as soon as he switched on his computer and began jotting down notes.

"Will I owe you anything?"

"Just your first born." He smiled. "I'll take it out of our winnings."

Jen laughed. She liked his confidence. "Thank you!"

Claus returned his attention to the screen, as if thinking of strategy. When Jen left she felt good, but once she was back on the street her anxieties returned with a vengeance. It was easy to confess to a stranger, especially someone who had a vested interest in your success. They were all on the same team, right?

But telling Luna, and worse, telling Susie, her client and her friend, that would be a lot harder.

She hoped Susie wouldn't find out.

Inside Luna's office Tuesday morning, Luna sat and stared at nothing in particular. She just looked older, a waning moon.

"What's wrong?" Jen asked. She now didn't want to tell Luna anything. Luna didn't look like she was exactly reeking with empathy.

"Election today," Luna said. "You know I'm up for retention, but I just got the poll numbers back. I'm going down."

"I thought retention was automatic," Jen said. "You're just running against the word 'no.'"

"Not with my luck."

Jen looked at Luna. These days Luna was as nervous as she was. "But I thought you wanted to resign anyway, to help with the case?"

"I just got the memo from a polling group. The news is not good. I got voted out in a recall election when I was D.A. You know that whole story. Not a good feeling. I want to leave on my own terms. Having the entire world vote you out is not fun. I've been there before."

"I can hang with you as you watch the returns."

"You sure you want to?" Luna asked. "There's a party at a hotel downtown. I've got to make an appearance; my 'duty to the party.'"

"Can you get out of it?" Jen asked.

"I wonder about you sometimes," Luna replied with a smile. "My duty to the party is that I'm about to get utterly humiliated in public."

"I'll be there," Jen said. "Misery likes company. I get humiliated in public all the time."

# Our Duty for the Party

JEN TOOK A CAB to the Hotel Andaluz near the convention center. This was the first Hilton Hotel in America, according to the plaque on the wall. The Hilton's had long since moved on, but after a serious renovation, this hotel had developed a nice boutique following. The main party for the political masses took place there, and the power players had rooms in the hotel. Jen hoped that she would be invisible, but once she entered the lobby every eye stared in her direction, as if she was naked.

"There she is. She's that murderer."

A lawyer who took the oath with her approached, and motioned that he wanted to talk to her privately.

"Is it true?" the lawyer asked out loud.

Jen failed to find an escape route; there wasn't one. "Is what true?"

"That you're a *multiple* murderer." The lawyer frowned. "Every lawyer in the New Mexico Bar got an e-mail about you. Every single lawyer. We got it yesterday."

"I was acquitted. Charges dismissed. Everyone knows that."

"You don't understand. Someone released audio tapes of you confessing to other murders. You sounded like you were under hypnosis or something."

Those damn tapes from Dr. Romero's file.

"But that isn't all," he said.

"What could be worse than that?"

"A video tape shows you dancing at a party with Susie Song and your bra pops open. It's up to a million hits on YouTube."

Jen looked at the floor. The vertigo returned, along with the nausea, but while her world was spinning, there she was, standing still.

Before she could reply to the lawyer, her mom called. "Jen, I want to invite you for Thanksgiving. The whole family is going to be there and you can invite anyone you want."

"That's great!" Jen had a vision of her mom's usual feast.

"But I just got the weirdest e-mail. There was a link with our name to something on YouTube. Should I click on it?"

"Ah . . . no."

Jen finally found Luna, after taking the elevator to the seventh floor. Luna had rented a suite with some other judges who were up for election, but had retired to the bedroom and shut the door. Luna had her daughter Dew with her. Dew was a year younger than Denise, but was a genius. Luna had never revealed who Dew's father was, not even to Jen.

"Is Mommy going to lose again?" Dew asked.

Perhaps having a genius brat daughter wasn't the best thing.

Jen waited with Luna in silence. Dew eventually fell asleep. At seven, the news did the first sweep of the election results. Preliminary results indicated Luna would not be retained. She would be the first district court judge in this district to lose a retention election in years.

Luna began to cry, and Jen felt herself tearing up as well. Dew had woken up and was trying to comfort her mother.

One of the other judicial candidates came into the room. "We've got a lot of people coming in to celebrate. Do you mind if we use this room?"

The prospect of drunken candidates and constituents coming in was too much for Luna. "I can't stay here," Luna said to Jen, "but I don't want to go home."

The door had only been open a crack, but a throng of the other judge's campaign workers came in. They were already drunk. The other judge looked a little toasted himself.

"Mommy, can we go home now?" Dew asked.

"That might be best," Luna said.

"Is there anything I can do?" Jen asked.

Luna shook her head. "By the way, I got an e-mail about you."

Jen shuddered. This night couldn't get any worse, could it? Just then, Jen's phone rang. It was Susie.

"We need to talk," Susie said. "I just got an envelope."

Jen backed away from the open window before she jumped out of it.

# Geisha Hospital

JEN'S GUT TIGHTENED AS she rode up the elevator at the hospital. She felt like she was going to the top of a rollercoaster and was not going like what she found on the other side. If Susie fired her, she really had no more reason to live.

Susie was wide awake, propped up in bed watching the election results on TV. Susie wore a UNM sweatshirt, as if she had resigned herself to being here for the duration. The weights were strewn on the floor, had she thrown them in a rage?

Jen's worst fears were realized when she saw the envelope on the table addressed to Susie. It had been hand delivered.

"Someone dropped it off when I took a bathroom break," Ariana said.

Susie did not greet Jen. "Open it," she said. "Check out what's inside."

Susie gave Ariana a stare, and the woman left the room.

Jen opened the envelope to find a hard copy of the e-mail that had gone out to the entire bar. The complete bar complaint was there as well. Even worse, there was the "wardrobe malfunction" pic with the words YOUR LAWYER scribbled on it.

Jen felt her heart practically fall out the window. She rushed into the bathroom and vomited.

"Am I still your lawyer?" she asked when she emerged.

"You missed a spot." Susie paused as Jen wiped her face. "Is all of that stuff true? That you have multiple personalities?"

"Technically, I only have *one* other personality. I'm on meds now."

Jen regretted lying. She feared that all of her meds had left her system. Her body betrayed her at that moment, and she shook involuntarily.

Susie frowned.

"I don't know."

Jen was about to vomit again. "I can quit as your lawyer you know," Jen said at last. "You don't need me at this point. We have other guys who are doing the work for you."

"I don't know Jen, let me think about it. I keep hearing about Sir Ian going bankrupt, so I might not need a lawyer because there will be nothing left."

Jen wanted to say something more, but her stomach remained unsettled.

"Just leave me, Jen. I want to be alone right now."

# November Pain

WHEN JEN WOKE UP the next morning there were several e-mails and texts from the Fellowship about Lyon Corporation's precarious financial condition. No one knew what to do next.

Jen had nowhere else to go, so she walked to the hospital to find out Susie's verdict on keeping her as her lawyer. Jen no longer cared whether or not she kept her license; the only opinion that mattered to her right now was Susie's. Susie wasn't in her room. Had she been moved?

When Dr. Ghandi walked by on his rounds, he said, "I heard you were here."

"Is everything all right?"

"Susie's on the balcony. It's down the hall."

Jen hurried down the hall, but hesitated when she came to the door that led to the balcony. The last thing she wanted to do was face the open air this high up. This was the sixth floor. It was loud up here, because there was construction going on for a new pediatric wing. With every jackhammer, Jen winced.

The balcony was about the size of a handball court, and Jen wished that there were four walls around her to block the hard

November wind. Susie sat in her chair draped in Navajo blankets, soaking up the fresh air. Ariana stood behind her.

Susie was going through the news on her iPad. "It keeps getting worse for Lyon Aerospace," she said.

A cold gust blew, and Jen shivered in the crisp air. She had a great view of the Sandias, which were fully illuminated in the morning sun. Several balloons had ascended to the north.

"So. Am I still your lawyer?" Jen asked.

"I don't know."

"What do you mean?"

"We got some bad news," Susie said. "My insurance company wants me to move out of here and into a rehab center in Tucson. Maybe I'll just get someone out there. I'm going to have to get someone to deal with my finances anyway. Besides, the lawsuit is pointless. I know Sir Ian won't have to pay me a dime after he declares bankruptcy. That's what they're saying online."

"What's the latest?" Jen asked, trying to buy herself more time.

Susie played with her iPad. On an international news channel they found news about Sir Ian's impending bankruptcy. Assed had dropped out, but the Wagatsuma group had formed an alliance with the Zhang group, a Chinese industrial conglomerate. They were prepared to swoop in.

The small screen showed Zhang's wheelchair factory outside of Shanghai. It looked like a propaganda tape as smiling workers stood by their product. Even the people in the wheelchairs were smiling.

Susie's eyes were riveted on the tiny screen as she clicked on a photo. The screen showed Zhang's latest model, which featured some magical alloy. The wheels on the chair looked like shiny flying saucers as they glistened in the sunlight. But, the reporter pointed out that the company had received some bad press after a notorious Colombian drug lord decided, after his own shooting, that he favored that particular model.

"Can you help me?" Susie asked. "My fingers are a little slow in the cold."

Jen clicked on the links on the iPad with her slim fingers. The iPad now showed other Zhang corporate activities. It had manufacturing concerns all over Asia. Jen clicked on one link that detailed the Wagatsuma organization and its research into robotic limbs for the elderly, currently in prototype stages. Wagatsuma had problems with marketing. They had the technology, but no one had ever heard of them.

On the iPad's tinny speakers, an English reporter discussed how Lyon Aerospace's stock price was affordable again in light of its recent setbacks in rocketry and its lack of financing since the Assed deal went sour. He said that talks had resumed between Wagatsuma and Lyon Aerospace, assuming that Lyon didn't go through with its proposed bankruptcy.

Susie frowned. The screen continued to show the video loop of Zhang smelting steel, Wagatsuma building computers, and then Lyon Aerospace launching rockets.

"Unfortunately the Zhang Corporation has had some recent set backs because of their toxic waste disposal problems," a reporter added on another link.

"It's all over," Susie said. What did she mean? The case, their lawyer client relationship, or even worse, their friendship? Jen knew she would have to act fast.

"I know a thing about China," Jen said, as she stared at the whirling corporate logos. "The symbol for crisis is the same as opportunity."

All the images on Susie's iPad seemed to melt together in her brain. "Maybe there's a way to work out a deal where Zhang buys Wagatsuma who buys Lyon. One of those corporate deals where Sir Ian pays you with other people's money."

Jen had taken the one required course in corporate law at UNM and remembered a little about assuming corporate debt and stock swaps. Jen had a brainstorm. Having a brain with ADD was sometimes a good thing; it made you see connections other people missed.

"Let's say Zhang buys Lyon Aerospace," she mused. "Who would be the ultimate spokesperson for Zhang, a wheelchair company that makes most of its money making weapons while it pollutes the water of poor people?"

"Who?" Susie asked.

"You!" Jen said. "You're the perfect PR person. That's got to be worth a billion to them, at least!"

"So what are you saying?" Susie asked.

"They need you," Jen said. "All of them. Sir Ian probably can't close the deal until he settles the case with you. We can use this; somehow get all those companies together to work out a deal, even if Sir Ian goes down."

Susie smiled. "Well, you're the lawyer, Jen, you figure it out."

Susie hadn't said that Jen was "*my* lawyer," but still, it was something.

"I'm on it, Susie."

"Try to get it done before I lose everything."

# Corporate Menage a Trois

JEN RAN BACK TO the Caddy Shack and started the ball rolling by e-mailing the Fellowship about the potential three-way deal. Black did most of the heavy lifting, working the phones between Zhang, Wagatsuma, and Sir Ian's people. Claus didn't have the corporate contacts, so they kept him out of the loop.

The dust finally settled a few days later and Jen was able to talk to Black on the phone.

"Talk to me as if I'm a five-year-old," Jen said when they were connected.

Black obliged and talked slowly. "I call it a corporate *ménage a trois*. That's a French term for—"

"I know what *ménage a trois* is," Jen said.

Black continued. "Well, in this deal, Wagatsuma uses Zhang's money to buy Lyon Aerospace on the cheap. That gets around some corporate problems about Chinese companies owning American defense contractors, although technically Lyon is a British corporation. Lyon will declare bankruptcy, but they will not discharge any debt to Susie."

"What does that mean to us?"

"We structure the deal so Zhang loans money to Sir Ian to pay off his debt to Susie for the law suit against him, personally, here in New Mexico. Here's the cool part, even by paying a couple of hundred million to Sir Ian, Zhang has access to Lyon technology much cheaper than they could get even a few weeks ago. Sir Ian could wait another year and try to get more money, but he'd still have the lawsuit hanging over his head, and the bankruptcy could sour the deal if a trustee doesn't let him out of his personal debt. He needs money now, regardless, because the Assed financing fell out. You understand the *ménage* so far?"

"*Mais oui.*"

Jen tried to call Claus to share the news, but he was out of the country.

Jen visited Susie that afternoon and told her the news in person. Susie's bed was up. She was in her chair stripped to a sports bra, lifting weights with a grim determination. Yesenia, the personal trainer, yelled encouragement. Jen now knew how her cousin was able to hit golf balls so far.

Unfortunately, Susie's lower half was covered in blankets, and still frozen in place. Sweat from her upper body stained the cloth, but Susie didn't seem to care. She finished a power set before stopping. Yesenia nodded and excused herself.

"Susie, you're inspiring me." Jen said. "And, it's all going to work out. We're figuring out the deal and Zhang is thrilled to have you as their spokesmodel."

"Spokesmodel?" Susie pointed down to the sweaty blankets. "How do I walk the runway in a wheelchair?"

"There's no walking involved. Basically, you appear with scientists and demonstrate their wheelchair technology. The scientist does all the real work. But with you there, the press goes wild when you push the button or whatever, and the government passes the bill and gives them money."

Susie thought for a minute. "I could be the good guy for the bad guys. Maybe I can convince them to do some good stuff for a change, like help the poor people that they've screwed. I could be like Angelina Jolie but more like a spokes person for the underdog."

Jen called Black and put it on speaker. "How much are we talking about? Altogether?"

"We're still not sure," Black said. "The people at Wagatsuma want us to come to their American headquarters in Los Angeles, in Century City. They want to meet Susie in person."

Susie frowned. "I could barely make it downtown to the zoo. I'm still recovering."

Ariana had returned to the room. "That's not going to happen," Ariana said. "Not on my watch."

"Maybe you can Skype her," Jen said. Perhaps they could even set this up before she got disbarred.

After they hung up and Ariana had left the room, Susie looked like she wanted to jump out of her chair right there.

"I'll be the bionic woman!" she said. "But would they have to chop off my old legs or just put in new circuits?"

"I have no idea," Jen said. "But one thing you have to understand. All of that is years away, if ever. You will still never golf again at the professional level."

Susie flexed her muscles. "I can live without professional golf," she said. "How about consortium? Will I still lose my consortium? Maybe they can build me a robotic consort?"

For the first time since the morning in the balloon, Susie smiled like a seventeen-year-old girl. She had forgotten her condition for a moment. Then she looked down at the sweaty blanket and began to cry.

"Don't cry, Susie," Jen said. "There's always hope. If this deal comes through, maybe you can help these people out."

"So I would be a spokesmodel in a wheelchair?"

"I guess so. You'd go to corporate events, and maybe do lobbying on Capitol Hill or in Tokyo, Seoul, or Beijing. That sort of thing."

"That could be okay, I guess."

Jen looked at Susie. "You know something. My life pretty much sucks right now. You're all I've got. I've had moments when it was about money, but I would give all the money I ever made if I could just see you do one thing: walk."

# One Knight in K Town

IT TOOK SOME MORE wheeling and dealing, but the big meeting would go down right before Thanksgiving. That would still be within the thirty-day window for Jen to respond to her disciplinary complaint, so she would hopefully still be a lawyer, regardless of the outcome of the meeting. Well, assuming the deal closed and money actually made its way into her pocket.

She tried to contact Claus again, but he was still out of the country adopting another child, this one in Kazakhstan. His "away message" indicated that there might be some difficulty reaching him. Jen didn't want to go without him, but the other lawyers insisted that the window was closing.

Black and Taranto arrived in Los Angeles that Monday. White, the tax lawyer, was already in L.A. on business. The Fellowship decided Claus wasn't needed.

"Too many people can queer a deal," Taranto said in a conference call.

"How about me?" Jen asked. "If Susie can't come, don't you think they need to see an Asian face?"

There was more bickering, but finally everyone relented.

"Why not?" Black asked. "Hopefully when they look at you, they think of Susie. You're just like her shorter, older clone."

Jen almost didn't go after all. Money was tight, and when she booked her flight it was too late to get a good rate on Southwest Airlines. Her first two credit cards were denied. Only her emergency one went through.

She took the only flight she could get, a red-eye to Burbank via Las Vegas. She sat in the middle seat over the wing and insisted that her neighbor close the window shade. She was nauseous, and threw up several times.

The flight from Vegas to Burbank was filled with losing gamblers and a few already lost prostitutes who were heading to the San Fernando Valley for a porn shoot. Jen had never seen so many big blonde women of all races. Jen recalled the well-known comparison between lawyers and prostitutes.

Her seat mate confirmed her thoughts when she told her about working on a ranch. "You sure you didn't use to work there? I know a girl who looks like a Mexican version of you."

"I'm sure that's a story for another time," Jen said. Were they talking about her half-sister Selena?

Jen arrived in Burbank after midnight. She rented the cheapest car she could find and looked for a reasonable motel near downtown. For some reason she figured the neighborhood around USC would be safe.

"South Central L.A. must be like a college town, just like Boulder or Ithaca," she thought to herself. She figured the hotels would be filled with moms and dads from Iowa who were in town for parents' weekend to see how little Jimmy was doing at film school.

Jen saw motel signs on Figueroa, and stopped at the first one. It had a very reasonable rate, even less than a motel in Albuquerque. Unfortunately a sign announced that the rate was *hourly.*

"Is it safe for me as a girl here?" Jen asked the clerk who waited behind bulletproof glass.

"We get a lot of girls like you here," the clerk said. "We get girls here all the time."

With the hourly rate, the motel would be far more expensive than she thought. Jen hurried back onto the road. She made a few turns and somehow ended up going north on Western Boulevard, past the Interstate 10.

Jen soon found herself in Koreatown, a.k.a. "K-town," the largest settlement of Koreans in the world outside the "land of the morning calm." If Jen had kept track of her Korean relatives she probably could have found a second or third cousin in the neighborhood.

Jen suddenly felt at home, even though she never had been to Korea or to K-town before. She couldn't even read Korean. Still, in Albuquerque, she always felt like an outsider. Considering her mixed race status, she never felt entirely at home anywhere.

K-town wasn't what she expected. She had hoped for a smaller version of the Mega-Tokyo of the geisha comics—a Mega-Seoul, so to speak. She wanted her relatives to live and work in the city of tomorrow. Unfortunately, K-town looked like any other bustling part of L.A. This part just had Korean signs.

However, Jen soon smiled. K-town was so alive, even this late at night. Land of the Morning Calm? Hardly. This was the land of the late evening bustle. Every business, bank, liquor store, and even bail bondsman catered to Koreans. Many stayed open late at night. North Korea was called the Hermit Kingdom, but she sure didn't see any hermits here.

Jen's heart beater faster every time she saw a billboard that portrayed a healthy Susie holding up a product, whether it was an energy drink or a vacuum cleaner. This Susie looked as if she could jump right off the billboard and do nine holes right there. Unfortunately, Korean graffiti defaced Susie's billboard for bottled water. Jen couldn't help but laugh. Korean was a language that was not meant for graffiti, and how could anyone not like bottled water?

She pulled into the parking lot of a motel on Western Boulevard. It wasn't that nice, and could pass for a larger version of Coronado's Caddy Shack. Still, it was well lit, and the sign for "vacancy" had all the letters.

"*Annyeong haseyo,*" she said to the clerk, her one phrase in Korean. A formal hello.

The clerk was shorter than her mother. He smiled and spoke rapidly in Korean. She then had to ask him to speak English. She pointed to a framed picture of Susie on the wall.

"I'm Susie's cousin," Jen said with pride.

The man shrugged. "Everybody say they Susie's cousin," he said as he checked her ID. Song was a popular Korean name but Jen took out a picture of her with Susie. He gave Jen the benefit of the doubt. She was his only customer not staying by the hour.

"Such a tragedy," he said.

"I know," Jen said, "but she's handling it very well."

For one brief moment the man teared up. He muttered something to himself in Korean, and then said, "I can't believe I'm crying for a woman I don't even know."

"She's gonna be all right," Jen said.

"I love her," he said. "We all love her here. She means so much to all of us."

He pointed to a picture of a young Korean girl. "My daughter Moran. She was getting into bad things, but she met Susie just once, and turned her life around."

"I feel that way too," Jen said.

The man smiled, as if giving her a special deal. "Since you are a Song, park your car in the back. That's so when the people try to break in I can see them and fight them off."

Jen sighed. Apparently he only did this for special customers. The others were left to fend for themselves. Jen wondered what would have happened if her last name was Goldberg.

The man apparently didn't do as good a job of guarding the motel rooms. Her walls had bullet holes on one side. Jen heard gunfire in the distance and the sound of helicopters overhead. She felt like she was at the DMZ, on the border of North Korea, and wondered if she was under surveillance. Her phone needed a charge, and she wanted to call Susie as a precaution in case anything happened to her. The motel phone didn't work; it required an extra deposit. She sure didn't want to go back out into the night to see the clerk.

Jen tried to sleep on the rock hard mattress but the sound of broken glass pulled her out of bed. Was someone breaking into her car? She cowered in her room, between the bed and the wall. Some geisha she was. Sure enough, she heard the little clerk go out and shout. "You get away from that car! That car belongs to nice girl. Don't mess with Susie Song's cousin!"

"Susie Song?" the burglar asked. Apparently he came here every night looking for cars to burgle, and usually, the clerk didn't object.

Susie's name worked wonders. The would-be burglar moved on, in search of someone else's car.

"Thank you, Susie," Jen said out loud. "I won't let you down."

# Nakatomi Plaza

THANKFULLY, JEN'S CAR REMAINED unharmed the rest of the night, but the car next to hers had a broken window. Maybe Susie's name had gotten around to all the potential burglars in K-town and they stayed clear. Jen noticed the area looked a little worse for wear in the daytime, but K-town still pulsated with energy. Her people got up early to head to work. She realized she was a stranger here in her own land.

After driving nearly to the Hollywood sign, Jen finally found the 101 South. She then headed toward downtown Los Angeles. She used the tall round building in the middle as her point of reference; thankfully it had survived the alien attack in the film *Independence Day*. Jen found I-10 West, but didn't know which exit to take to Century City, so she got on the 405 North, exited on Santa Monica Boulevard and headed east. By backtracking, she probably made things worse.

On Santa Monica she passed the beautiful Mormon temple. To her surprise, a few blocks later she arrived in Century City. She recognized the corporate headquarters of the fictional Nakatomi Corporation featured in *Die Hard*.

Jen wanted to park under the massive building, but the hourly parking rate was comparable to the hourly rate at her motel in K-town. At least at the motel they threw in a pot of coffee, a bed, and some movies. Jen couldn't calculate the length of the meeting. She couldn't depend on the other side to validate her parking ticket either, if negotiations broke down. If she stayed for more than three hours, she would not be able to cover it. She saw a bank nearby; perhaps she could take out a parking loan.

Jen frowned. She was here negotiating a billion dollar deal, but couldn't afford to park.

"Is there any place cheap to park?" she asked the attendant. The handsome Hispanic man looked like an actor who was portraying a valet, rather than a real one. He laughed at her. "Just park in the Century City Shopping Center. That's where us Mexicans park."

The underground lot beneath the Century City Shopping Center was gigantic, probably even bigger than Albuquerque itself. Jen entered off Santa Monica Boulevard and took her ticket. She smiled. She had three hours free. This billion-dollar deal shouldn't take much longer than that. She would be fine.

Jen had a theory: if you remembered your parking space you'd forget an important childhood memory. Thankfully, once she exited, the *Die Hard* building towered over Century City to the east, only a few blocks away through the outdoor mall. A few saleswomen dressed in black stared at her as they smoked cigarettes outside their doors. They shook their heads at Jen's fashion choices. Albuquerque was at least ten years behind the times when it came to fashion. Jen coughed through their smoke.

She was self-conscious and sweaty when she checked in at the building's security desk. The guard told her to go up to the twenty-second floor. Many of the office workers entering the building were beautiful, and the building could be a casting couch for a romantic comedy. They, too, all wore black. Black was apparently the new black.

By the time she entered the room, the meeting had already started.

"What took you so long?" Taranto asked.

"Traffic was a bitch."

She hoped that people would smile, but all eyes looked at her with ninja stares. One elderly translator at the Wagatsuma table was confused. "That's not Susie Song," he said. Apparently they thought Susie would be here, rather than the cheap knock-off. What had Black told them before she arrived?

Jen took a moment to figure out where to sit. The conference room was big and modern, and could pass for a hip Pan-Asian restaurant in Beverly Hills. The Wagatsuma brain trust must have figured the perfect feng shui for the big, long table. Jen was intimidated by the view out to the Pacific even before she caught sight of the bloody Samurai paintings behind the Wagatsuma contingent.

On the other side of the room, a huge flat screen revealed the Zhang boardroom in Shanghai, the Shanghai skyline behind them. They must be on the hundredth floor of something, as they were on the same level as the top of the famed Shanghai

Pearl Tower. The Pearl Tower resembled the Eiffel Tower with an attitude. Even the televised image of the building intimidated her.

An unsmiling Japanese intern brought Jen a deliberately tiny chair. The intern even put her at the "kid's" part of the table. She sat with young staffers, a few feet below Taranto. White and Black sat against the window. Man they were high up. She forced herself to look at the Pacific several miles away.

Don't look down!

Jen turned her head away from the window and focused on the interior of the room. She recognized the chairman of Wagatsuma sitting at the head of the table like a shogun emeritus. A Samurai sword hung on the wall behind him, and he could easily grab it if things got out of hand. He apparently didn't recognize her. Either that or he made it a point to ignore her. Jen figured either way was just as well. No need to embarrass everyone here.

Sir Ian and his lawyer were visible on a smaller screen near the window. He looked smaller than in life, and the screen was blurry. Sir Ian wore a ski sweater. Maybe he was at his home in Aspen? Even through the blurry screen he looked considerably worse for wear after the excitement of the last few weeks. His face was redder than normal, his eyes bloodshot and watery. The stress of the lawsuits and the mergers must have taken a pound or two of his pale, English flesh.

Black said nothing as Jen sat down. She tried to adjust her chair, but they had placed her too low to the ground. Everything seemed deliberate. She swiveled in the chair like a whirling Dervish. She wanted to turn away to avoid looking out the window, but some force kept drawing her back. Black shot her a glance that indicated she had better stop swiveling, and then responded to a series of questions from Wagatsuma's number two.

Jen sat still and focused on the inside of the boardroom as she recalled *Die Hard*. Alan Rickman had shot the nice Japanese boss in the movie. This would be a good room for someone to get shot in and then thrown out a window. Jen wondered if the windows were bulletproof—or at least *body* proof.

Apparently the discussion focused on whether to make the pay off before or after the New Year.

"Our New Year or the Chinese New Year?" Jen asked.

No one looked at her. Black gave her another dirty look and didn't bother to acknowledge the question.

Jen watched Black in action. He was nice enough on the surface, and certainly smart, but she didn't trust him. He was too glib. He had arranged this meeting and she wondered if he had ulterior motives. The Wagatsuma folks nodded a little too quickly at his every word. Were they all in cahoots?

Jen heard the word "*hai*" several times, Japanese for "yes." Yes was good word, right?

The inevitable impasse came, and everyone stopped nodding. Zhang and Wagatsuma were on the same page, well, adjacent pages, but Sir Ian was angry.

"Why should I pay that tall bitch anything?" he muttered, not realizing his proximity to the microphone and the power of Japanese technology.

Jen's blood boiled. No, she wasn't a superhero, but she was a lawyer. For now, at least. Maybe because she was so high above the ground she channeled a bit of Pink's dark side. The room shimmered for a moment, as if it was about to turn sideways. No one talked about her client, her cousin, her *friend*, with words like that.

"This isn't about you." She stood and walked in front of Sir Ian's screen and made eye contact with the tiny webcam. "This is about Susie. Your son ruined her life. He was drunk when you gave him the keys, but you didn't care. She can't walk, she can't swing a golf club and she'll never be able to—"

Jen was about to say "have sex" but caught herself just in time. "—be with someone unless these good people from Wagatsuma can come up with a medical miracle."

The Wagatsuma people smiled. Jen had scored a point with them. Still standing, she pointed to the Wagatsuma table and then to the Zhang screen. "To the Zhang people, this is a business deal. They can buy your company cheap right now and still pay off your debt to Susie. What do you call it—corporate synergy? I don't pretend to understand all of it."

Jen waited as the Zhang translator worked his magic out in Shanghai. She could tell something was lost in translation. Even the Pearl Tower looked dimmer.

"Synergy?" Jen said again. No, that wasn't the right word. "Feng shui," she amended.

It must have meant something. The Zhang folks nodded. The Pearl Tower looked brighter.

Jen now stared directly at Sir Ian. "But let me tell you about Susie. Even in a wheelchair, she has more heart, more guts, and more brains than you have in all of your rockets."

She now turned back to the Zhang screen. "You are getting the public relations coup of the century. Every girl in Asia, every girl in America, looked up to Susie Song. Still does. You will forever be remembered as the company that helped this disabled young woman. This is not just about your Chinese business. Susie will help you break through to the American market. Right now, when people think of your company, all they think of are peasants drinking toxic water caused by your factories. If you do this deal, people will think of Zhang as the wonderful people who saved Susie Song and who will someday save my daughter if she ever gets injured. Talk about great public relations."

Jen actually believed that Susie could force those bastards to clean up the dirty water. She really could be the good guy for the bad guys.

She finally looked at Mr. Wagatsuma, who sat only a foot away from her. "And your company does robotics. If Susie Song walks again because of your technology, it's worth far more than a billion dollars."

Mr. Wagatsuma stared at her. Jen could tell he finally recognized her as he mumbled something in Japanese to one of his cronies.

"Everyone in this room has sins," she said to Wagatsuma. "But Susie Song is a symbol of survival. I don't know if your stock price will soar because of Susie, but I'm betting it will. You probably earn more in one week on the various markets you've invested in than you'll pay us. When you lobby for relaxed air quality standards for your manufacturing plants here, lawmakers will remember that you were the ones who helped Susie Song, so you can't be *all* bad. She can help you in ways you cannot even imagine. Corporate *Feng Shui.*"

They nodded. The translator smiled at Jen.

She now turned back to Sir Ian. "What your son did to Susie is a crime, and you were an accomplice. You probably bought your way out of charges, but people in Albuquerque rarely *stay* bought. You do not want to be sitting in court in Albuquerque for a year as your stock price tanks and these people buy out some other billionaire who has less baggage."

Jen paused. She wondered if the alliteration translated well in Chinese. It did ring with Sir Ian. He actually looked pensive.

"Sir Ian, here's your chance to buy your way out of your own hell," she said. "The guilt is something you will live with for the rest of your life. But today you have the opportunity to buy your way out of this hell with other people's money."

Jen sat down. She was spent. She realized that this was the first speech of her legal career, and it wasn't half bad. She wanted to think that her speech closed the deal. It didn't. The discussion went on for several more hours. The Wagatsuma people actually called for take-out before it was finished.

Jen couldn't remember all the particulars of the deal, except one thing—six hundred million dollars would be paid to Susie as part of the three-way merger. Six hundred million divided by three meant *two hundred million* for the Fellowship.

"We can wire the funds to your trust account," the Zhang translator said.

"You can wire it to my account," Black said, a little too quickly. "I can handle the distribution to the client and the rest of the legal team."

Taranto had been silent the entire time. "That might not be the best idea." He punched Black in the shoulder, a supposedly friendly punch, but the punch was a lot harder than it looked. Black winced.

"May we have a minute?" Black asked.

Jen could read his mind. Despite her lofty words of a moment ago, she felt the same feeling in her gut that Taranto did. Two hundred million dollars was a lot of money to put in a stranger's bank account.

The Fellowship retired to another room, this one with a picture window facing west. The sun had now started to descend over the Pacific a few miles away. Jen wasn't used to seeing water instead of desert to the west. She could feel the tension in the room. Were these guys packing heat?

Taranto got in Black's face. "We can't do an electronic transfer to the trust account," he said. "How do we know you won't then transfer the money to Brazil, or Switzerland?"

"You have my word as a lawyer," Black said. "And I checked on you Taranto. You've had more disciplinary complaints than a dog has fleas. The fact that you're sleeping with Susie's mom shouldn't entitle you to shit."

"Who I'm sleeping with is irrelevant," Taranto said. "For two hundred million dollars, I bet you can break your word. I'd sure as hell break mine."

Black pointed out a few tax concerns that ignited further discussion. Jen remained silent; she was afraid one of the men might throw her out the window. But, she finally had an idea. She remembered something else from *Die Hard*. "What exactly is a bearer bond?" she asked.

Black and Taranto smiled at exactly the same time.

When they returned to the meeting room, the Wagatsuma contingent looked pained. The Zhang folks looked worse, or perhaps it was the light on the screen. As for Sir Ian, on his screen, he kept glancing at the snow that was falling behind him.

"We've come up with a solution," Black said. He explained about bearer bonds. Someone mentioned gold, but bearer bonds made more sense. They could be counted right there in the room. After more haggling, the group set a date for the transfer, December 21st, the winter solstice and the shortest day of the year.

Sir Ian actually smiled. "I'm glad we can put this behind us before Christmas, and we will still have enough time to close by New Year's."

Jen didn't understand corporate tax. She had thought criminal law was filled with criminals, but she now realized that the real stealing took place in the boardroom. They bickered some more over the location of the closing. Wagatsuma wanted Los Angeles, Sir Ian wanted Colorado, and the Fellowship wanted Albuquerque.

Jen knew she needed to jump in again, before this got out of hand. If money went anywhere other than New Mexico, Susie might not see a dime of it. "We filed the law suit in the Second Judicial District State Court in Albuquerque. We can get an emergency setting there at any time. A judge's signature would settle the case once and for all."

"I like the words 'settled once and for all,'" Sir Ian said. "But is it safe?" He sounded a lot like Sir Lawrence Olivier's evil dentist in *Marathon Man*.

Jen wanted to defend the honor of her courthouse. "It's a secure facility with guards everywhere, just five minutes from the airport. I think you could even take your helicopter in and land on the roof."

Sir Ian smiled. "In, out. No one gets hurt."

The Fellowship shook hands with the Wagatsuma people and bowed to the Zhang screen. They didn't know what to do with Sir Ian's screen, so they just nodded.

Sir Ian smiled. "Miss Song, you're becoming a real lawyer after all. I apologize for any *miscommunication*."

"Let's just get this matter settled," Jen said. "I don't know if I will be a real lawyer after that."

As Jen went down the elevator with the other members of the Fellowship, she felt her high slipping away with every floor. "By the way, my mom makes the best Thanksgiving food ever. You're all welcome to come."

Black and Taranto smiled for a change. "Jen, it would be an honor," Taranto said.

"I agree," Black added.

"Woo Hoo!" she said, just before the door opened.

# T'rial of the Century

JEN TRIED TO GAGE her emotions as she walked up Avenue of the
Stars north from Nakatomi Plaza. Avenue of the Stars, hell
yeah! She was a star, after all. She looked at Century City's
massive twin towers, filled with entertainment lawyers.

"I'm going to make more than you," she said out loud.
"And I only went to UNM Law School."

She could learn to like being a lawyer. Even if it was only
for a few weeks before the Bar pulled her ticket. Jen dialed
Susie to tell her the good news.

Ariana answered. "Susie can't come to the phone now."

"Is Susie all right?"

"I don't know yet. No one tells me anything."

After a grueling flight, spent mainly in the airplane lavatory,
Jen did a quick scan of her home when she arrived and noticed
nothing out of the ordinary. It was just as sloppy as before. In
her medicine cabinet she found one pill bottle with one single

solitary pill. She didn't care what it was. She just took it. Thankfully, she fell right asleep. Even better, she didn't remember her dreams.

When she woke up the next morning, before dawn, she called Claus on his cell. He was finally back from his trip abroad.

"Why didn't you wait?"

"I called you. Time was of the essence."

There was silence on the other end.

"You still there?" Jen asked.

"I'm fine. I'm just not sure if I can trust the Fellowship anymore. Well, everyone except you."

"Still, you gotta be happy we closed the deal!"

"They didn't cut me out, did they?"

The man seemed a little paranoid.

"We're going to get the money. Don't worry, you'll get your share, too." Jen then explained the particulars of the closing.

"Thank God," Claus said. "I've got another mouth to feed. We're adopting another child."

She could hear a baby crying in the background. "I don't think you'll have to worry about baby food for a long, long time." Jen hesitated before she brought up a final item. "What's going on with the disciplinary complaint? I haven't heard anything."

"You'll probably be on supervised probation when all the dust settles," he said. "As long as a licensed attorney supervises you it will be okay. I can supervise you myself."

Jen felt better. "I'll still be able to keep the money, lawyer or not?"

"Definitely," he said. "By the way, we're having our Thanksgiving dinner early in the day. You should come by to meet our new arrival, assuming I change this diaper and live to tell the tale."

"My mother always has Thanksgiving. It's usually later in the evening though."

"Come on," Claus pleaded. "You can do both. You're like family to us."

Jen felt she was barely family to her own family. Oh well, she would just have to eat two dinners. Jen decided she would fast for the next few days, just in case.

"That does sound great," Jen said. "I'll try not to eat too much. You're not serving mutton, are you?"

"Don't worry. I think you'll be pleasantly surprised."

Jen visited Susie to tell her the good news. Unfortunately, Susie suffered from what Ariana termed a relapse.

"Her physical therapist is killing her," Ariana said. "You've seen how hard she works out."

On the bed, Susie had her Navajo blankets pulled up to her chin and was under heavy sedation.

Jen tried to tell her what had happened, but Susie didn't seem to understand.

"We've won," Jen said.

"What have we won?" Susie said.

"The case! You're going to get four hundred million dollars."

"Four hundred million? What can I do with four hundred million if I am locked in a room?"

Had Ariana poisoned Susie? Jen hoped this setback was only temporary. But Susie was right. What had they won? The

Wagatsuma miracle limbs were years away, if they ever came at all. Money wouldn't make Susie herself again.

"Well, at least we know Sir Ian will never be so irresponsible again," Jen said.

Susie smiled. "That's something."

Susie then whispered something. Jen couldn't hear, so she came closer.

When Jen approached, Susie moved her neck a fraction of an inch to kiss Jen on the cheek. "I love you, Laser Geisha Pink," she said. "You're going to save me."

"I love you, too, Laser Geisha Gold."

Jen arrived at the Claus compound at noon on Thanksgiving Day. One of the kids asked about watching a football game, but Claus reminded them it was a "family day."

"No TV!" he said. Everyone was in the midst of a whir of activity. Jen watched the entire family set the table, as Claus helped his Navajo wife with the cooking. "Mrs. Claus" ran the kitchen like a general commanded a battalion—everyone had a specific assignment. They set the table and cooked the meal like they were planning to invade Poland.

"We raised the turkey ourselves," Junior said.

"I got to kill it," said Troy.

"I carved it up," said Rock.

"I'm just going to eat it," said Jen.

"No," Mrs. Claus said. "Everybody works around here."

She was an intimidating woman who obviously wore the pants in the family, extra big pants. That's might be why Claus worked so hard to avoid making her angry.

✦

"I'm giving you the easiest task," Mrs. Claus said to Jen. "Just look after the new baby." Jen had thought that Kazakhs had Slavic features, like Borat, but Claus's baby looked as if she was from Mongolia.

Jen did her best to play mommy as the family prepared the feast. Mrs. Claus had prepared side dishes from each child's native country, including fry bread from the Navajo reservation. Jen would have to force herself to limit it to one bite.

When the meal was ready a little after one, Jen nearly grabbed the food before Mrs. Claus shot her a nasty look. Claus said grace, and then directed each child to say everything they were thankful for. All told stories of hardship back home and how thankful they were to have a loving family.

But Jen sensed they weren't entirely thankful. Times were still a little tough. The boys wore blazers that must have come from the Goodwill, and the boys' roughhousing had taken its toll on the house; there were many dents in the walls that hadn't been repaired.

Claus spoke of the impending good fortune. "I can *finally* give all of you the life you deserve. We'll get a bigger house."

"Our own beds?" Troy asked.

"Maybe," Claus said.

"Troy needs his own room," Junior said. "He needs his own darn house, the way he eats beans."

"You're the worst, Rock," Troy said. "You could blow the whole house down."

Everyone laughed, except for Jen.

"I just will be glad when we don't have to worry so much," Mrs. Claus said at last.

Finally they came to Jen, and she took a second to collect her thoughts. "I'm thankful that I have you for my family," she said. She was slightly embarrassed that she would see her real family in just a few hours. "I appreciate your taking me in."

"Amen," Claus said with a smile. "We're good to go."

They ate the rest of the meal in silence except for some mumbling between the triplets, and the occasional punch between them. The food was good, there just wasn't that much of it for all the people at the table. By the time Rock got his portion of the turkey, Claus could only give him a bite or two. Junior and Troy laughed before Claus gave them a look. Jen gave him most of her portion while the others weren't looking.

Jen didn't know if she fit in here after all.

After the meal, Claus invited her back into the workshop. He showed her pictures of himself with his wife as she flew a helicopter in Afghanistan.

"I am so afraid of heights," she said.

"Well, enough of that," he said, as he put the picture away.

"My kids are each expecting their own car and my wife wants a new house. But, when it comes to the deal, I don't know. I still think Taranto is going to screw us."

"He had that look," she said, "but the other guys are worse."

"I did all the work," he said.

"I know. I'll make sure you don't lose out."

Mrs. Claus came in holding Asia. Jen gagged on the stench.

"The baby's sick," she said. "I think we have to take her to the hospital."

Claus shook his head. "That baby's going to be the death of me." He listed all the various ailments the child had. If little Asia was a used car, he had bought a lemon. "And, we don't have insurance any more."

Jen felt uncomfortable. She looked at her watch. "I have to go to my mom's now. I think Black and Taranto will be there, so let me know if there's anything you want me to pass along."

"Tell them not to forget about me," he said.

"We will all have to get ready for the blessed event."

"Other than taking the money to the bank, I don't think there's much that needs to be done," Jen said.

"I hope you're right," Claus said.

Jen smiled at the baby. "She's adorable."

"I forget," Claus said. "Do you have kids?"

"I have one," she said. "Although it feels like I have two."

# Home for Thanksgiving

JEN WAS STILL FULL by the time she made it to her mom's house. She also felt nauseous because she was off her meds, but she forced herself to remain mentally stable. Unlike the Claus home, her mother's house was chaos. Inside, it could still be a group home filled with kids. Nurse Song had not completed the meal, yet she refused help from everyone.

"My kitchen, my rules!" Nurse Song said, declaring a DMZ around the oven. Everyone steered clear.

The living room already held a few people. Black and Taranto were there, and Taranto brought Jae Lee.

"We're family," Jae Lee said.

"Sure we are," Jen replied.

In the backyard her other half-sister Selena, a law student from Boulder, was talking with her boyfriend, Mayhem Moreno. Jen went out to say hello, more out of a sense of obligation than anything else.

"I better leave before Luna gets here," Mayhem said as Jen walked up. "She represented me on some things years ago and I don't want to ruin your dinner."

Jen hadn't spent much time with Selena and realized how little she knew her half-sister. The boyfriend hurried out the door like a frightened puppy.

"Just remember what I told you," he said to Selena.

Selena shook her head after the door closed. "Can you help me study for my criminal law class? *I* might have to represent my boyfriend, too."

"I'd like to, but I don't remember anything about criminal law, Sel," Jen said with a smile "I'm a civil lawyer for the duration."

Selena frowned. "You know, sometimes I feel like I've been written out of your life."

Back inside, Denise sat on the couch like a statue, watching football. Luna's daughter, Dew, sat with her. Jen tried to hug her daughter, but the girl pushed her away. So much for bonding. The television was just too enthralling for Denise's young mind.

"I don't think she's sick," Dew said, apropos of nothing.

"So what do you think?'" Jen asked the girl.

"I talk with my mom all the time," Dew said. "We think Denise just doesn't want to talk to anyone until she has something really important to say."

"Do you have anything to say, Denise?" Jen asked.

Denise shook her head and pointed to the TV. At least she understood things.

"The time has to be right," Dew said.

Taranto sat in a folded chair next to Jae Lee. Jen tried to catch up with her aunt, but the gap was too great.

"Do you like being a lawyer, Jen?" Jae Lee asked, again . . . and again. Jae Lee was already drunk from a bottle of *Soju*, a Korean rice wine that she pulled out of her purse.

"I guess," was the only response Jen could muster after the third time and Jae Lee's third consecutive swig.

A knock came on the door and Jen hurried to answer it. Luna arrived escorting their father, Dr. Mondragon. He wore civilian clothes and looked quite dashing, considering the circumstances.

"I got a furlough from jail," he said. "Four hours. Let's make it count."

Once you looked past the nice suit, her father looked like a zombie. He sat with Dew on the couch and she soon crawled onto his lap as they watched football.

"On third and long they need to start passing more on crossing routes to confuse the secondary," Dew said. Apparently she was an expert on football, too.

Denise sat next to them. While she didn't speak, it was clear that she didn't care for football. No, the time was not yet right for her to speak.

"Can we eat now?" Selena asked. "I'm starving. I hope we're having turkey."

"Actually, we're doing something different tonight," Nurse Song said. "We're having pheasant. A traditional Korean recipe."

"Peasant?' Dew asked. "We're eating poor people?"

Everyone groaned in unison.

"I'm kidding," Dew said.

"I like Romanian peasants best," said Selena.

"I've always liked the Transylvanian peasant," said Luna. "You know the ones with the pitchforks that burnt down Frankenstein's castle."

Nurse Song didn't smile. Thanksgiving was a big deal for her and no one knocked her cooking choices. "We're waiting for one more," Nurse Song said, changing the subject. "It's a surprise."

They looked around. Who else could be coming? The house was filled to the brim.

As if on cue, the door rang. Jen was in the kitchen when she heard a voice yell, "Can someone give me a hand?"

Luna hurried outside, and soon returned with Ariana and Susie. Panting slightly, Ariana wheeled Susie into the room. Susie had recovered from yesterday's setback, but still looked faint, even in her signature outfit—polo shirt and baseball cap with the logo. She wanted to reclaim the Susie Song of old, although she had five layers of blankets on top of her.

"I hope you didn't wait for me," Susie said. "I don't want you to have cold turkey."

"Pheasant," Nurse Song said. "And we wouldn't dream of starting without you, Susie Q."

Nurse Song smiled at her own lame attempt at humor. Everyone at the table started singing the song, "My Suzie Q," and Susie blushed.

The pheasant was worth the wait. Nurse Song put in her usual Korean touches like a side of *kim chee* to spice up the traditional meal.

"I like my food the way I like my women," Dr. Mondragon said with a smile. He forced himself to drown the *kim chee*. "Extremely spicy."

Everyone laughed with nervous laughter. Despite the spices, everyone dived in like they were blitzing over the thirty-eighth parallel. Her father hadn't eaten good food for months, so he gorged. Denise ate with her hands, but no one wanted to stop her. Jen didn't want to touch anything after the feast at Claus's but her mother kept prodding her.

Jen sat next to Susie and was surprised how well Susie was able to feed herself.

"I'm almost there," Susie said. "Every day I'm getting stronger with physical therapy. I lost a lot of muscle tone from lack of exercise. It's weird, but a few months ago, I wanted to be the first woman to win a men's tournament. Now my goal is to push my own wheelchair."

The good feelings didn't last, of course. The discussion turned bloody by the end of the first course. Black and Taranto argued privately over something, taking their meals with them to the TV room, and Denise joined them.

Jae Lee tried to get back into Susie's good graces, but Ariana stopped Jae Lee from getting close to her daughter. "She doesn't want to talk to you, mother or not."

Luna learned that Selena's boyfriend had been there earlier. "I'm glad that bastard left."

"I love him," Selena said.

"He's only going to lead you to ruin," Luna said. "But it's your life."

Dessert came, and then coffee.

"Decaf," her father said. "Brewed decaf. They're going to test me when I get back. In jail, it's illegal to use caffeine."

No one laughed, except Jen. "I would be so busted."

Jen was embarrassed by her own laughter. She figured she had better save the moment. "I almost feel like we should say a prayer or something," she said at last.

They all looked at her as if she was from Mars. She realized that she would have to speak the words.

"I look at all of you," Jen said. "I'm related to some of you. I'm friends with some, and some I barely know."

Everyone kept their glasses raised.

"But we're all here for Susie, and hopefully next month, we'll be able to help her get part of her life back. So let's drink up to Susie."

They drank up.

"And more peasant!" Dew shouted.

Everyone except Denise laughed.

The blood bath over, everyone declared a truce. Susie finally talked to her mother. Luna, Selena, and Jen also agreed that law sucked no matter where you were on the food chain, while the men watched a thrilling football game.

One of the Cowboys made an amazing catch, which was replayed endlessly. "I want to play football someday," Dew said. "Maybe Mom can get me on steroids."

The Cowboys defense sure needs steroids," Black said. "I don't like the Cowboys."

The talk shifted to how people chose their sport teams.

"I hate teams from states where people have broken my heart," Luna said, "so I hate California teams."

"Everybody's broken your heart. I don't much like your football. For me, real football is the world cup," said Selena, who had grown up in Mexico.

"I cheer against dictatorships," said her father. "Unless they're benevolent dictatorships and I can get a good point spread. I always bet the *under*."

"I always cheer for Mexico," said Selena.

"They aren't doing that well in football this year, real football," said Jen.

"I could never cheer for North Korea," said Nurse Song. Her levity about Susie Q was her last joke for the year; her seriousness was back with a vengeance. "Too many people died under that regime."

"So would you cheer for Dallas over North Korea?" Jen asked Black.

"Yes," he said. "You wouldn't even have to give me points."

"Normally I cheer against Japan and China," said Susie. "But now Japan and China are saving my ass."

"So money can buy your love, Susie?" asked Jen.

"A couple hundred million buys a lot of love," said Susie. "And a lot of cheering."

Everyone agreed with that.

"To Susie," every one toasted.

Jae Lee finished her drink first, of course.

Even Dr. Mondragon, who wasn't supposed to drink while on furlough, downed a hearty toast to Susie. He smiled at breaking his conditions of release. "What are they going to do, keep me in jail?" he laughed. "You're worth an extra year in jail, Susie."

"Hell yeah," said Jen. "Maybe two years."

"That could only happen to you, Jen," Selena added. "The clients are the ones to do the time, not the lawyers."

"You're the one dating the criminal."

Susie looked around at the love in the room. She had a tear in her eye. "I don't know what to say."

The discussion kept going and Jen found herself enjoying it in spite of herself. Black was charming. Selena was quite sharp with her retorts, and Dew was wise beyond her years. Even Luna smiled, happy to be with her father for a change.

Jen felt like she belonged here in the chaos, far more than at the Claus residence. Here the tension was out in the open. Her mind was naturally at chaos. Why shouldn't her family be the same?

"Can I sleep here tonight?" Jen asked her mom. "I know you have a lot of empty rooms."

"If you help with the cleaning," Nurse Song said. "You know the rules of my house."

"Sure," Jen said. "Just like old times."

"Don't break anything like you did in old times," her mother said. She didn't smile when she said that. Nurse Song was indeed limited to one joke a year.

Jen did a great job with the dishes. After the last dish, she was finally alone with her mom Denise, Luna, and her father. Denise didn't even protest when they turned off the TV and she actually cuddled with her mother.

Ariana called the hospital to tell them Susie would be back a little later than planned. Whoever was on the other end apparently didn't protest.

"Almost ready for bed, Denise?"

Denise nodded.

"I'm ready for bed," Jen said, taking a deep breath. "I've survived Thanksgiving."

Had she? For one moment everything had been perfect. Jen closed her eyes to savor the moment, to take in the lingering smells and sounds of true laughter. The other guests excused themselves. Black, Taranto, and Jae Lee waved good-bye and headed out the door. Selena took a phone call, and then followed them out. Jen smiled at Luna, at her mom, and at Denise and Dew. Yes, life was good all right. She had a family for real.

Suddenly, they heard a gunshot, and then a scream.

Someone pounded on the door. Before anyone could open it Selena rushed inside, blood dripping from her face. Selena screamed in pain as blood dripped off her hands.

Jen looked everywhere on Selena. She couldn't see a wound, but Selena kept crying as if she had been shot.

"What happened?" Jen asked. "What happened?

Finally Selena could get the words out. "They shot him in the head. I couldn't see who. Hurry! He might still be alive!"

Before they could get out the door, a bullet sailed through the window and the glass shattered.

# Bullet the Black Sky

ANOTHER GUNSHOT, ANOTHER CRASH of glass.

"Everybody, get down!" Luna yelled. Denise didn't move, so Jen grabbed her and pulled her to the floor. She wouldn't let those bastards get her baby. Everyone else huddled near the couch as if it was bulletproof.

Once Denise was safe, Jen and Ariana helped Susie out of her chair and brought her safely to the ground, as if they were Secret Service agents protecting the President.

"Would I take a bullet for this girl?" Jen asked herself. As she hid on the floor, Jen tried to tell herself that this wasn't *it*. She knew she would live at least until she fell from the top of the district court building. But that didn't mean other people couldn't die right now, today—especially Susie. Jen hugged the poor girl.

"I'd take a bullet for you, Susie," Jen said. "Don't worry."

Luna called the police substation on her cell and gave the address, adding. "This is *Judge* Luna Cruz. We're under attack!" Jen saw real terror on Susie's face.

"This wasn't supposed to happen," she said.

"What wasn't supposed to happen?" The greatest golfer in the world, lying paralyzed on a floor in a converted group home in Albuquerque?

"Are we going to be all right, Jen?" Susie asked. "You'll save me, right? Nothing was supposed to work out this way."

Nothing Susie said made sense to Jen, but Jen wanted to say something, anything, to make Susie feel better. She wanted to say that she would save Susie. But she didn't want to make a promise she couldn't keep.

"It's going to be all right," Jen said at last.

Susie didn't look convinced and started to cry.

Heavy footsteps circled the house. Perhaps the Dallas Cowboys themselves were out there. It sure sounded like it. A cold breeze blew through the broken window and cut through them, just like a bullet.

"I wish I was back in jail where it's safe," her father whispered.

No one moved. Footsteps came toward the door. Jen was about to wet her pants. Instead, she threw up on her mom's clean floor.

"You will clean that up," said Nurse Song.

Thankfully, Nurse Song lived close to a police sub-station, and sirens sounded moments later. As the sirens neared, the footsteps hurried away. As the police cruisers arrived more shots were fired.

"Sir Ian wants you to drop the case!" a voice yelled, before it trailed off into the darkness.

✝

An APD SWAT team quickly secured the area and Jen recognized Officer Bebe Tran as soon as she entered the house.

Officer Tran was obviously not convinced of Jen's innocence. "Is there any reason someone would want to shoot the man outside?"

"There are a billion reasons," Jen said. "Well, at least six hundred million reasons. They're after Susie."

Denise had returned to the couch. She sat in front of the blank television screen, seemingly oblivious to the commotion.

The officers did a quick sweep of the area. "All clear," one officer reported to Tran.

"What's the status of the wounded?" Tran asked.

"We don't know yet. But the Asian woman is dead."

Susie gasped. Her mother was dead.

"Did you get the shooter?" Jen asked.

Officer Tran consulted with the other cops, then said, "We think there were multiple shooters. They disappeared into the residential neighborhood across the street. Probably some gang thing. They probably confused you with someone who owed them money in a drug deal."

Jen looked at her mom, who now cuddled with Denise and Dew. No! No gang kids would be after her mom. Her mom gave her a dirty look. Jen cleaned up the glass, and then reluctantly cleaned the vomit on the floor. Then she wiped everything down one more time, just to be safe.

Ariana and Jen helped Susie back into her chair, and then Ariana arranged her legs. That felt too intimate for Jen to do.

Susie began to cry big tears. She had lost her mother, and even though it was a troubled relationship, her mom was still her mom. Susie said a quick prayer, and then wiped away her tears. Then Ariana helped Susie put on her baseball cap with that funky logo. In that instant she became the Susie that Jen loved so much.

"It's going to take more than the death of my mother to stop me," Susie said, as Ariana wheeled her out the door.

# Black Friday

JEN DECIDED TO SPEND the night in the safest place she could imagine, in a cot in Susie's room at the hospital. The hospital added several big, burly guards as security. Jen felt as safe as possible under the circumstances.

Ariana didn't look happy to be responsible for Jen's security as well.

"You'll protect Jen just like you'd protect me," Susie said.

Ariana just grunted. Dr. Ghandi came in and gave Susie a shot, and she was out like a light.

Later that evening, as Jen went to the bathroom, she realized that every milligram of medication had exited her system. Her body was starting to shake. It had grown worse every day, but in light of the disciplinary complaint, she felt she was under an electron microscope. She didn't want to get any pills because then she'd have to face the stares of a doctor, and then a pharmacist. She would have to do it on her own.

"I don't know how much longer I can pretend I'm all right," she said to herself.

She wasn't Jekyll any more. She was all Hyde and the excitement had worn off what little veneer that she had.

Jen returned to the cot, but could not sleep on the uncomfortable bed. By midnight, Susie's snoring had gotten so loud that it ceased being "asnoreable" and crossed the line to annoying. Jen's shaking grew worse. She really needed some pills. She got up and wandered the hallway. Maybe she'd find a doctor who would give her a prescription. But, the halls were empty. Ariana was nowhere to be seen and the beefed up security was gone as well.

A female nurse came over to Jen. The nurse wore a gauze mask, so Jen couldn't see the lower half of her face. That seemed strange, but maybe she'd just come from surgery.

"Can I help you?" the nurse asked.

"I'm Susie Song's cousin. I'm staying with her tonight."

The nurse nodded. "You look a little agitated. Is there something I can get you? I have some medication that you don't need a prescription for. I have some stuff right here that will make you really relax," the nurse said.

That sounded too good to be true. Jen looked down at her hands. They were shaking. "What have you got?"

"Let's go into the bathroom," the nurse said. "I think I know just what you're looking for."

Something didn't seem right, but off her meds Jen's mind wasn't working on all cylinders, especially after the shooting. She was so desperate she might do whatever it took to get a fix, anything to take the edge off.

Jen didn't have time to think things out before the nurse grabbed her by the arm. Jen was too weak to resist as the nurse pulled her into the bathroom. Then she felt someone grab her from behind and cover her mouth. The nurse took out a needle and injected her.

Jen lost her balance and nearly hit her head on the sink before the nurse grabbed her by the neck. The door opened and two men dressed as orderlies grabbed her in a most un-orderly fashion. These guys were big.

The orderlies wore surgical masks over their faces so she couldn't recognize them. That wasn't good, but Jen was powerless to resist. They lifted her onto a stretcher. Her head was covered. She didn't see the covering move at all. Was she breathing? Was she even alive?

Jen realized that she kept breathing, just slower than she ever had. She wanted to push open the blankets that covered her. "I'm alive!" she wanted to say, but her lips wouldn't move.

Jen expected to have an out-of-body experience, but her eyes focused on the coverings. The orderlies took her down a back staircase and, at one point, nearly dropped her, but managed to catch her.

"Sorry," one said.

At least he sounded polite. Polite people don't kill, do they?

"Shut the fuck up," the other said. That didn't sound good.

"What about Susie?" Jen asked, somehow getting the words out. "What about Susie?"

"Susie will be just fine," the nice orderly said.

"She's still up?" the mean orderly asked. "I thought you took her out."

"I gave her enough to take out a horse," the nurse said. "She must have a tolerance."

"Well do something," the mean orderly said. "She's got to be unconscious for the ride."

"I don't want to go on a ride," Jen said.

"Don't worry, I got something else for you," the nurse said.

She felt a shot in her arm. "Make sure you don't kill her," were the last words she heard before losing consciousness. She might also have heard the word "yet."

# Tramway to Heaven

WHEN SHE WOKE UP, Jen shivered. She still wore her street clothes, but it must be below zero here in the darkness. If it weren't for the cold and the headache, she would have thought this was still a dream.

But, as she struggled against the ropes around her, she knew this was very real. She had rope burns on her wrists and ankles. Had she struggled in her sleep? To make things worse, the ground beneath her was vibrating. Was she in a helicopter? No, it felt like a train going up a windy track that was about to derail.

"Where am I?" she asked.

"She's up," the nice orderly said, but he didn't sound so nice right now.

Her eyes were uncovered and she could finally scan the two masked men. Were they Snape and Jean Claude? The men wore parkas with hoods over their orderly scrubs, so she could not tell for sure.

Her muscles struggled against tight ropes as the room kept moving.

"Right here is the highest point," the mean orderly said. He pressed a button and talked into a speaker on the wall. "Stop us here."

Suddenly the room came to an abrupt stop.

The mean orderly then touched a radio on the side of the wall and she heard static.

"Get out of the case, Jen," the voice said through the intercom.

She couldn't place the accent. The static disguised it, but the voice sounded familiar.

"Which case?" she asked.

"You know which case," the static voice from the speaker said. "Drop out, Jen, or we'll drop you."

She wanted to come up with a great one liner but she wasn't as clever as Selena, or as optimistic as Susie. Superpowers sure would be nice right now.

"Well?" the nice orderly asked. "We're trying to help you here. We don't want to hurt you if we don't have to."

"Screw you," Jen said. "This is about Susie."

"Are you sure?" the nice one asked. "We can help you help her. You can save yourself; she'll be all right on her own."

"You can't mess with the Laser Geishas!"

Why did she just say that? She wasn't Laser Geisha Pink; she was just a new lawyer about to be disbarred during her first few weeks on the job.

"Do it," the voice said from the other side of the intercom.

Do what? Jen wanted to ask.

The bad orderly picked her up, while the other one opened the door.

"Take a look," the mean orderly said. "Look down. The first step is a doozy."

"Where am I?"

"You're on the tramway to heaven," the nice orderly said. "We don't have to do this if you help us out."

"Come on, take a look," the mean orderly said.

Jen suddenly realized that she was on the edge of a blue car on the Sandia Peak Tramway. The mean orderly pushed her head out the door while the other held her legs. She could gauge her altitude from triangulating the lights of Albuquerque down below. The tramcar hung about thousand feet above the ground, held only by a single steel cable. Here, nothing but thin air lay between her and the forest and rocks below. They could not be serious, could they?

For a moment she thought Pink would take over, but the nurse had pumped her with something really nasty. Even Pink had her limits.

Why couldn't they just shoot her? That would at least get it over with. Why all this?

In the distance she saw the twinkling lights of the exclusive suburb of Sandia Heights. It was adjacent to the base of the tram. She had been there once with Denise's father, the late Paul Dellagio. The man had had a mansion on top of one of the hills. Now, she could still make out the outline of his watchtower, which was really more of a minaret that he adopted after a trip to the Middle East.

She forced herself to look away from the ground below and tried to shift her head to focus on the full moon. In one of her visions she'd seen a golden disk, something rotating quickly, flickering. She wanted to reach out and grab the moon right there, and hold on for dear life.

"Just think about it," the nice orderly said. "All you have to do it drop out."

"And we won't drop you," the mean orderly said.

Jen said nothing. She kept looking at the moon. Did the moon just wink at her?

The nice orderly checked her feet nervously. "Are you sure you measured the rope right?"

"Does it matter?" the mean one said. "It's not like we need her any more, no matter what he says."

Who was "he?"

"You guys don't have to do this," Jen said.

"Yeah, we do." The mean one said.

The nice one piped in. "This is your last chance to save yourself."

Jen tried to move her legs, but the rope that was tied around her ankles held them fast. She couldn't tell if it was a bungee cord or regular rope. She tried to see if the rope was attached to anything, but it was too dark to come to a conclusion about that.

She would have to act on faith. She'd probably only fall a few feet and then they'd pull her back. She could suck it up for Susie. "I'm not dropping the case."

"Sorry you think that way," the nice orderly said.

The bad orderly took a deep breath and pushed her out with all his might. "*Sayonara* bitch," he said with a snarl.

"I'm Korean, damn it," she said, but she was already falling into the air.

"Hope the rope holds," the nice orderly called after her.

The wind cut through her as the air rushed up toward her from the earth. It was as if an avalanche of air flowed up and raced through her lungs and then into her capillaries. Jen tried to reach up, but her hands were tied, her feet were tied. All she could do was stare at the moon.

"Luna," she cried. No. It had nothing to do with Luna, nor Selena. It was all about Susie. Off to the east, she saw the first glimmer of the sun on the furthest reaches of the horizon. It's always darkest before the dawn, right?

Jen wiggled her legs but the tight ropes limited their movement. Maybe this *was* a bungee cord, but then again, she was dropping down a thousand feet, and would hit terminal velocity. She remembered the good orderly worried about the other's calculations.

That didn't sound good. Jen craned her head and eyes to the ground below. She tried to focus on the rapidly approaching rocks. She headed straight down, toward sharp spires, a low rent version of the Garden of the Gods Park in Colorado Springs. She tried to cheer herself up. This wasn't *it*. She would die in district court, right?

She looked up. The moon winked at her again, and Jen became unstuck in time.

The blackness faded. When the lights came back she was in the past again, in the anime world of her memory, floating above a tower. It took her a moment to recognize Paul Dellagio's mansion in the foothills of Albuquerque. This thirty-foot Arab minaret was part of his adobe castle on the rocky knob of a hill. In the sharp angles of the anime world, the minaret could be Rapunzel's tower. How much money did this guy have to pay to beat the covenants to build a tower this high?

Jen floated just above the minaret as she looked down at the rocks far below. If someone fell out the window, they'd have less than a fifty-fifty chance of surviving. She looked into the open window. Pink stood there with Paul Dellagio, the father of her child.

Jen vaguely recalled events leading up to the scene. Dellagio had called to talk about something. They'd gone to the minaret to talk and have a drink. Then he attacked her, threatened her, and did the worst possible thing: shoved her against the wall and turned her head so she looked over the edge.

"I'll throw your ass over," he said. "I know you're afraid of heights."

That's when Pink took over. Pink pushed him away, and then punched him so hard that he fell to the floor. Then he chased her around the house before she found his gun and shot him. Twice. Pink's heartbeat didn't even rise.

It was justified murder. Self-defense, right?

Pink stayed in control. She knew just how to arrange the body to make it look like suicide. Then she wiped away her powder burns with a cleanser. There was a legal term for those actions. It was called tampering with evidence.

"You're not me," Jen said. "You're a multiple personality."

Pink stared at the floating Jen and shrugged. "Are you sure?" she asked.

"I'm the good guy," Jen said.

Pink laughed, and said again, "Are you sure?"

The avalanche of cold air continued unabated through her lungs. Jen opened her eyes to find she was falling even faster. She had fallen another hundred or more feet. She felt an increasing pressure from the line and then heard the sound of it tightening. Must be a bungee cord, she thought, as she would have been jerked hard by a traditional rope. Would the bungee cord hold? They're just scaring me, right?

Jagged rocks rushed toward her. Her eyes became super acute, even in the darkness; she could now make out individual trees. Depending on the wind, she'd either hit a pine tree or a rock formation. Would she turn into Pink? No, the nurse had injected too many drugs into her system. It was almost as if they knew. Jen was stuck being Jen, but this wasn't *it*. This was not the end!

The wind blew her to the left, toward the rock pinnacle. The pinnacle stood maybe thirty feet high. Unless he had majored in differential calculus, or took wind speed into account, the bad orderly had failed to figure it in.

Jen looked once again at the sunrise over the Sandia Crest. If the sun could save her, now sure would be a good time. Just inches from the pinnacle, Jen felt the tug of the bungee cord, the cord strained under her weight and velocity. She could almost kiss the granite when suddenly she ascended like a rocket. The moon definitely smiled at her now.

Jen ascended nearly all the way back to the tramcar, when she started falling again. Just as fast as before. Maybe gravity wanted her more the second time around. She descended even more rapidly this time.

# ACT III
## Lone Geisha

JEN AWOKE IN A cramped broom closet that reeked of death and
ammonia. It took a second for her to recognize that the solid
object lodged against her back was indeed a broom and not a
gun. She was able to move her hands and legs, and the ropes
were gone.

Her hangover felt like Sir Ian's rocket had exploded inside
her head, over and over again. For one brief moment, she
hoped that the fall was all a dream, but sure enough she felt
the rope burns around her legs and wrists. All of her muscles
ached, just as if someone had gone medieval across her entire
body. Without her meds, she was shaking even more than she
had the day before.

Jen touched her arm, felt the pin-prick wound of the shot,
then felt another, and another. How many shots had they given
her?

The smell of ammonia forced her into consciousness. She
used the broom for support to hoist herself up. Thank God, she
wasn't tied up any more, but the rope burns remained.

She stumbled toward the door. Thankfully, the door opened to her slight touch. Two orderlies pushed a body past her, ignoring her. Both listened to iPods, earphones in their ears, and shuffled to a Spanish rap beat. Their faces were uncovered. Jen had a moment of panic but quickly realized that these men were much smaller than her kidnapers, and were definitely not the same guys.

"Hello!" she yelled.

The two men kept moving along, keeping time to rap in Español, something called the Burque beat. Jen had a bad feeling about this. She heard a bell ring, but the men didn't respond to that either. She looked to see if some angel had just got his wings. The orderlies neared the end of the hall. One said something about how the hot chick beneath the sheets had been a dancer.

Jen freaked. She ran over to them; she just had to see the corpse. This wasn't the afterlife, was it? Without a word to the men, Jen opened the sheet to reveal an attractive African-American woman.

"What the hell did you do that for?" one orderly asked, not turning off his music.

"You're not supposed to be down here!" the other said, grabbing her.

"You can see and hear me?" Jen asked. "I'm not dead?"

"No, you crazy bitch," the orderly said. "But if you keep it up—"

"Where am I?"

One orderly angrily explained that she was in the hospital, on a lower floor near the morgue. The other summoned security.

Jen was confused. Maybe it was the drugs. "What day is it?"

"Saturday," one orderly said. "November something or other."

That's the day it was supposed to be, right? Jen was about to ask what year, but she didn't want to push her luck.

Upstairs in the lobby Jen explained the situation to Officer Tran, who was already in the building looking for her. "I'm head of the Jen Song task force," she said.

"Don't you mean Susie Song?"

"No, we're more interested in you right now."

Jen knew she shouldn't say too much, but she had to talk to someone. Tran escorted her into a private waiting room where, thankfully, there were no windows. Tran stopped being a cop and tried to play therapist. She listened patiently for an hour, peppering Jen with questions.

"Why didn't they kill you?" Tran asked again and again.

"I don't know," Jen said. "They just kept telling me to drop Susie's case."

Needless to say, no nurse or orderly matched the descriptions Jen gave.

"Are you going to press charges?" Jen said. "This would be assault, right? They definitely kidnapped me once they moved me against my will. Tying me up would be false imprisonment, and the nurse who drugged me would be conspiracy."

"Who should we press charges against?"

Jen said nothing. "This has to have something to do with Susie's case."

Tran didn't change her expression. "I'll ask again. Who, or is it whom, do we press charges against?"

"Sir Ian," Jen said.

"We checked," Tran said. "He's in Aspen."

"What about his henchmen? Snape and Jean Claude?"

"They're in Aspen with him. They're actually skiing right now on two feet of new powder."

"Couldn't he call someone? Couldn't he get local dudes to do his dirty work?"

"Dirty deeds done dirt cheap," Tran said. "If you can bring in a dirty deed doer let me know."

"So what should I do?"

"Don't go anywhere," Tran said. "You're still a person of interest."

"Interest in what?" Jen asked.

Tran's phone rang and she excused herself.

Jen waited fifteen minutes before she decided to look down the hallway. Tran was nowhere to be seen.

Jen texted Luna, and her sister met her minutes later in the lobby. The two headed over to the Starbucks on the grounds. Over a hot tea with the soothing label of "Zen," Jen told Luna what had happened.

Luna seemed more nervous than Jen as she gulped a double espresso. "Are you sure you're all right? We're in a hospital. You can stay here."

When Jen assured her that she was fine, Luna updated her on what had happened to the people involved in the shooting. Black had died on the way to the hospital, as did Taranto. Jae Lee had died instantly.

"This is more serious than I ever imagined," said Jen.

"There's more," Luna said. "White, the tax lawyer, got whacked in his home in Vegas. Police there say it was a contract killing. And your friend Claus's house got shot up. He has some minor injuries, but should be all right. Thank God his wife is an EMT who could fix him up."

"Poor Claus," Jen said. "He's a nice man. Is his new baby all right?"

"I don't know," she said. "I didn't know he had a new baby. He's your friend, not mine."

Luna related a sliver of good news. Nurse Song and Denise had gone to a police safe house. Selena and Dew had joined them.

"Dad returned to jail, in solitary. He is probably the safest all of us right now."

"Solitary confinement sure sounds good," Jen said. "I feel responsible. I brought all of them into this mess."

"I'm sure it has nothing to do with you, Jen," Luna replied.

"Do you think it was Sir Ian's people?" Jen asked.

"Who else would it be? Maybe he doesn't want to pay up."

"So what do you think I should do?"

It's your call, Jen. No case is worth dying for."

After she finished with Luna, Jen stayed at Starbucks, had a refill of Zen, and called Claus. She didn't tell him about the incident last night. The man probably had enough on his plate.

"Are you all right?" she asked. "I heard you were shot too."

"I'm fine," he said. "I got hit in the leg, but just grazed. Someone's trying to take us all out."

"I bet it's Sir Ian. I bet he's using his goons."

"No doubt. Are you safe?"

"I'm waiting it out in the hospital with Susie until I know more."

"What do you mean? Do you want to stay on the case after all this?" Claus asked.

"Luna told me that no case is worth dying for." Jen took a deep breath. The Zen tea stopped working abruptly. For a brief moment, she felt vertigo again, even though she was there on the ground in a Starbucks.

"I don't know," she said to Claus. "I'm going to talk to Susie."

"What are you going to tell her?"

"I don't know."

Jen hadn't decided whether or not to stick with the case when she went upstairs to check on Susie. Thankfully, armed APD officers had been assigned to stand by Susie's room in shifts, around the clock. Jen was relieved to see someone other than Ariana.

"I need to see Susie," Jen said to the officer. "She's my cousin, and I'm her lawyer"

Ariana then came out of the bathroom. She frowned at Jen. Jen frowned back.

"Could you keep it down?" Ariana asked. "She's asleep, still on meds. She hated her mother, but losing her is still taking a toll. She's had a bit of a relapse."

"Is there going to be a funeral for Jae Lee?"

"The people at the crime lab are still looking at the body. If there's going to be any funeral at all, it will be in Arizona and

Susie can't travel there yet. I have a feeling that Jae Lee Song is not going to be missed, so I doubt that there will be much of a ceremony."

"Still, it is sad. Susie lost her mother. I lost my aunt."

Ariana shrugged. "You can choose your friends. You can't choose your family."

"You're right about that."

Jen didn't trust Ariana. This probably had been an inside job, and Ariana was the most inside person here. Dr. Ghandi poked his head in. Jen didn't entirely trust him either.

"I think we need to settle things," Ariana said.

"I think so, too," Jen replied.

"Come back at noon," Ariana said. "You can talk to Susie then and we can sort everything out."

"High noon," Jen said.

It was barely ten o'clock. Jen had two hours to decide if she wanted to stick with the case. After the elevator door closed, Jen had a moment of panic as the elevator eased down. She held her breath as her brain tried to ponder what had happened during the past twenty-four hours. None of it made sense. Why hadn't her kidnappers killed Susie?

Why hadn't they killed Jen either, for that matter?

When the elevator door opened on the first floor, Jen gasped at the fresh air. She had a moment of relief when she remembered that her destiny would be to die falling from the seventh floor of the courthouse. For the moment, she was immortal. But in her vision, she most certainly did not have gray hair or wrinkles. There wasn't much time left.

When Jen emerged outside, she glanced at the Sandia Crest. The sun had risen over the top. She couldn't see the tram from this distance. Just as well.

Jen took another deep breath. Maybe she should get out of the lawsuit. It wouldn't be that big of a deal, she could just type up a one page piece of paper, sign it and file it. Claus could take over. Besides, he needed the money.

Jen would be disbarred, of course. Probably just as well, but she'd be alive, which counted for something. She could always hide in K-town and blend in. Maybe she could become a floozy like her late aunt Jae Lee and find an endless succession of rich lawyers to live off. No, she was getting too old for that.

In any event, Jen didn't want to decide anything right now. She sat there in front of the hospital on a stoop. The smokers stood there with her, puffing away.

Jen could see the obvious irony of doctors and nurses smoking out in the cold. Jen bummed a cigarette from a handsome doctor.

"I'm not supposed to do this," he said with a smile.

"There are a lot of things, I'm not supposed to do either," Jen said.

Jen sat there smoking, bumming cigarette after cigarette from doctors and nurses. She really had no idea what she wanted to do any more. She felt bad about putting her friends and family in danger. Denise could have been killed.

Claus called. "How are you?" he asked. "Just wanted to tell you that I should have the answer to your disciplinary complaint filed by Monday."

"I don't know if I still want to be a lawyer," she said.

"I can type up a withdrawal of counsel form," he said. "If your heart isn't in it, it isn't fair to your client for you to stay on."

"If I decide to go that route I'll do it myself. It only took a handwritten letter to get me on the case. It will probably only take a scribble on a napkin to get me off."

Jen decided to visit her mom and daughter. They were staying at a cheap motel on Central, a few blocks from the university. Jen didn't say a word to her daughter, but Denise came over and hugged her while Jen held her tightly.

"I love you, Denise. I hope I never lose you."

Denise actually had a tear in her eye. She thought once again about falling over the balcony at district court. This case would kill her. She knew it in her heart.

All the more reason to drop out.

Jen checked her watch, then walked back to the hospital and up to Susie's room. This was it. High noon.

"I need to talk to Susie," Jen said to Ariana, who was waiting outside the room. "Alone."

Jen walked to Susie's bed. There was a picture of Susie's mother on the nightstand. Blood was blood after all. Through the window, Jen could see the Sandias in the distance. She couldn't believe she'd been there only hours before.

"Susie, I don't know if I can do this," Jen said.

Susie said nothing and her monitors indicated no change.

Jen took another deep breath. She wondered what a monitor would say about her own pulse right now. She took another glimpse at the Sandias. Damn, they were high.

"I don't know if I am really a lawyer."

Susie moved her left hand to touch Jen's.

"You *are* a real lawyer," she said. "I don't know Claus. I never knew any of these guys. I only know you."

"Susie, you're the only good thing in my life right now. I feel responsible for getting you into this mess."

"I got myself into this mess. You don't know the half of it."

They stayed motionless for a few minutes.

Susie grimaced, and then moved her right hand to grab

Jen's. "I couldn't have gotten this far if it wasn't for you. I need you, Jen. I can't do it alone."

"So what do you want me to do?"

"Don't leave me. Don't give up on me. Keep being my lawyer."

Jen looked at Susie's big brown eyes. It was like looking into a mirror. Susie was her blood. Susie was her friend. Susie was her love, but this case was too big for her as a lawyer. There was no doubt in her mind any more. "I don't want to be your lawyer anymore," Jen said at last. "It's too dangerous, people are dying."

"What?"

"I said, I don't want to be a lawyer. You don't need a lawyer. A lawyer can't win your case. A lawyer can't save you."

"What are you talking about?"

"I don't want to be your lawyer," Jen smiled. "I want to be your Laser Geisha. I want to do whatever it takes to win. I'm ready to kill these bastards if I have to, if that's what it takes to save you."

A slow smile spread across Susie's face. "Laser Geisha Gold," she said firmly.

"Lawyer Geisha Pink," Jen replied.

# Jingle Bell

DECEMBER PASSED QUICKLY. THERE were memorial services out of town for members of the Fellowship—Black, White and Taranto—but Jen was not invited. Probably just as well. She sent flowers to the funeral homes.

Jen had never met Black's widow, but the woman left a nasty message on Jen's phone. "This wouldn't have happened if it hadn't been for you."

The days grew shorter as the sun hesitated to rise over the Sandias until the last possible moment, yet hurried to set quickly over the volcanoes to the west. Jen went to bed earlier and earlier as the weather changed. Albuquerque had some real snow for a change, and the snow actually decided to stick around without melting by mid-morning.

So much for global warming, Jen thought.

Without the others, it was just Claus and Jen. Thankfully, Claus recovered from his injuries due to of his wife's quick response and her training as an EMT. He made regular calls to Sir Ian, Wagatsuma, and Zhang, to make sure the deal stayed on track.

After Jen told Claus that she had a change of heart, Claus repeatedly asked her if she wanted to continue with the case, and she assured him every time that she was all in.

He shrugged. "Okay. I guess it will all work out the way it's supposed to work out."

Claus hated wandering around on crutches, so he let Jen change Asia's diaper during one of their sessions. Unfortunately, she absent-mindedly reached for the nearest paper at hand, one of Claus's motions *in limine*, a request to a judge before the start of a trial that certain evidence be admitted . . . or not.

"So that's what you think of my writing?" he asked with a smile.

Jen swapped the motion for the appropriate paper towels and managed to clean the crying Asia. Asia took a while, but finally adjusted to Jen's touch.

"That wasn't so hard," she said with a smile. "Being a mother isn't such a big deal after all."

Claus showed her the answer he had filed regarding her disciplinary complaint.

The man was good. He had answered every point.

"Thank you for being there for me," she said. "I've decided that I don't care what happens, as long as I'm still a lawyer when the deal goes down. I really don't care after that."

"I'll take care of you being a lawyer," he said.

On December 20th, the day before the solstice; Jen took her mother and Denise to ABQ Uptown, the Albuquerque equivalent of Los Angeles's Century City outdoor mall. They were not alone. Done with school up in Boulder, Selena tagged along. She had aced her finals for the semester.

And, after considerable begging, Susie was able to meet them there, with Ariana as her chaperone. Officer Tran was off duty and acted as a bodyguard. Susie would have a few hours before she had to return to the hospital.

Once they emerged into the cold, Susie donned her Navajo disguise and covered herself in blankets. She no longer had to wear a neck brace, but still had scarves around her neck.

"Being Navajo is like being Asian, without the math scores," Selena said.

Both Susie and Jen stared at her. "Just because you're Hispanic, doesn't mean that you can't be racist." Jen said.

"I have a Navajo accountant who is a lot smarter than I am," Susie said.

"And the math thing is a total stereotype," Susie said. "Both Jen and I are terrible at math."

"As a lawyer on a contingency case, all I need to do is to divide by three," Jen said.

"You might not even have to do that," Susie said.

Jen wasn't sure what she meant by that. She couldn't read Susie's cryptic smile.

As they walked through the faux streetscape of stores, Jen figured the developers had been shooting for something out of the Italian Alps. She waited next to a bookstore with Susie as Denise went to sit on Santa's lap. Jen shivered. The cold did seep in when they stopped moving.

"Remember when malls used to be indoors?" Jen asked.

Susie smiled. "I love the cold air," she said. "I love any air at all these days."

A teen chorus sang a hip-hop version of Jingle Bells. Jen looked at their collection hat. A sign read HELP SAVE TROUBLED YOUTH.

"I'm a troubled youth," Susie said.

"Well, I'm helping you." Jen said. "What do you want for Christmas?" Jen pointed at the bookstore behind them. "An author is doing a signing. I can get you a signed book."

Susie smiled. "I could write a book myself someday. It doesn't seem that hard. God knows everybody else is doing it. But being on a book tour seems like the most humiliating thing in the world, especially around Christmas. Imagine sitting alone at a store next to the open door as strangers walk by and ignore you."

She pointed to her legs under the blankets. "I think you know what I want. I'll settle for hundreds of millions of dollars, however. How about you, Jen? What do you want for Christmas?"

At that moment, Denise ran away from Santa, crying into Jen's arms. Jen was secretly glad that Denise had chosen her instead of Nurse Song.

"You two are getting closer every day." Susie smiled. "By the way, I have a present for you."

"For me?"

They were next to the outdoor mall's fifteen-foot tall Christmas tree. Jen could almost pretend they were in Vermont.

Susie pulled a manila envelope from under her blankets. Jen was surprised to see it was a legal document that Taranto had prepared before his death. "You're not my only lawyer, you know," Susie said. "I have a lawyer in Arizona, too."

Jen panicked. Susie had an Arizona lawyer, other than Taranto? That couldn't be good. Would the case become even uglier and more complicated?

Jen scanned the document, which bore a caption from the Pima County District Court in Tucson. Her heart raced. It took her a moment to understand the legalese, but the judge had ordered Jae Lee Song to cease and desist in acting as the official guardian of Susie Song. It listed the cause as embezzling the trust account. Taranto was also subject to a disciplinary complaint, so he was not entitled to any remuneration.

"I don't get it. Your mom is dead. So is Taranto. Don't they appoint a trustee or something? Does this mean you are making my mom your guardian?" Jen asked.

"I checked with the people in Arizona and they told me that the document Luna signed was not binding, since she did not sign in it her judicial capacity. As I am an Arizona resident, or was at the time, it wouldn't be binding on an Arizona court."

"What does that mean?"

Susie smiled. "Keep reading. Turn to the next page."

There was a second document, this one bearing a New Mexico seal. It declared that Jen Song was now the official guardian of Susie Song, until she reached the age of majority. It took a moment for Jen to figure it out.

"Jen Song?" Jen asked. "Do you have another relative named Jen?"

Susie laughed.

"So you are my mother for the next few weeks—until my birthday," Susie said.

Jen knew there might be problems with the document. Talk about the appearance of impropriety during a pending lawsuit. But wow, no one had ever asked her to be a mother before.

"So what does that mean in terms of the lawsuit?"

"If anything happens to me in the next few weeks, every-thing goes to you."

Jen should have felt happy, but a chill passed through her, as if she was falling again.

She now felt that she had an even bigger target on her back.

"Ho, ho ho," Santa yelled from in front of the book store.

# The Shortest Day of the Year

DECEMBER TWENTY-FIRST CAME at last; winter solstice, the first day of winter and, of course, the shortest day of the year. Jen thought of all the pagan rights that had preceded Christmas. It had snowed that morning, so everything was now on a two-hour delay. But warm winds arrived after noon, as if the ancient pagan gods wanted to take back Christmas.

Was this *it*—her last day on earth?

Probably not. All she had to do was avoid getting thrown off the seventh floor atrium and she would be just fine. Court was on the fifth floor.

Jen arrived at one o'clock dressed in a gray suit with a sweater vest. Like her outfit from the swearing in, she had bought this at the Brooks Brothers outlet in Santa Fe. The vest had a pink argyle pattern that didn't quite work with her gray pin stripes, but it would have to do. It was better to be warm than to look good.

Jen waited outside the courthouse for everyone else to arrive, both friend and foe. While she was standing there, the war between the winds grew noticeably fiercer. First the hot wind made an assault and then the cold wind responded in kind. Would these be her last few breaths of fresh air?

She took a call from Luna. "Good news and bad," Luna said in a soft voice. "Apparently the response to the D-board got lost in the mail. Claus did tell them he would resend it, however. You will probably be suspended for non-disclosure after the first of the year. Dr. Romero's disappearance is also a bad thing. Appearance of impropriety and all that."

Jen shivered along with a sudden gust of wind. "But Claus said it would all work out. I saw his brief; it was amazing."

"I don't know what to tell you. But as I said, there is also good news."

"I'm being disbarred in a few days, or at least suspended. What could possibly be the good news?"

"You are a lawyer at this very moment. Assuming the deal goes down today, you do get to keep the money. I could hold it in trust for you if you want."

"No thank you," Jen said. "If it's mine legally, I want to keep it. I kinda liked this whole being a lawyer thing."

"Well, enjoy it while it lasts."

Jen smiled at the bustle of the courthouse. She would miss this. Even the lawyer line was long today. She couldn't just flash her card and get through; everyone ielse had already tried that.

"No one gets through without passing through security," a guard said. "I mean no one, no how, no*body*!"

She asked a clerk about the location of the hearing, just to make sure. Thankfully, court would not be on the seventh floor. As long as she avoided that floor, she would be fine. Actually, since she'd be taking a vacation from law for a while, she'd never have to go there for the rest of her life.

Jen enjoyed another few moments of equilibrium—until Selena arrived.

"I wouldn't miss this for the world," Selena said. She wore a black suit with a green bow. "How you say, Laser Geishas forever, and all that?"

Jen forced a smile. Was this too little, too late with Selena? "Laser Geishas united and all that right back at you," Jen replied.

"Parking was a bitch," Selena said. She hurried inside.

Jen quickly saw the reason for the lack of parking. A host of media trucks began to pull up alongside the courthouse. Then a van with Chinese lettering pulled up along Fourth Street and parked in a no parking zone. It had the Zhang corporate logo on the side.

After a moment, a ramp came down and Susie wheeled down in a motorized chair and proceeded on her own power. The golden chair was the one they'd seen in one of Zhang's promotional videos, shiny and new. It looked like something out of *Transformers*, like maybe it could transform into a giant robot.

Ariana hurried behind, guarding Susie's flank. Jen hurried to greet them.

"Susie, do you have a comment?" a reporter yelled.

Susie stopped the chair, and almost had whiplash. She was not used to the new technology. "I want to thank the Zhang Corporation," she said in a carefully rehearsed voice. "As a show of good faith, they've given me this amazing chair, the latest model of the Ziyi 6000."

Photographers took pictures of the chair and were as enamored with it as if it had been a racecar. Susie smiled as if she was a fashion model. She still had a blue scarf where the neck brace used to be. "Make sure you get my good side," she said, tossing the scarf over her side.

"Pimp my chair," Jen muttered to herself. But the chair was pimped in all senses of the word, even the Zhang logo in English and Chinese looked like a garish pimp's medallion.

Jen looked at her watch. "We've got to get up there."

Susie motioned for Jen to join her by the magnificent chair. "I'll be glad when this is over," Susie said in her grown-up voice. Then she looked down at the Navajo blankets that covered her legs. "I guess this might *never* be over."

Jen fought a tear when Susie said that.

Suddenly all the cameras pointed at Jen, and Jen wilted under the lights.

"Susie, is it true that your lawyer was an accused murderer, a former exotic dancer, and is currently in trouble with the Bar?" a young reporter asked, as if Jen was the client and Susie was the lawyer.

Jen covered her breasts instinctively with her arms, as if they could see right through the pink argyles. She wanted to say that she had been a *waitress*, but was sure that wouldn't work.

"My lawyer is my lawyer," said Susie. "And that's my business."

Susie held Jen's hand in a loose grip and Jen wondered if she embarrassed Susie. Jen gathered her resolve and said, "We've really got to move."

The crowd just stood there, even when Ariana gave her women's prison stare to the photographers. It wasn't enough. Thankfully, Officer Tran came out of nowhere and flashed her sidearm. The photographers and reporters finally backed off. Susie pressed a button, and the golden chair moved forward. Jen walked along side.

The chief judge had banned media from inside the courthouse on high profile cases like Susie's, so the camera crews waited outside the building.

"Good luck, Susie!" a cameraman yelled.

"I have faith in my lawyer!" she yelled back.

Inside, security was brutal, worse than an airport and a prison put together. *Con Airport.* The guards checked every inch of Susie's new chair.

"I'm clean," Susie said. She pointed at the chair again, as a guard checked under the motor's hood. "Chinese technology combining comfort and speed."

"Shut up, Susie," Jen said. "This isn't an ad."

Susie just smiled. The cousins finally made it through and waited on the other side. The delay had caused the line to snake out the building.

Just then, the head deputy stopped the line to make an announcement. "There will be no, I repeat no, weapons past security. And by the way, Merry Christmas."

Jen looked past the deputy. The opposing parties had arrived.

The deputy looked at the Zhang contingent. "You first!" she said.

The Zhang people made it through quickly, as if they dealt with security and metal detectors regularly. The Wagatsuma people, however, were not so lucky. One man dressed in black carried a big briefcase that was handcuffed to his body. He looked like a real ninja; his face was uncovered, but he displayed no emotion. His briefcase beeped as he passed through the detector.

"You!" the deputy said. "Open it. And slowly. Keep your hands where I can see them."

The ninja slowly opened his case. The deputy could not believe what he saw and summoned his superior to verify the contents

"Is that what I think it is?" Officer Tyson, the head deputy asked the ninja. Tyson resembled the famous boxer. He did not sport any tattoos on his face, however.

The ninja did not say anything. Tyson shrugged and waved him through. The ninja closed the case and waited by the elevator.

Wagatsuma's personal bodyguard beeped repeatedly and had to undress to his underwear. He had several tattoos that honored the yazuka, the Japanese mafia. Tyson touched every inch of the man's body, including his crotch.

"He's clean," Tyson said. "Next!" Tyson pointed toward Sir Ian and his group.

Sir Ian walked through the detector. He had a sterling silver ballpoint pen that he had forgotten. "I can't sign the bloody deal without a pen," he said. "Take it if you want."

Tyson let him through, after searching the pen to make sure it wasn't a weapon.

"This wouldn't have happened if you'd let me land my helicopter on the roof," Sir Ian said. "In, out, nobody gets hurt."

"No landings today," Tyson said. In fact, there had never been a roof landing, but it was technically possible to land on the courthouse's flat circular roof. "Winds will kill you."

Sir Ian's personal lawyer, Gupta, followed behind him. Gupta didn't beep at all, despite cufflinks and jewelry. "It's a new alloy," he said in explanation.

Snape and Jean Claude brought up the rear. They wore matching long black leather jackets. Snape had a particularly nice Beretta that the guard removed from him. "If you scuff it up, you better use it on yourself," Snape said to the guard, "because I will bloody kill you, mate."

Tyson didn't flinch.

Jean Claude mumbled something in French when his weapons were taken.

"Can we hurry this up?" a woman asked. "People are trying to get divorced here!"

"You'll have to wait your turn like everyone else," the guard replied.

"Screw it, I'll just stay married," the woman said. She turned and walked toward the door, then grabbed her soon-to-be ex-husband from further back in line.

"True love waits," Sir Ian said, forcing a smile at the woman.

Claus came at the very end of the line, limping slowly on crutches. They weren't made of any special alloy and had trouble supporting his heavy frame. Still, he tried to make the best of it by sporting a red Christmas tie and his blue polyester suit. Jen thought it might be his only suit.

Claus had brought the triplets with him: Junior, Troy, and Rock. They really did look like an offensive line, except for the matching red Christmas ties that were identical to their dad's.

Plus, all three boys had their long curly hair tied back in a ponytail.

"You again?" Tyson frowned. "This is the fifth time today. Do you live here?"

"It's my home away from home," Claus said. He beeped. "Like I keep telling you, I had surgery and have a metal hip."

Unfortunately, his briefcase beeped as well.

"Not again," Tyson shook his head.

"Like I told you the last four times," Claus said as he opened the big case to reveal legal papers. "I'm an attorney."

Claus had the original of the settlement agreement. If he didn't get in, the whole deal fell apart. Jen had a moment of panic. She didn't want to lose her last chance at happiness because of an overzealous metal detector.

"He's with us," she said to Tyson.

Tyson looked at Jen. He didn't trust Jen's word about vouching for the man. Thankfully, Luna came over to intercede. She walked to Tyson and flashed her district court card. She only had a few more days as a judge but she still had some clout.

"You expire next week," he said. "As a judge."

"I'm valid now," she replied. "And that's all that counts. We need him on the case on the fifth floor before Judge Salazar."

She looked directly at Tyson. "I can hold you in contempt if you don't let him in."

"All right, let him in," Tyson said.

The triplets followed their father. One of them beeped. "A brace for my ACL," he said.

Tyson shrugged, tired of it all. "Whatever," he said, and waved him through.

✝

The line for the elevators was long, and Jen felt claustrophobic crowded in with everyone else. She waited until the others had gone up before she got in her own elevator. When Jen emerged, the floor was strangely empty. Something was wrong. Where was everyone? Perhaps she had taken the elevator to a parallel universe by mistake.

She walked toward the glass of the atrium and realized that she had exited on the fourth floor by mistake. She couldn't help but wander out to look at the atrium lobby. She walked past the sculpture in the center of the bulls-eye tiling.

"Are you coming?" Susie asked, looking down from the fifth floor.

Jen was pretty sure that nothing could happen from if she fell from the fifth floor, just one floor up.

"Hello?" Susie shouted. She had taken off her blankets, and was now dressed in white. Like an angel.

The fifth floor was where the other disk was. It was just a weird dream, right? Jen looked up at Susie. She could still back out, let Claus handle the case. Jen knew once she got back on the elevator there was no turning back. This was for Susie.

Jen smiled at her cousin. "I'm on my way up."

She took one last glance around. Would she be on her way back down soon?

No, a one-story fall from the fifth floor wouldn't kill her. Today wasn't the day.

Or was it?

# The Dotted Line

JUDGE DANIELLE JOHNSON-SALAZAR was one of the newer judges. She was a pretty blonde who had married a prominent criminal defense lawyer. In an earlier generation, her husband would have bought her a card shop. These days, spouses bought their partners judgeships. But Judge Johnson-Salazar surprised everyone by becoming one of the finest minds on the New Mexico bench. She was a no-nonsense woman, perfect for a tough case like this.

The airy courtroom was already packed when Jen and Susie arrived. Claus sat at the plaintiff's table on the left. Sir Ian and Gupta sat at the defendant's table on the right. The Wagatsuma and Zhang folks sat in the jury box, as if passing judgment on the others.

Luna and Selena sat in the gallery. Each wore grey Brooks Brothers outlet suits, but Jen noticed that Selena's had a green bow, while Luna's had a blue one. They were undercover geishas. Jen's pink argyles completed her own Geisha effect. Susie wore several pieces of gold jewelry, so that should count for something.

They all looked so proud of Jen, even Luna. Jen nodded at each of them as she joined Susie at the plaintiff's counsel table on the left. Claus sat at the edge of the table, next to the space between the two tables and did most of the whispered exchanges between the parties.

"It's funny," Jen said to Susie. "This is a billion dollar deal and each side keeps penciling in final corrections."

Due to security issues, Officer Tran acted as the bailiff today. Jen was happy to see the big gun on a holster around her tiny waist.

"Are you ready?" Tran asked.

"Not yet," Claus and Gupta said simultaneously.

They then initialed each correction, and then initialed the corrections to the corrections. It stayed heated, over whether to use the word "a" or "the." Susie grew impatient, as did Jen.

"Can't we just get this settled?" Susie asked.

"It's the shortest day of the year," Jen said for no reason.

"Sure doesn't feel like it," Susie replied.

"Just a second," Claus said.

Claus showed the final draft of the paperwork, complete with all the scribbling and initials to Susie. Susie made a cursory look, due to the lateness of the hour.

Jen made a point to show the "guardianship and "power of attorney" pages to all concerned.

Sir Ian's lawyer, Gupta, said, "It doesn't pass the smell test. But let's get this over with."

Jen then realized that she had misplaced her pen and asked Gupta to hand her Sir Ian's pen.

Sir Ian shook his head while he stared at Jen. "I've never heard of a lawyer who didn't have a pen. Are you sure you're really a lawyer?"

Jen ignored him.

Sir Ian was about to make another comment concerning Jen's "real" occupation, but a look from Gupta silenced him. "Sir Ian, there's no need. I've heard that she's disbarred as of the first of the year anyway."

Jen ignored the slight. She waited for one moment, and then took a deep breath. This would be her first and last time signing a legal document. She wanted to savor the feeling.

The pen didn't work at first, then ink dripped out as if it was blood. Jen could barely remember how to spell her name. Should she sign her legal name Chan Wol Song or Jen Song? Or perhaps she should sign it as Laser Geisha Pink?

She went with Chan Wol Song, a.k.a. Jen Song, then handed the document to Claus.

Claus signed quickly, almost too quickly, before he passed the document to Gupta. Gupta took one more cursory glance, checked the initialed phrases, and checked the power of attorney page one more time. He then looked at the Wagatsuma people who nodded at him. Sir Ian whispered in his ear, something along the lines of make them sign first.

Gupta gingerly brought the pages to Mr. Wagatsuma, who signed. Gupta then gave the document to Sir Ian.

"Could I have my bloody pen back?" he asked Jen. "You're already sticking it all the way up my arse-hole."

Jen passed the pen back to him.

As the defendant, if Sir Ian didn't sign, the whole agreement fell apart. He looked at Susie as if he wanted to say something profound.

Jen felt the weight of his stare.

"Are you sure you want to do this, Susie?" he asked.

Susie nodded.

"Yes," Jen said. "She does."

"Shite," he said at last, and signed. He went out of his way to sign all of his noble titles, several of them in foreign lands. "Tell the judge we're ready."

Jen smiled. This was it! She had a moment of triumph. She would live to see this after all.

Claus had gone out to the gallery with the triplets. Each one of them gave him a hug.

"Remember, it's not official until the judge signs it," Jen said to Susie.

Officer Tran took the agreement with her. "I'll be right back," she said.

Jen stared at the ninja who held the briefcase. In moments she would have her share of the contents. Maybe she could go to Hawaii and drink Kona coffee and learn to hula dance. She wanted to sing or do a hula dance right there in the courtroom. Hell, she'd even give Sir Ian a hula lap dance just for spite. She felt positively giddy. This was all going to work out. Once the judge signed off, everything would be okay.

There was a sound from the other side of the door and everyone jumped up. Unfortunately, it was only the judge's trial court assistant, Beverly, who came out from a door at the back of the courtroom. Beverly was beautiful, but one glance from her indicated that things were not going smoothly.

"Just be patient," she said. "The judge needs to go through it line by line. We really wish you had given us the agreement beforehand."

Everyone mumbled, and Beverly disappeared through the back door.

Jen had a moment of panic. Perhaps the judge would throw the whole thing out, including the power of attorney and guardianship. Her paranoia deepened. Something was definitely in the air that afternoon, something sinister.

"I'm on the fifth floor," she whispered under her breath, over and over. "Nothing can happen to me on the fifth floor. can it?"

Beverly emerged once again. "The judge is taking a conference call," she said. "On a wrongful death case. Death takes priority."

That didn't sound good.

Beverly noticed their impatience. "Trust me. She wants to get this over with as quickly as you do."

Ninja fidgeted with his briefcase.

It was nearly five o'clock when Judge Salazar herself finally came out.

"All rise!" Officer Tran shouted.

Susie made a pretense of lifting herself out of her chair, but Tran indicated she could stay seated.

The judge took a long moment to get comfortable. "Merry Christmas," she said with a smile. "I think we'll finally have a white Christmas this year."

"Merry Christmas." Everyone, even the Wagatsuma folks, replied in unison.

Jen wanted to mention the solstice, but thought better of it.

"I understand that there is a settlement in the case of Sun Song a.k.a. Susie Song versus Lyon Aerospace which is consolidated with Song versus Sir Ian Lyon in his personal capacity, so today will be a presentment hearing."

Claus seemed pre-occupied. He nodded at Jen to play quarterback for the final dive.

"Jen Song, *attorney* for the plaintiff, Susie Song," she said with all the authority she could muster.

Damn that felt good to say. This was the proudest moment of her life. Jen was actually a lawyer arguing for a client. "There is indeed a resolution in this matter your honor."

Jen looked at the gallery. Luna and Selena nodded at her.

"Let me read the proposed agreement," the judge said. "I, of course, reserve the right to reject it, if anything is inappropriate."

Read it? What the hell had she been doing back there? Jen bit her tongue. She certainly didn't want to piss Judge Salazar off now, at her moment of triumph.

The judge scanned every line and verified a few initials. Everyone grumbled. It was now well past five o'clock and the rest of the courthouse had long since emptied. Judge Salazar squinted at the last of the scribbling then finally signed it with a sterling silver ball point of her own. She smiled again. "I guess this really will be a merry Christmas," she said. "Well, it will be for some of you."

"Yes indeed," said Jen.

"I understand that the disbursement of funds will now take place right here in the courtroom," the judge said. "I don't think I've ever seen this much cash, excuse me, this many bearer bonds, actually change hands before."

Sir Ian pretended to howl in pain. "Tell me about it your honor."

Gupta got up. "That is correct your honor," he said. "Mr. Nakamura from the Wagatsuma Corporation will now disburse the funds through his designee."

Wagatsuma nodded at the ninja who walked over to the plaintiff's table, opened the briefcases, and showed the contents to Jen and Claus. He made them sign a receipt in both Japanese and English.

Claus checked the briefcase carefully to make sure the bonds were in there and that there were no booby traps. After a moment, he smiled.

"We're good to go," he said as if he was a Marine. He smiled at his boys.

"Good to go," Junior said.

Jen was about to hug Susie, but Susie was frowning. Claus took the case with him and headed toward the back.

Jen smiled. "Good to go," she agreed. Claus kept walking and handed the case to Troy.

"Uh . . . excuse me," Susie called to Claus. She didn't even know his name. Jen just realized the two had never actually met. "Where are you going with *my* money?"

"Is something wrong?" Jen asked.

There was some commotion and Jen had trouble figuring out what the fuss was all about.

"What the blue blazes?" Sir Ian shouted.

The triplets had arranged themselves around the room. Junior blocked the door and Troy stood behind Sir Ian. In front of the courtroom, Rock had a gun in his left hand pointed at Officer Tran. He quickly took Tran's gun out of her holster with his right and aimed it at the judge.

A gun? How did—

Jen remembered the guard saying Claus entered the court-house five times that day complaining about his metal hip. He had probably hidden the guns in a false bottom in his briefcase.

"Shite!" Sir Ian said. "They've got guns."

Indeed, the triplets and Claus all branded semi-automatic pistols.

"Don't fucking move or I'll execute every mother fucking last one of you," Rock said.

Jen recognized the voice. He was the bad orderly. Jen had never liked the triplets, and it was obvious that they didn't like her. Jen remembered that they had talked about a job last summer. Their summer job must have been at the tram.

Claus had thrown his crutches down, like a cripple who was saved at a revival meeting. Now he took one crutch, pulled out a gun, and pointed it at the ninja. What was going on?

Alarms went off and Claus shot a bullet at the alarm, silencing it instantly. He was a good shot.

"Everybody get down!" he shouted.

"You're robbing us?" Jen asked.

Without hesitation, Claus fired at the ninja's forehead. He went down hard. The head wound made a sucking sound, as if air was flowing in. Jen shuddered.

"I said get down, face first!" Claus yelled again.

Everybody got down, face on the floor. Susie couldn't move of course, but one of the boys took her out of the chair, and helped her lie face down.

Jen lay next to Susie's wheel and held Susie's hand tightly.

"Please don't move," Troy said. "I don't want this to be worse than it has to be."

Troy must have been the nice orderly that night. That didn't make Jen feel any better. Junior made Luna and Selena lie next to Jen. The geishas had already lost.

"You'll never get out of here," Sir Ian said. "The whole building is surrounded."

Claus went up to Sir Ian and pointed a gun at his head.

"What are you going to do?" Sir Ian said. He might be an asshole, but he had no fear.

"Sir Ian," Claus said. "I suggest you call your helicopter to come pick us up on the roof."

Sir Ian jerked his head. "My helicopter? They'll shoot you out of the sky."

"Not if you're in it with me," Claus said.

Jen did the math, forcing herself to stay in lawyer mode despite the pain in her gut. Susie might be worth more as a plaintiff, but Sir Ian was the wealthiest man here and worth the most as a hostage. If Claus took someone from Zhang or Wagatsuma, he risked an international incident with the Chinese.

The gun at his head, Sir Ian reluctantly picked up his phone and spoke into it. "It can be here in ten minutes," he said. "It's coming from the airport.

"Should we take Susie?" Junior asked. "Could be a bonus."

"I don't want to fucking carry her," Rock said. "The chair weighs a ton."

"She won't fit," Sir Ian said. "Not with that chair. Especially if you want to take all of your boys with you. She's just dead weight."

"That's my choice," Claus said. "Not yours."

Claus walked to Susie and looked at the chair. He kicked the shiny golden tires, and then lifted it. "This thing does weigh a ton." He rubbed the gun against Susie's forehead.

Susie whimpered and then wet her pants. Fluid washed over the tiles of the floor. She shivered, embarrassed. She looked absolutely beaten down, like an infant.

"This wasn't supposed to happen," she said.

"Not the reaction I expected," said Claus. "We've got room for one more, but I don't know if I want to deal with a cripple. We could just put you out of your misery."

Jen tried to toughen up. Could she jump over and take the bullet for Susie? She wanted to, but without superpowers would she make it in time?

"Don't take Susie. Take me," Jen said. "Take me!" she said again. "If I am there, maybe they'll think you have Susie. All us Koreans look the same anyway to you, right?"

Claus pulled the gun away from Susie's head. "Good idea. We take the bitch. As insurance."

"Yeah, let's take her," Rock, the mean one said. "She's lighter than Susie and they won't figure out what's going on until it's too late."

Claus smiled. "By the time they figure it out, we'll be in the air."

Jen frowned. Who was this whore Claud mentioned? Her answer came quickly.

Rock picked her up as if she was a football shoulder pad. He raised a fist to her head. "Don't fucking move!"

Shite.

Jen looked at Claus and suddenly it all made sense. She had once seen him at the mental health center; he had been there for his *own* mental illness.

"I thought we were friends," Jen said.

"We were never friends," Claus said. "You were just a means to an end."

"Why?"

"I've had nothing my whole life, and I have a family to support. The bar was gonna take my license too, once Dr. Romero released my medical report. If you're expecting me to give a long speech, I'm sorry to disappoint you."

Claus started toward the door, keeping his gun pointed at the crowd. A semi-automatic, it could take all of them out in seconds.

Troy squeezed her so tight she couldn't breathe. Thankfully, she didn't have to pee.

Rock stayed behind for crowd control. Troy squeezed her again just for good measure. She gasped for breath and nearly blacked out.

They entered the elevator and started to ascend. Jen's stomach tightened further. She was a hostage and they don't kill hostages, right? She would be safe on the roof. She was only in danger on the seventh floor.

Hopefully they would go right to the roof. She would live if they went to the roof.

The elevator had made it to the sixth floor when Junior said, "Damn it. This elevator doesn't go to the roof. We have to get off on the seventh floor."

*Seventh floor?*

Jen's stomach knew what that meant before her brain did. So much for being a hostage. This was definitely it. She wasn't going to make it. Her courtroom career would last only a few hours. For her, this would indeed be the shortest day of the year.

They all waited on the seventh floor for Sir Ian's helicopter, and would go up the stairs at that time, and not a moment before. Claus had Troy and Junior with him. Rock had stayed down below to enforce crowd control with the remaining hostages.

Jen sat on the floor with Sir Ian.

"Why don't we wait for the helicopter on the roof?" Jen asked Claus. Anything to get off this floor.

"They're going to have snipers," Claus said, trying to remain calm. "I don't want to give them a chance to aim until the helicopter is there."

The courthouse must have had great sound-proofing be-cause it was deathly silent there on the seventh floor. Through the windows, though, Jen could see police lights everywhere.

"Stay in the corner," Troy said. "Hands over your head, and don't move a damn muscle."

"You were the guy in the tram," Jen said. "How did you get access?"

"We all worked there during the summer. Thought you knew that." He shrugged. "We kept the keys and the codes. This time you won't get a rope to save you if we throw you out of the helicopter."

"You're not going to throw me out of the helicopter," she said. Why was she so certain? Because she knew that death waited for her here, on this floor.

Jen looked out the big glass windows on the other side of the atrium. Spotlights scanned the building, as if this was a Hollywood premiere. It was now snowing and the snow dif-fused the beams. How would they ever get the helicopter in place?

Jen squirmed as a light passed over her. Could they see her? She hoped not.

"So why didn't you kill me on the tram?" Jen asked.

"The deal hadn't been signed yet," Claus replied. "And without you, there's no Susie. I just wanted you to drop out of the case. I really thought that you were going to sign it all over to us."

"And Black and Taranto?"

"Let's just say my boys learned about guns while growing up on the islands. In case, you're wondering about the other lawyer, White, we hired someone to take him out."

"Dirty deeds done dirt cheap," Jen said.

"Not that cheap," Claus sighed.

They waited. Tension was high. Claus checked the door to the roof and found it jammed, perhaps intentionally. He sent Junior back up to open the door with a blow torch. A blow torch? They must have been planting stuff in here for weeks.

"Why are you doing this?" Sir Ian said. "Is it about the money?"

Claus smiled. "Your company has exploited aluminum miners in Africa, and Wagatsuma and Zhang both oppress their workers in Asia. Your father did radioactive tests on the islands where my sons grew up. In fact, each of my children comes from an embattled region that these corporations have trampled upon."

Jen looked at Claus. He was serious. This was the man she had admired so much. So this was all for a noble cause, the poor. He was trying to make the world a better place. She felt a tinge of Stockholm syndrome. And for a moment, she actually believed him. Perhaps, this nice man wouldn't kill her after all.

Then Claus changed before their eyes. "Fuck that," he laughed. "This is about the money. It's all about the money. "

"Money?" Sir Ian asked. He had done a lot of evil things in his life, but most of them were for fame, pride, lust, or revenge. Nothing was merely for money.

Claus shook his head. "This is about the money. I'm just a poor working man trying to feed his kids."

It was apparent that Claus wanted to go on about his family's needs, but he checked his watch. "Any minute now."

Claus called the security desk down below. "No one comes up here, or Sir Ian dies. Susie Song, too. Let the helicopter land on the roof and give me, Sir Ian, and Susie free passage to the spaceport."

The spaceport? From there he could catch a plane or a rocket that could take him anywhere in the world. Where did he adopt his last child? Was that a place he could get asylum? Wasn't his wife was a pilot? Jen didn't think the man would risk taking a rocket, but things had become crazy. She didn't know him anymore.

"If you do not follow my orders," he continued, "I'll kill Sir Ian and the hostages, one by one. Now put me through to the pilot."

An operator patched him through, and Jen overheard some back and forth about how many people the helicopter could carry.

"We're hauling a lot of equipment," the pilot said. "It's locked in and will take about an hour to unload. We can only take five passengers max."

Claus frowned.

"You won't have room for all of us," Sir Ian said, sensing an opening. "You'll have to leave someone behind."

"You can't leave Rock behind," said Troy. "They'll kill him."

"You all knew what you were getting into," Claus said.

"If we have Sir Ian," Troy said. "Then we don't need them to think we're taking Susie. We don't need the whore."

What did that mean? Her answer came in an instant.

"The whore is afraid of heights," Troy said. "You should have seen her in the tram."

Jen cowered in the corner, hoping she could develop the ability to disappear, or better yet, walk through walls.

Claus then picked Jen up, and threw her over his shoulder as if she was a bag of Christmas toys. She had lost weight due to the stress of the deal, so it was effortless for him. "Don't make this hard on yourself."

What was the point? It was inevitable from here on. This was *it*. The past and present were about to collide.

"I thought you were my friend," she said as he carried her toward the railing. "I thought I was part of your family."

He laughed. "You really expected me to believe you were just a waitress?"

"I was!" Jen said. "I was!"

"I read your psych files," he said. The mystery of the missing files was now solved. Claus had taken them. "I knew you were nuts when I saw you at the clinic. You're a killer, too. I'm doing the world a favor."

She expected him to give a big speech, but then they heard the helicopter. Claus didn't bother talking over the noise. This was real life, not a James Bond movie. Claus would get this over with quickly, without much fanfare. One quick toss of a hundred and ten pounds of Jen Song over the railing. This was it. It all ended here.

Jen wanted to start praying, but her mind was frozen. She could not save herself. She tried to form the words to the Lord's Prayer in her head, but it had been too long. No one would save her, in this world or the next.

Or would they?

She heard rumbling below, from the fifth floor. Were those gunshots coming from the courtroom? Outside, she heard a second helicopter and could see a police 'copter on the other side of the building. It shined a spotlight directly into the atrium.

This was her chance. Jen kicked Claus as hard as she could. Nothing.

Shite! It was fate; there was no way to avoid this moment. Claus lifted her up over his head as if she was a barbell.

More gunshots came from below. A rescue attempt now would actually make it worse for her. She would be the last person to die. She expected Claus to say one more thing, a word of wisdom, or perhaps even good-bye, but he said nothing.

He wavered for one moment, during which Junior shouted, "Dad, they got Rock. The hostages are free!"

Claus raised Jen even higher, as if she, personally, had killed his son. More commotion came from below.

"Dad, the hostages are getting away!"

Claus grabbed her from behind. More gunshots. The police helicopter hovered outside, its spotlight now scanning the building.

"It's over, Claus," Jen said. "Just put me down."

"You're going down all right."

Before Jen had a chance to defend herself, Claus picked her up and tossed her off the balcony. Jen looked down and saw the floor, which was arranged in a giant bulls-eye that pointed toward the glass sculpture with the shiny metal rim.

She started to fall.

# Invisible Sun

JEN OPENED HER EYES as she looked down. And she saw it, the golden disk, that little rotating sun. I've got to head toward the light, she thought. The light was there on the other side of the railing on the fifth floor. If she had superpowers, now would be the time to use them.

"Laser Geisha Pink!" Jen shouted.

Then everything changed.

There might be a logical explanation for what happened next. Perhaps a tremor in some yet unknown fault beneath Albuquerque shifted the position of the building a few feet to the northeast. Perhaps a solar storm momentarily shifted the earth's orbit ten feet. Or, the helicopter outside could have forced air into the intake valves and a sudden gust of air could have pushed the falling woman toward the railing.

Or, perhaps Jen Song did indeed become Laser Geisha Pink.

As Jen glided toward a shiny disk on the fifth floor, it came into focus. It wasn't a sun, but whatever it was, it spun rapidly in the police spotlight.

"I've got to get there," Jen thought, but she had no control. Pink ruled her body now, and Pink only had so much control over gravity in this world.

For one brief moment, Jen feared it was over. Then Pink grabbed the side of the balcony to stop her fall. Unfortunately, Pink's grip was wet, and she started to lose her hold. Then she felt a firm grip on her wrist that stopped her momentum. Jen dangled over the atrium floor.

Time started moving again.

"I'VE GOT YOU, JEN," a voice said. "I've got you."

Before Jen could recognize the voice, she felt the grip loosening, but other hands quickly grabbed her. Within seconds, Luna and Selena hoisted her up and she was back on the fifth floor.

Jen looked at the shining "sun." The shiny spinning object had been a golden wheel from Susie's chair glistening in the spotlight. Susie had saved her.

"We escaped," Luna said. "Jean Claude is fighting that Samoan kid."

Jen wanted to smile, but she hadn't yet resumed control of her body. She realized that the world was anime again, but this time she was awake—a houseguest in her own brain.

There were more gunshots.

Typically, Pink only went away after all of the danger was over. Well, the danger *was* over, wasn't it? Maybe not. Pink headed toward the courtroom.

"What are you doing?" Jen asked Pink, but Pink did not reply.

Pink was going to see if Jean Claude needed help, but the elevator door open behind her.

"I can't get to Rock, but I can get Susie!" Troy yelled into his phone. Then, without another word, Troy grabbed Susie out of her wheelchair and dragged her into the elevator.

Pink didn't bother to open the door into the courtroom, but instead turned around and started her pursuit.

"I'll let you handle this one from here," Jen said to Pink.

# Laser Geisha Pink

IT WAS TOO LATE. The elevator door closed behind Troy and Susie. Pink didn't follow them. Instead, she hurried to the stairs down the hallway. These stairs led to the roof. Pink hurried up the stairs with fast strides and didn't bother to stop for breath, as Jen would have done.

Jen didn't float above Pink as she had done other times. This time she was right there inside Pink's brain. Jen panicked. She should have died in the fall. She was on borrowed time.

The door to the roof was locked, but Pink pulled it open without straining a muscle. She emerged onto the big round roof of the district courthouse, several hundred feet above Albuquerque. It was the perfect heliport on a calm day, but today was hardly calm. Albuquerque was having a rare blizzard. It would be a white Christmas after all. With the swirling winds, the snow actually flowed upwards. Through Pink's eyes the snowflakes were bigger and the building seemed taller, like they could be in Mega-Tokyo.

Sir Ian's helicopter tried to land on the roof, but the wind and the snow made it almost impossible. The pilot probably would have abandoned the try if he hadn't seen Claus point a gun to his boss's head.

"Stop!" Pink yelled.

Claus fired a shot at her.

The wind must have blown the bullet off course, but Pink wasn't afraid of a mere bullet.

"Try to duck at least!" Jen wanted tell Pink, but she had lost control of her mouth. "You're not bulletproof!"

Pink didn't care much about life or death. She was on a mission.

Perhaps the cold and his nervousness were ruining his simple plan. Claus was now shaking. Or maybe, Claus was just not someone who knew how to improvise.

The district courthouse now glowed from the many spotlights from the police and news helicopters that were orbiting the building. Someone in a police helicopter fired a shot at her. Pink didn't duck as the bullet ricocheted off the metal of the building.

"I'm a good guy!" Jen tried to shout.

But was she?

Jen felt like a tourist in her own brain as Pink calmly continued toward the helicopter, which was now about fifty feet away.

Another gust almost knocked the helicopter over the edge, but the pilot finally guided it to a safe landing and opened the side door. He hadn't been kidding about the supplies inside. No, they wouldn't have been able to fit Rock in.

Claus boarded first. Then he grabbed Sir Ian and pulled him inside. Troy threw the briefcase up and together, Troy and Junior struggled with Susie's bulk. Troy got in first and they took a moment to figure out how to load Susie.

"Let's go!" Claus yelled. Pink was still twenty feet away. She wouldn't make it in time.

"Close the door!" the pilot yelled.

"The door's jammed!" Claus yelled. Susie held an arm in the doorway.

The helicopter rose in the swirling winds, but then a gust pushed it down. Jen thought of the exploding rocket. Sir Ian's technology was not the best. To make it worse, Susie kept struggling. She used her arms to try to roll her weight around. That made the helicopter even more unstable.

Sir Ian got into the act. He smacked Claus hard, as hard as he could muster.

The helicopter descended, and the pilot managed to keep it hovering inches above the ground. Claus slammed Sir Ian, and tried to close the door. Unfortunately, while Susie's arm had been moved, the briefcase had gotten free and now blocked the door.

Pink approached the helicopter, not even bothering to duck from the rotor blades. Jen had long since given up hope of telling Pink to bend down. Police helicopters now adopted a tighter orbit around the perimeter of the building.

"Take off!" Claus yelled. "Or I kill Sir Ian. And I got Susie Song as insurance."

The helicopter could barely muster any gain in altitude. It held just two feet off the roof.

Sir Ian punched Claus again, but Troy grabbed him hard. The door still wasn't shut, but the helicopter finally rose another foot. Unfortunately, it now also moved in random directions, like a drunken bull at a rodeo. The helicopter jerked closer to Pink and a rotor nearly took her head off. Pink still didn't duck.

Claus punched Sir Ian, and blood splattered everywhere. Sir Ian slumped, down for the count. Claus reached for the briefcase. When he had it in his hand, he started to close the sliding door. Just then, the winds died suddenly, as if God himself was giving clearance for take-off.

"We're good to go," Claus said, looking directly at Pink.

"Do it!" Jen shouted inside her head.

"Help!" Susie shouted. "Save me."

Claus turned and said something to the pilot. He was about to close the door when Susie bit him on the leg. He howled in pain and dropped the briefcase. After another lurch, the briefcase slid next to the door.

Pink saw her opening. No one on the helicopter paid attention to her, even though it was at the level of her waist. Claus stopped trying to close the door, and turned his attention to Susie.

"You've got to save Susie," Jen said to Pink.

"Don't you get it?" Pink said out loud. "This has nothing to do with Susie."

Pink leaped toward the helicopter and landed, half in and half out. Her dangling weight upset the balance on the helicopter. Another gust carried them over Lomas Boulevard, two hundred feet below. Jen wanted to look down, but was glad that Pink was in control. Pink showed no fear, and didn't even bother to look.

Claus stepped on Pink's hands. "Get the fuck off my flight!"

Another gust took the helicopter back over the roof.

Pink slugged him and he went backward.

"The briefcase," Susie shouted. The briefcase was now free of Claus's grip and slid away with the next lurch, taking the helicopter back over the courthouse roof. It would be an easy jump from here.

Pink knew she could take the case or take Susie, but not both. The helicopter bucked again. There was no telling where the next gust would take it. She had to act quickly.

"Save Susie," Jen said inside her brain. "Screw the money!" Pink hesitated. Pink was her dark side. Pink was all about the money. Please let me be a good person, Jen thought. Please. Pink kept hesitating and Jen could see terror in Susie's eyes.

"Screw you, Pink!" Jen said. With sheer force of will Jen resumed control over her own body.

"I'm back!" she said. She grabbed Susie and pulled her out, just as the helicopter bucked again. She and Susie fell into the thin air. Claus grabbed the briefcase and let them go.

Jen tried to look below and saw only street. Where would they land? She hugged Susie tight. "I'm sorry I couldn't save you, Susie," Jen said. "I love you."

Susie's eyes were closed. Had all the stress been too much for her?

Sir Ian managed to get up for one more round. He now locked himself with Claus in a death grip. The helicopter bucked again, and spun out over the street. Claus could have knocked Sir Ian out, but he saw the briefcase nearly fall through the still open door. He and Sir Ian both jumped toward it, and that movement upset the balance of the helicopter even further.

A news helicopter finally got too close. That, along with another gust of wind, and the helicopter went down. It fell straight down onto Lomas Boulevard and exploded. Bearer Bonds flew into the air. Some of them seemed to spontaneously combust.

Jen's mind went blank. Pink was gone.

Where was she? Where was Susie?

Were they still alive?

# EPILOGUE
## Merry Solstice

JEN AND SUSIE HUDDLED through the explosion against the chimney. They had somehow landed on the roof. The world was back to its old boring self, and Jen was glad that the colors were muted.

She smiled. "I'm myself again. Pink is gone."

There had to be a logical explanation as to why they landed on the roof and not on top of the burning helicopter below. But who knew what it was?

"Maybe I have superpowers on my own," Jen said. "Who needs Laser Geisha Pink?"

Susie didn't respond.

Hundreds of the fiery bearer bonds now floated in the air, like flaming snowflakes. Wind carried the bonds in all directions. How much was one bond worth? Several thousand? Jen wasn't sure. She would never be good in math, but it didn't matter.

A bearer bond floated right by her. Only one end was burning. Maybe she could save it.

But, right as she grabbed it, a sudden gust fanned the flames and burned her hand. God must be telling me something, Jen thought. Other bonds floated by her, some not even burning, but Jen didn't reach for them.

"Laser Geisha Pink!" Jen shouted.

"Laser Geisha Gold," Susie said faintly, opening her eyes.

"Are you alright?

Susie huddled against Jen for warmth. "I think so." She looked up at the burning bonds. "The money? It's all gone."

Jen shrugged. "This was never about the money."

Susie smiled. "I know. I love you Jen."

"I love you Susie."

Susie propped herself up. "Don't tell anybody about me peeing my pants. It will cost me my endorsements."

"Don't worry," Jen said. "Let me see what happened to the helicopter."

Jen went to the edge of the roof and looked down at the burning wreckage. An explosion came as a fuel tank erupted. More debris billowed in the air. For an instant, Jen thought about jumping into the hell below. She had been Laser Geisha Pink one last time. She was off her meds. Could she return to being plain old Jen again? Especially now that she would no longer be a lawyer?

She spit down on the volcano of burning debris, as if testing the winds.

"Jen!" Susie shouted.

Jen turned. No she wasn't a good person. But as her Dad said, she wanted to be good. That should count for something. She turned back toward Susie.

Thankfully, Luna and Selena hurried up to the roof and gave them a hug. They also helped carry Susie.

Luna shook her head. "You saved everybody, Jen. You're a hero."

Selena was even more surprised. "You're a tough act to follow, Jenita."

Jen smiled. "I could learn to like this lawyer thing."

Susie laughed. "She's not my lawyer, she's my geisha."

# There's No Place Like Home

THE GEISHA GIRLS HAD a Christmas party at Nurse Song's home, a few days later. Nurse Song cooked an amazing meal, her famed pheasant again, and it was agreed that there could only be five pheasant jokes. Selena was only allowed two, which was fine by her. Dew kept telling jokes of her own, but she was a kid genius who got away with just about anything.

They were glad that they had an unexpected guest. Dr. Romero was indeed alive and well. Claus had taken mercy on her and told her to go to Mexico. She revealed that Claus also had dissociative identity disorder and would have lost his license in a few weeks anyway.

"I had been treating him for years," she said with a frown. "If you think you had problems," she said to Jen. "This guy made you look sane."

"What brought on his other personality?"

"You did."

"Huh?"

The doctor revealed that she learned that when interviewed by the police in juvenile jail, the surviving triplet, Rock, told about his father's obsession with Jen. Apparently his computer was littered with pictures of her and he listened to the stolen tapes with his door shut. The boy also said that they heard heavy breathing coming from Claus's room along with the sound of her voice on the tapes.

Jen shuddered when she heard that. Best of all, it turned out that Susie would get her money after all. The Wagatsuma folk weren't stupid. They had insurance on the bearer bonds. She would be set for life. In a press conference, Mr. Wagatsuma stated that with the improved limb technology, she might even walk again in ten years or so. As Jen had predicted, Wagatsuma's stock price went through the roof.

"We bought Lyon Aerospace for a 'song,'" he said. "We really did."

By dessert, Luna had taken Jen aside and given her some good news. "I talked with the bar," Luna said. "They'll let you continue to practice law if you are under the direct supervision of another attorney."

Jen frowned. "What attorney is ever going to hire me?"

"I will. I guess you heard the voters recommended that I go back into private practice."

She then had a mischievous smile. "But I lied to them," she said. "I won't really be supervising you, we'll be partners."

Jen gave Luna a hug. "This is the best Christmas ever. The very, very best."

She did a mental check-up. Pink was gone forever. Somehow her triumph had exorcised the demon from her personality. "I'm cured," she said.

"It gets better," Nurse Song said as she brought out the dessert—a pumpkin pie with exotic Korean spices. Jen wondered if the spices were legal.

"I have a surprise," Nurse Song said after they all dug in. "Denise has something to say."

Denise?

Little Denise sat on Jen's lap and gave her a kiss. "I'm so proud of you Mommy," Denise said. "I love you."

Jen was shocked. She hadn't known whether her daughter could talk at all.

"I could learn to love this being a mother thing," Jen said.

"One more thing," Denise said.

"She can't shut up now," Dew said.

"God bless us everyone," she said.

Jen had a tear in her eye as they all sat silently and demolished the spicy pumpkin pie. When they finished, Jen got up. She knew her mother would yell at her if she didn't do the dishes.

"Stay seated Jenita," Selena said.

Her mom laughed. "Heroes don't have to do the dishes."

Dishes finished, they sat at the table. No one wanted to leave.

Susie now smiled. "There's something I want to try."

She pushed herself up and attempted to rise. It was a great effort. She was able to pick herself up just a bit. But the effort was too much and she scrunched back down. She started to cry.

"You'll get it next time, Susie," Jen said.

"Next time," Susie said. "I love you Jen."

"I love you, too, Susie."

In the corner, Denise got on top of a chair and then jumped off. She then did it again.

"Denise, stop that!" Jen said. Maybe being a mom would be a handful.

"Don't call me, Denise," the girl said. "My name is Pink."

# One Scene Too Many?

IT WAS NEW YEAR'S Day, just a week later—Susie's eighteenth birthday. She ran around UNM golf course. No one recognized her in her hooded sweatshirt and big sunglasses. She had checked out of the hospital and moved into Sir Ian's old place at the vineyard. She had wanted to run along the river, but she didn't want to slip on any ice and wind up getting wounded for real.

It was amazing that she'd gotten away with it. The plan sure hadn't worked out the way she thought it would. No one had counted on Claus, but in some ways it worked out for the best. She would miss Sir Ian, but that was collateral damage.

Susie had known since she was thirteen that she would never have a real career as a golfer. She was strong to be sure, but even when she was in rehab that first time, she knew she would always have nerves, and whenever she took medication to deal with them, it just made her worse. She knew she'd have to quit before they found out.

She had told Sir Ian about it at the Lyon Invitational Tournament over a year ago.

"I need a way out," she said.

"So do I," he answered.

He had hinted that he wanted to make moves on her there, but she wasn't ready.

"Wait a year," she had told him. "I'm only seventeen."

"You're worth waiting for," he said. "We're two of a kind."

"What do you mean?"

"I hate my life, too."

"There's got to be a way to work this so I can quit golf and you can sell your company. What is the way that people deliberately want their company to lose money?"

"Selling short," he said. "I'll think of a way to sell short on both of us."

She smiled as she ran the golf course. Sir Ian's plan had been a little too complicated. Jean Claude would rig the Mountain Lyon. They'd fake the injury, file a bogus lawsuit, and she'd get the money from Wagatsuma. Once the situation got messy, the Zhang people had to be brought in, but that still worked out. All while he sold the stock short of a company that made defective helicopters and rockets that were billion dollar lawsuits waiting to happen.

She'd never have to golf again. Sir Ian had explained about the weird corporate *ménage a trois* stuff, but she hadn't really grasped it then, and still didn't now.

Basically, Sir Ian explained, all his corporate holdings were shams. His rockets would never be able to take people into orbit without massive investment. This way he would be able to use Zhang's insurance proceeds to pay for everything, and Wagatsuma was just along for the ride.

Jean Claude had driven the Mountain Lyon that night. She hadn't even been in the car with the strapped in Hal. She didn't realize that he wanted to kill his own son and eventually set her up as his heir.

Hal had been making noise about Sir Ian killing the boy's mother, threatening to take it public, so Sir Ian felt he had no choice. She could have loved Hal, he sure was cute, but he was just a boy and Sir Ian was a man. And with Hal gone, she'd get it all.

She ran a bit faster now as she came up a hill near the monolith wall of the Court of Appeals. Her knees still hurt from the months of faking. Sir Ian brought in his own doctors, of course, like that jerk Jen called Dr. Ghandi. She could never pronounce his name either. He'd given her a few shots to make sure her legs stayed numb.

Dr. Ghandi falsified all the reports and made sure no one else got to see her. Sir Ian had bribed the hospital staff to stay out of the way, of course. That only took a new pediatric wing built on his dime to shut up the hospital board.

She had to put up with that bitch Ariana, but that was just the price she had to pay. Ariana had drugged her a few times, just to show her who was boss.

Susie was supposed to get an inexperienced local lawyer they could manipulate, and Jen was the worst lawyer in the world. They'd give her a taste, and she was supposed to disappear. Sir Ian nearly blew it when he assaulted Jen. She would never forgive him for that. Thankfully, she wouldn't have to.

Why did Jen have to bring Claus into it? Claus turned out to be psycho. No one counted on Claus. The man looked like a polyester Santa for God's sake.

Perhaps it was a good thing that Sir Ian died after all. She wouldn't have to sleep with him, thank God. He was handsome, but he was old enough to be her grandfather.

Susie decided to sprint for the home stretch, right past the Court of Appeals. It was nice and level. She took a final look at the hospital. Thank God, she would never have to go there again. She chugged the last of her Gatorade. Would they still sponsor her if they knew?

Everything had worked out after all. She got her money. Even better, she now had Sir Ian's money, even the offshore accounts. She would never have to golf again. Oh, the Wagatsuma people would use her for show and tell a few times to get funding for their artificial limbs. Then a year from now, two at the latest, she'd be able to walk again in public. All hail the miracle cure produced by Japanese technology.

Susie laughed. In essence, she was a pawn of multi-nationals so they could get increased funding from their governments. Still, this pawn was getting a boat load of money at eighteen. She got back in a new and improved version of the Mountain Lyon and closed the door before anyone could see her. Jean Claude smiled. "Where to *Mademoiselle*?"

"Home," she said. "But first, go past Jen's house on Stanford Street."

"As you say, *Mademoiselle*. I work for you now." As Jean Claude drove her past Jen's house, Susie saw Jen out getting her mail. Jen noticed the vehicle, but the windows were too dark and she wouldn't be able to see inside.

"Susie tells you hello," Jean Claude shouted. "She's already back in Arizona."

"Tell her hello, too," Jen said.

Susie was sorry she dragged Jen into it. Jen had become her friend, after all. She would tell Jen someday, but not now.

Susie felt another tinge of guilt. Yes, she had the money, but was it worth it? She sometimes wondered if she herself had two personalities, but that was ridiculous. She remembered the stories she'd heard about her grandmother, Un Chong, the crazy one. She was the one who started all the craziness. Maybe it had been passed down through the generations. The whole Laser Geisha Gold thing couldn't possibly be real.

Or could it?

THE END

# AUTHOR'S NOTE

Second Judicial District Court in Albuquerque is accurately depicted. There is indeed a three-story drop that could potentially lead to a fatal injury, and there is a statue of Lady Justice at the bottom of the fourth floor. The balloon fiesta is accurately portrayed, although individual balloons are fictional. The neighborhood around the law school is realistically described—the UNM hospital, mental health center, law school, and Court of Appeals are all within walking distance, although Jen's home and the "group home" are not based on any actual structures. As of this writing, there is a spaceport under construction near Upham, New Mexico and it has already been the site of several tests. All corporations are fictional.

Jen Song is not based on any individual. There is an indeed a "Not-for-the-Top" scholarship sponsored by the late Mary Han. Meanwhile, there are numerous successful Korean golfers, but none of them form the basis for Susie Song. An English billionaire has been linked to the spaceport, but otherwise, Sir Ian Lyon is totally fictitious.

A law suit such as the one portrayed here would probably be more complex and time consuming to resolve than indicated, and the recovery from the accident would also probably take more time than portrayed.

The Laser Geishas are fictional.

For now.

## ABOUT THE AUTHOR

Jonathan Miller is an award-winning author and attorney who practices criminal law in New Mexico. He is a graduate of Albuquerque Academy, Cornell University, the University of Colorado Law School, and the American Film Institute.

Author photo by Rima Krisst
Cover medallion photo by Stella Conklin

# READER QUESTIONS

1. Is Jen Song good or bad? What about Susie?

2. Where do the Laser Geishas come from?

3. If you had the opportunity, would you go into orbit? Why or why not?

4. How prevalent do you think mental illness is among lawyers?

5. Do you think Susie Song really could have sued Lyon Aerospace for a billion dollars?

7. In your opinion, could multiple personalities be a defense to murder?

8. Do you think a fear of heights could trigger a psychotic break?

9. How did the Jekyll/Hyde myth come into play in this story?

10. What other literary works and/or stories do you think influenced this book?

11. How do you think Luna keeps in such good spirits after all her defeats?

12. Do you feel that Sir Ian Lyon should be liable for damages caused by his seventeen-year-old son's drunk driving?

13. In your opinion, is Jen a good role model for Susie?

14. In what ways do you think Jen is a good or bad mother?

15. Ultimately, who is the dominant party in the friendship, Jen or Susie? Why?

16. Do you think Susie will ever tell Jen her secret? Why or why not?

17. How does becoming a lawyer make Jen's mental illness both better and worse?

18. Do you think Jen's fear of heights is a metaphor for something? If so, what?

19. Do you think Laser Geisha Pink is real or just a figment of Jen's imagination? Does it matter?

20. How do you think the friendship between Susie and Jen is real? How about false?

## IF YOU ENJOYED THIS BOOK, YOU MAY ALSO ENJOY THESE, AND OTHER, AWARD WINNING BOOKS FROM COOL TITLES.
### Learn more at CoolTitles.com

Santa Fe attorney Dan Shepard has made it to the top; but his girlfriend, Ophelia Paz, may have killed the governor's wife and dumped her in a ditch. And after Ophelia reveals the governor's dark secret, Dan would like to ditch Ophelia. Dan wants to help, but needs attorney Luna Cruz to guide him. In the process he falls in love with Luna, putting the case at risk. Dan wonders how deeply he must descend into political muck to save Ophelia, and will he take Luna down with him?

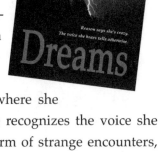

Human reason tells her she's crazy the voice she hears tells otherwise. Emerald McGintay experiences dreams and visions and is diagnosed with schizophrenia. When she stumbles upon a trail of hidden secrets, her father decides to send her away to a special clinic. She flees her luxurious home in Philadephia to a safe haven in the Colorado Rockies where she meets a rancher who suggests he recognizes the voice she hears. Battered by a relentless storm of strange encounters, Emerald struggles to discover her reality.

When retired movie star Glenda Dupree was murdered in her antebellum mansion in Tennessee, there was much speculation. Prior to leaving life on earth, Glenda had offended everyone, including her neighbor, a (mostly) law-abiding horse trainer named Cat Enright. Cat finds Glenda's body, is implicated in the murder, and also in the disappearance of a ten-year-old neighbor, 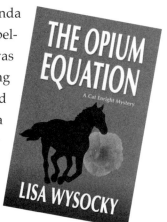 Bubba Henley. An unpopular sheriff and upcoming election mean the pressure to close the case is on. With the help of her riding students, a (possibly) psychic horse, a local cop, a kid named Frog, and an eccentric client of a certain age with electric blue hair, Cat takes time from her horse training business to try to solve the case and keep herself out of prison.

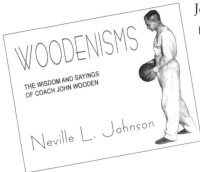 John Wooden was arguably the greatest coach, the greatest leader, of all time. These Woodenisms, a collection of his wisdom and sayings, inspire, motivate, and prepare you for any challenge. Woodensims provide common sense, assist you in being a leader and a team player, and also give you strength. Many of these Woodenisms have been distributed individually. They have also been used in print, and in presentations by Coach and other speakers. Now they are collected here, yours to cherish and enjoy as you strive for success.